CANDLELIGHT
Ecstasy Supreme

"YOU NEVER ANSWERED ME," SHE SAID. "ARE YOU MARRIED?"

"No." He stepped closer.

"How do I know you're not lying? You lie like a rug."

"This hasn't been a lie," said Paul as he pressed himself against her. "My wanting you is real and true."

"It—it's not the same," she objected breathlessly. "You know it's not. I—being lied to—it's made me feel—vulnerable."

He bent to kiss her but she turned her head away. He buried his lips in the side of her neck. He could feel her heart beating against his. He could feel the heat of her breath. Flames of desire licked through his blood and for one agonized moment he wished he could go back and start all over with her. He wished he could court her with champagne and flowers, deck her in diamonds, take her without all the lies.

D1446791

CANDLELIGHT ECSTASY SUPREMES

LOVERS AND PRETENDERS

Prudence Martin

A CANDLELIGHT ECSTASY SUPREME

Published by
Dell Publishing Co., Inc.
1 Dag Hammarskjold Plaza
New York, New York 10017

*To Tom and Sharon
with thanks for all the encouragement*

Dell ® TM 681510, Dell Publishing Co., Inc.

Candlelight Ecstasy Supreme is a trademark of Dell
Publishing Co., Inc.

Candlelight Ecstasy Romance®, 1,203,540, is a registered
trademark of Dell Publishing Co., Inc.

ISBN: 0–440–15013–2

Printed in the United States of America
First printing—August 1983

To Our Readers:

Candlelight Ecstasy is delighted to announce the start of a brand-new series—Ecstasy Supremes! Now you can enjoy a romance series unlike all the others—longer and more exciting, filled with more passion, adventure, and intrigue—the stories you've been waiting for.

In months to come we look forward to presenting books by many of your favorite authors and the very finest work from new authors of romantic fiction as well. As always, we are striving to present the unique, absorbing love stories that you enjoy most—the very best love has to offer.

Breathtaking and unforgettable, Ecstasy Supremes will follow in the great romantic tradition you've come to expect *only* from Candlelight Ecstasy.

Your suggestions and comments are always welcome. Please let us hear from you.

Sincerely,

The Editors
Candlelight Romances
1 Dag Hammarskjold Plaza
New York, New York 10017

CHAPTER ONE

Christine barely noticed the customer slouching in the shadows at the corner table. The light was too dim and hazed with smoke, the air too packed with the rise and fall of voices crowding in on one another above the continual drone of the Muzak. She had no time to notice one man. Saturday was her busiest night and tonight was busier than usual.

She plopped her round tray on the bar and snapped, "Two rum and Coke, two Buds on tap, and a Scotch on the rocks." Henry nodded and she picked up a tray laden with a colorful assortment of glasses. She quickly looked them over, checking the orders and mentally reviewing what went where even as she began to turn from the counter.

When she'd first started as a hostess, Christine had told her sister The Scarlet Lady was like a shoebox stuffed with garish ornaments. Brass gargoyles decorated the wooden counter that ran the length of the rectangular room, and yawned grotesquely at the edges of the mirror that lined the wall. A murky gloom mercifully obscured most of the brass and glass fixtures scattered throughout the room, but here and there crimson tulips hung upside down, providing a faint vermilion glow through which smoke perpetually wisped. One end wall was dominated by a full-length portrait of a lusty lady decked out in a lush scarlet gown, coyly waving a red feathered fan. Fortunately the six months she'd worked there had dulled Chris to the horrors of her surroundings.

Unfortunately it hadn't dulled her to the repugnant facets of her work, to the smoke and the noise and, worst of all, the drunks. Threading her way around the maze of tables, she managed to summon up smiles; it was harder for her to ignore the leers down her bodice whenever she bent forward.

It wasn't that the décolletage was so low. It was simply that the red leotard with spaghetti-thin straps criss-crossing her bare back clung so tightly, seeming to thrust her firm, full bosom at the leering men. Those who weren't trying to grab her snugly outlined rear or run a hand down her shapely black-hosed legs, that is. She'd drawn the line at the spike heels that the other hostesses wore, defiantly lacing her feet into black ballet slippers each night, despite the fact that the spikes were excellent weapons when a drunk got too inclined to grab. As many of them invariably did. God, how she hated this!

Her favorite fantasy involved flinging her skimpy "uniform" in Don Rosta's face and striding out of The Scarlet Lady for good. But she couldn't afford to offend the owner until she could afford to live without her job. She'd tried to find something more suited to her temperament, but night jobs that paid as well as the tips she earned here, thereby allowing her the luxury of going to school in the daytime, simply didn't exist. She knew; she'd looked for them.

Grimacing tightly at a pair of middle-aged men who were ogling her openly, she made her way to the next table. "Anything else here?" she asked with her leave-a-good-tip-fellas smile. She leaned across the table to collect empty glasses, then jerked back as one man reached forward to finger her breasts. "Those real, little lady?" he asked to the guffaws of his two table partners.

She longed to smack his head with her tray. One of

these days, she promised herself, she'd do it and the job be damned. For now, she contented herself with moving out of range, pretending not to hear their demands for another round. She slapped the lone whiskey glass on the small corner table. "Two-fifty," she said without looking at the man seated there.

Long fingers curled around the glass as he lifted it and downed the contents in a gulp. Still holding the empty glass, he dug into the pocket of a pair of smoke-gray slacks and waved a bill he peeled from a thick roll. Christine took it and raised her brows. It was a fifty.

"Bring me a bottle," he ordered shortly.

His voice was perfectly steady. Even, thought Chris, quite pleasant. But she hesitated. A prickling, a premonition, something she couldn't define, delayed her. She tried to count the number of glasses she'd previously brought him, but she couldn't recall. Without realizing it she stared at his face. Though the smoky light veiled his features, she had the impression of dark coloring and unhappy lines.

"Something wrong?" he said, startling her out of her reverie. This voice wasn't pleasant at all. It was sharply harsh.

"No—not at all," said Chris quickly.

"Then bring me a bottle."

She wheeled around and returned to the bar, skirting the table with the obnoxious lout and his two friends. Shoving the tray full of dirty glasses across the bar, she reeled off her next order, then handed Henry the fifty and asked him to give her the bottle of Jack Daniel's immediately. The bartender's oft-broken nose wrinkled, his broad jaw jutted forward, and his heavy lips split into a grin. Despite his enormous size and fearsome features, Henry was surprisingly shy and gentle. He rumbled to the storeroom behind the bar and Chris thought how absurd his hulking frame looked in the frilled red shirt Don Rosta insisted his burly bartenders wear. That man's taste, she

11

concluded, was all in his mouth. With a shrug she let her mind glide back to her customer in the corner.

She tapped a fingernail against the bar and wondered why she felt so reluctant to give that man the whiskey. Perhaps it was the way he'd downed that glassful. So resolutely, as if he had no other choice. A man who meant to get drunk. Or drunker. The kind of man who usually meant trouble.

An arm slid around over her hip, startling her. "Hey, Tina baby, what's goin' on? You got three guys back there that say you're refusin' to take their order."

Chris stood stiffly within Don's hold. His intimacies nauseated her, but it went with the job. If he'd singled her out for such attention she'd have quit the first night, but he touched all the girls. It was one of his privileges as owner and manager. She turned her head and looked directly into the pale spherule eyes set widely in his fleshy face.

"I'm not waiting on any creep who thinks he has the right to grope while I do."

The jowls on Don's cheeks fell heavily as he sighed dramatically. "Come on, doll. You know the score. These guys work hard all week, they deserve a little freebie now and again. Now, now," he said quickly, tightening his hold at her jerky protest. "Tina, baby, what's the big deal? They get a little kick, you get a bigger tip. That's the way it works. You keep 'em happy, they come back and spend more next week. Okay?"

"Sure," she muttered, lifting her tray as Henry set the Jack Daniel's on it. Although she didn't think that's the way it should be, Chris knew that's the way it was. Most nights she accepted it—to a degree—but tonight's rowdy crowd made it more difficult to do so. She didn't look at Don, but she felt his hardened gaze boring through her. His protuberant paunch shifted; he dropped his hand and she took a step away.

"Tina, baby," said Don, halting her.

12

"Yes?"

"Smile."

She plastered a smile in place, holding her lips so far up, her jaws ached. Being called Tina only irritated her further. Tina, Don repeatedly said, had more class than Chris. The fact was, she now thought, Don Rosta wouldn't know class if it walked through the door. She vowed to once again check the want ads.

When she reached the groper's table, she stood well back and positively beamed at the trio. "Did you want anything this go-round?" she asked, mentally adding a few choice epithets.

"Some service would be nice," said the groper with a sneer.

His friends snickered, she somehow swallowed back a retort, and he ordered another round of beer. Nodding curtly, she moved on to the corner table. She set down the bottle of whiskey. The man began pouring as she counted out his change.

"Keep it," he said.

Her hand wavered in mid-air. She held over thirty dollars. Steady voice or not, this guy had to be drunk. "But—"

"Keep it," he repeated. He tilted the glass against his lips and swallowed.

Chris followed the motion, noting that his hair had to be very dark; it melted into the shadows as he tipped his head back. The simple rippling of muscles down his arched throat strangely mesmerized her. She wished he were sitting nearer a light. She wanted to see more than the square line of his jaw, the broad outline of his nose, the tight set of his mouth. He thumped the glass down to refill it and all her original doubts about serving him returned. She laid the bills beside his hand. "I can't take this much, sir."

He did not seem to have heard her. He sloshed more whiskey into his glass, splashing a bit onto the table, then again drained the glassful. Chris couldn't stifle her protest. "You really shouldn't drink like that."

This time she got his attention. He shoved the money in her direction and growled, "Do you think your boss would enjoy hearing that? He doesn't seem too pleased with you as it is. Be smart. Take your tip and disappear."

Well, he couldn't be too drunk if he'd noticed the by-play with Don. Chris looked down at the money, then turned and walked away. By the time she reached the bar she was regretting leaving the money. What was she, stupid? And what did she care if this guy got drunk? As long as he kept his hands off her she didn't care if he drank the joint dry.

With a shrug she pushed the lost money from her mind. Instead, she turned her thoughts to school. The session had just begun and she looked forward to a fairly easy summer. She had only two classes; she might even have time to find another job. Feeling cheered by this ray of hope, she exchanged a quip with Joe behind the bar. Joe nearly matched Henry for size, but he was far more outgoing and delighted in making the hostesses laugh with his off-color brand of humor. He particularly liked to tease Chris because, he told her, the sight of a blush was so unique. Tonight, however, she was too wrapped up in her own reflections to produce the desired effect. She hardly even heard him, smiling and nodding without really listening before lifting her tray and moving on.

She passed from table to table, pausing to chat with the regulars, though only half-attending to what was said. She studiously avoided the corner table, but all her attempts to avoid thinking of the man there were to no avail. Again and again he intruded on her thoughts. He really wasn't like the usual clientele. The Scarlet Lady normally drew middle-class, blue collar workers from the surrounding south L.A. neighborhood. Occasionally college students from one of the universities dotted throughout the area would wander in, but they generally gravitated toward

14

more upbeat bars with dance floors and live bands. This particular customer didn't fit into either category. Eventually she yielded to the temptation to stop by his table.

Her eyes rounded as she noted the near empty fifth and the puddle standing beside it. She strove to keep her voice neutral as she inquired, "Is everything okay?"

Even white teeth gleamed as he smiled. It was a boyish grin, charmingly crooked, and despite her dislike of drunks Chris responded warmly to it.

"It is now," he answered with a slight slur that brought a crease to her brow.

She leaned forward. "Would you like me to call you a cab?"

"Nope. I have a car . . . and I'm not ready to leave," he replied, still grinning.

She shook her head and leaned closer still, intending to restate her offer. The words stuck in her throat. This close she could see the intensity of his snapping dark eyes, the satanic effect of his heavy black brows. They tilted oddly at the outer ends and emphasized the force of those eyes. Though clouded by drink, his gaze still had the power to hold her speechless. They were eyes she felt she could drown in.

"Wanna drink?" he asked, bringing her to her senses.

She straightened and regathered her breath. "I'm sorry, but I can't, not on the job. How about that cab? I'd be happy to call one to take you home. You really shouldn't drive."

His smile vanished. He reached for the whiskey bottle and examined it solemnly. He tipped it back and forth, watching the dark liquid swish against the sides. "I'm not going home," he stated decisively.

Chris opened her mouth to dissuade him from finishing the whiskey, when she was interrupted by a strident shout. "Hey! You! We want some attention!"

She glanced over her shoulder at the next table. The groper and his friends held empty beer mugs high. She

15

hesitated, then sighed and moved to serve them while mentally resolving not to let her mystery man drive home. "Another round?" she asked automatically as she glided past the trio.

An arm shot out, coming down like a roadblock in front of her. Startled, Chris gazed down into the pinched features of the groper. "We'd like a little personal attention," he jeered. "Like you give your boyfriend over there," he added with a jerk of his head toward the corner.

Having learned quickly that calm was the only weapon to use with an angry drunk, she tamped down her rising temper. "Let me get your beer," she said evenly.

"After we get some attention," he insisted. Before Chris realized his intent, he hooked his arm around her hip, digging his fingers into the soft flesh of her buttocks, and yanked her forward. The action took her by surprise. The tray in her hand was jolted, knocking over two glasses and spilling the residue of liquor down her bodice.

"Damn! Will you—" was as far as she got. With a fluidity that amazed her, the corner customer was beside her. He slid the tray from her grasp and thunked it to the table as he shoved her aside. She didn't have time to protest before the crunching sound of his fist whacking the groper's jaw reverberated through the bar. The groper toppled backward, his chair crashing with him. Voices instantly stilled, eyes riveted on the scuffle. The Muzak blared on.

Chairs scraped back as the downed man's two friends jumped up. Chris didn't stop to think, she just reacted to the sight of two ganging up on one. She grabbed her tray, tossing glasses and mugs to the floor with a splintering crash, and swung forcefully at the nearest foe's back. Her arms quivered with the impact. He spun around, swearing, his balding head agleam in the reddish haze. She aimed a second blow at him, but he ducked and her tray whooshed through empty air. A thwack echoed behind her. She whirled to see the other attacker stagger back-

16

ward. From the corner of her eye she glimpsed the cocky grin of her defender, then caught sight of the groper rising to his feet, preparing to pounce.

"Look out!" she shouted.

The man wheeled, fists raised. In the same instant a blur of red frills launched into view. Henry clamped his arms around one combatant. Joe locked the other within an equally constrictive body hold. Don swept the tray from Christine's upraised hands. The fight was over.

"Throw 'em out," ordered Don curtly. He jerked his thumbs at the one who stood sullenly rubbing his jaw. "Get out. Take your buddy with you."

A slow hum began, then built among the patrons as the brawlers shuffled out. The clink of glasses rose over the steadily swelling voices. Don glanced around, assessing the mood while surveying the damage. Apparently satisfied that all would be well, he finally turned to Chris. "What the hell was all this?"

She didn't hear him. She watched Henry and Joe hustle the two fighters down the narrow entryway toward the door. The fight would be continued outside and it wouldn't be fair, not three against one. Without casting so much as a glance at Don, Chris hastened after the exiting men. She halted Henry at the doorway, grabbing his elbow and pulling.

"Wait, Henry, if you throw him out now, he'll get clobbered. Even if those apes don't hang around to continue the fight, he's in no condition to drive home. Let me call him a cab. I'll send him off in ten minutes."

"I don't want a cab," he put in, speaking too carefully.

Chris ignored him. "Don't throw him out, Henry, please. I'll make sure he doesn't cause any more trouble."

Henry glanced once toward the interior of the bar and once toward the door. Then he shrugged his massive shoulders, released his prisoner, and ambled back to the counter. Joe reentered and shot them a quizzical look but continued on back to the bar.

17

"Let me get you a cab," said Chris. "You really aren't in any shape to drive home."

"I'm not going home," he said, sounding stubborn, petulant.

"Well, wherever. You just shouldn't be driving."

"You drive me," he suggested.

He took a step, missed, and rolled forward, pressing her against the wall. His body was warm and damp from exertion. His breath was moist and acrid from stale whiskey. Beneath the gray suit, his physique was hard, solid, overpowering. Chris searched for her missing breath, found it, and managed, "I can't. I'm working."

He swayed slightly, then stepped back. Her relief died stillborn. His gaze fixed on the stain spread over the front of her red leotard. Her heart began to thump painfully as he extended a fingertip. He traced the outline of the dampness, following the jagged rim over the curve of her breast, down the underside, back up and around. It was not as the other had fingered her, not crude and ugly with suggestion. His touch was lighter than the shadows flicking over her, lighter than the liquor sticking to her skin through the slick material. Not once did she consider knocking his hand away.

"That bastard. Look what he did to you," he muttered. Then with a harsh growl, he spun toward the door. "I'm going to teach him—"

Chris threw herself against him, clasping his arm as tightly as she could. "Wait! Please! I can't allow you to fight for me, for this." She glanced down at her wet bodice, then up at him. A discernible flash of desire flared in his eyes and she dropped his arm as if he'd suddenly burst into flame. "I'll go call that cab," she said as steadily as she could. She moved to the pay phone hanging on the wall and began dialing.

"I'll pay you to drive me," he said, coming up beside her.

She stopped dialing and held the receiver in mid-air. She

18

narrowed her eyes against the smoke to scrutinize his features in the dim light. "You'll what?"

"Here," he said, shoving his hand into the pocket of his gray slacks. He drew out a fat roll of bills and peeled off five, then thrust them at her. "Take this. I'll pay gas too."

Chris stared at the bills. They were hundreds. Five of them. She hung up the receiver and took them. Even in the poor light she could see the wad of money he was stuffing back into his pocket. What was he—a bank robber? If so, he was a robber with good taste. Those slacks and that perfectly tailored jacket had the unmistakable stamp of quality. She suspected the white-on-white shirt was silk and knew without doubt that the tie dangling untidily from a pocket was.

"I—" Chris licked her lower lip, not noticing the waxy taste of her lipstick. "Where?"

"Hell, I don't know. I don't care. Anywhere."

She sighed. Her brief surge of excitement ebbed. Of course it was too good to be true. He was in no condition to think rationally. She again·reached for the phone. His hand settled over hers, holding it still. The heat of his hand traveled through her skin to the pit of her stomach. She yanked her hand from beneath the warmth of his.

"I can't go home," he persisted peevishly. Suddenly he smiled, blinding Chris to the unreality of the situation. "Vegas. You could take me to Vegas."

The temptation was great. She studied the roll of bills in her hand, hesitating. She threw up her chin and eyed him directly. "Just drive? Nothing . . . more?"

"Just drive."

Her fist clenched over the money. She couldn't accept it, she knew that. After all, she knew nothing about this man or where the money had come from. Licking her lip again, Chris decided to be sensible and refuse.

"What the hell are you doing?" demanded Don, stamping up behind her. His jowls were bunched in anger and his swarthy face stained even darker than usual. "What d'ya think you're doing? Get back to work."

She very slowly turned to face him, watching the color suffuse his face. Five hundred dollars was more than two weeks net for her, tips included. It was stupid, insane, utterly ridiculous. And yet . . . Surely she could find a decent enough job in two weeks.

"You! I thought you were outta here. That damned Henry, why'd he—" Don was saying. He broke off as he realized Chris hadn't moved. He shook his pudgy fist at her. "Damn it, Tina, get back to work!"

Like a kaleidoscope falling into place, everything cleared for her at the sound of his growled order. "My name is not Tina," said Chris through her teeth. Tossing a directive not to move to the stranger, she strode to the hallway behind the bar, past the storeroom and Don's office to the small concrete cell with metal lockers where the hostesses left their personal items while at work. Don followed her, yelling with each step. "You're not goin' nowhere. You can't just walk out on me! What d'ya think you're doing?"

She didn't respond. She threw open a locker and pulled out a pair of jeans. Don stood, calling her a string of names, so she simply drew them on over her stockinged legs and threw her pale lilac cotton top over her drying leotard. The roll of bills, her jogging shoes, and two text-books were jammed haphazardly into the leather tote she called a purse. Finally she broke into Don's vitriolic con-demnation. "You want to know what I'm doing? I'm quitting, that's what. Take off for the broken glassware, then send what's owed me to my home address."

He followed her back to the foyer, his short stubby legs angrily matching her longer strides. She ignored his sput-tering threats and took hold of the stranger's sleeve. He grinned happily as she shoved him out the door. It swung shut on Don's last adjuration that she go to hell.

A feeling of victorious freedom exploded within her.

Chris felt like tap-dancing with joy to be free of The Scarlet Lady. She paused beneath the light that flooded the entrance to search the ink of night for the trio who'd caused her such trouble all evening long. She didn't see anything and turned to ask her companion if he did. Not a sound came from her suddenly constricted throat.

The soft corona of light haloed the thick blackness of his hair with a silvery sheen. Even somewhat glazed, his sloe eyes were darkly captivating. Though a bit broad, his nose was long and straight, defining that handsome face into two perfect halves. Now that he no longer held his mouth tightly, she could see his lips were sensually full, as if he'd just been thoroughly kissed. Chris pulled herself up short. To be thinking such unreasonable things disturbed her. She didn't know what it was about him—perhaps it was that odd upward slant of his dark brows, or the square strength of his jawline, or that passionate promise in the curve of his mouth—but whatever it was, it was having an effect on her she hadn't expected.

She hurriedly stepped from the puddle of light into the dark lake of the parking lot. Her car was behind the building, a battered old Maverick that ran mostly on spit and good faith. "Is your car locked up?" she inquired as she unlocked the passenger door. He shrugged and sprawled onto the torn vinyl seat.

Well, if he didn't care, she surely wouldn't. She got in on the driver's side and felt her brief elation vanish. My God, what was she doing? This guy could be a rapist, a murderer, an escaped convict. Streetlights licked eerily at shadowed pavement as she drove through the seedy neighborhood, her apprehension heightening. She cast several sidelong glances at him. He was hunched in the corner, arms folded over his chest and eyes closed, apparently asleep, but still her alarm grew. She castigated herself for being so trustingly naïve. She couldn't believe that it was she, calm, cautious Christine Casolaro, who had taken off

21

with a complete stranger. She must have been temporarily mad!

Turning into the nearest gas station, she parked and faced him. She extended her hand and gingerly tapped his shoulder, snatching her hand back as he abruptly sat up. "I'll be happy to take you home," she timidly offered.

"I told you, I'm not going home." He looked out the windshield, presenting her with a severe profile. The station lights spilled over his features, highlighting the unhappy grooves beside his set mouth.

"Well—uh—if you're serious about going to Las Vegas—"

"I am."

"I'll have to call my sister and let her know why I won't be home tonight." There. If he had any nefarious intentions, that should warn him off.

He slowly turned his head toward her. Her breath caught. An unexpected longing to wrap him in her arms and soothe away his hurt shook her. He looked patently unhappy. "I'll be right back," she whispered hoarsely and got out.

Using the pay phone on the outside of the station, Chris called her older sister. As she'd expected, Theresa didn't accept her explanation of driving to Vegas on a whim and after several fruitless minutes of arguing, Chris broke down and told her sister the truth. Theresa's screech could be heard over the rock 'n' roll buzz of the attendant's radio.

"You're doing what? Chris, for the love of Mary, be reasonable! What do you know about this man?"

"Nothing," she admitted, then added quickly, "except that he's very unhappy, in no condition to drive himself, and determined not to go home."

"Huh! It sounds to me like you've got a runaway husband on your hands," stated Theresa coldly, and Chris could visualize the agitated tapping of her foot and the annoyed sweep of a hand through her short black hair.

"Unhappy or not, you don't want to get between a man and his wife."

The notion of a wife in the background depressed her. Chris knew she was being totally ridiculous and spoke more forcefully than she'd intended. "He's not wearing a ring!"

"So? Does every married man wear one? I can't believe you walked out on your job with a man you know nothing about!"

Embarrassed that she'd admitted noticing whether he wore a ring or not, resentful that Theresa would raise objections she herself wanted to ignore, distressed over the clear note of concern in her sister's protests, Chris mumbled, "Well, I can't just leave him here."

"Oh, Chris, this isn't like you at all! You're usually so level-headed . . ." When Chris let the pause drag out, Theresa's heavy sigh huffed through the earpiece. "I'm sure you're making a mistake, but if you feel you must take care of this stranger—who could be a murderer or worse —for God's sake bring him home."

"Tony would just love that," said Chris with heavy sarcasm. Her brother-in-law accepted having Chris live with them only because the money she paid for room and board was needed. He had made it perfectly clear in the past that he wouldn't tolerate her having men over; he disapproved of her as it was. In Tony's view, any woman of twenty-six who was still unmarried couldn't possibly be "good."

She managed to calm Theresa, who muttered that she'd known all along she couldn't shake Christine from a decision, however stupid that decision might be. With a promise to call her from Vegas, Chris hung up, feeling further deflated. Perhaps she should give up her classes at Santa Monica Junior College for a semester or two and take a full time job that paid enough for her to move out. When Theresa had the next baby their small house was going to be overcrowded even without Chris there.

23

Getting back into the car, she pulled up to one of the pumps, got back out, and settled the hose into her tank. What was she doing? Theresa was right—she wasn't the type to give into impulses like this. Usually she was sensible almost to the point of *un*common sense. She was the type who never got into her car without first checking the back seat, who never went shopping without a complete list in hand, who never started a meal until all the necessary ingredients had been set neatly out. Growing up in one of the poorest sections of L.A., Chris had learned early on that if she wanted to survive, she had to be both prudent and pragmatic. She had learned to stretch one dollar into two, to get through a day with hunger roiling in her stomach, to sidestep any situation she couldn't control. Her background had taught her to be conservative and cautious, but it was also an inherent part of her nature to plan ahead, to examine, reflect, and analyze before proceeding with any course of action. Usually she did just that. Usually.

So what had happened to her tonight?

Chris doggedly refused to glance toward the front of the car as she flicked the hose out and turned off the pump. She just as doggedly refused to delve into the motivations behind her uncharacteristically impulsive actions. Her conversation with her sister had only reinforced her own doubts and yet, strangely enough, had stiffened her resolve to go ahead and drive the stranger to Las Vegas. The five hundred would be essential now, anyway, since she no longer had a job. She told herself it was the money, and not any interest in the man, that led her to purchase a map and check the highways to Vegas.

When she got into the car again she paused before turning on the ignition. "Perhaps you should call your wife and explain that you won't be home tonight," she said cautiously.

He still slouched in the seat with his eyes closed. He didn't stir, but told her, "I don't have a wife."

The wave of relief that flooded Chris was completely unwarranted. He wasn't married. She knew it shouldn't make a jot of difference to her, yet she couldn't repress the smile that touched her lips at his reply. He didn't have a wife. But why . . . ? She voiced her thought. "Why don't you want to go home?"

"I'm running away," he replied seriously. Then he flashed that grin that had dazzled her back at The Scarlet Lady. "I'm running away from home," he repeated. He laughed.

It was a deep rumble of bitter mockery that shivered along her skin. All the unhappiness she'd thought she'd seen earlier was evident in that laugh. She waited for an explanation that obviously wasn't going to come. At last she held out her hand. "If we're going to Vegas together, I might as well introduce myself. Chris Casolaro."

He took her hand, engulfing it in the smooth warmth of his. He looked beyond her shoulder, staring into the night. "I'm P-Paul," he drawled slowly. "Paul . . . Richards."

"Okay, Paul. If you're sure there's no one you'd like to call . . ." He shook his head and she started the ignition. Turning toward Harbor Freeway, she announced determinedly, "Las Vegas, here we come!"

CHAPTER TWO

Preston responded reluctantly to wakefulness. He rolled over, trying to disregard the sensation that the bed was spinning. Shifting, however, was a mistake. It called attention to the throbbing in his head. As he realized some mighty Thor was wielding a sledgehammer on the anvil of his head, Preston also realized he couldn't tolerate the taste of his own mouth. He plunged further into the stiffness of his pillow. It was as he wondered at the peculiarity of a stiff feather pillow that he heard the sounds of a shower running nearby. He opened his eyes.

Where the hell was he? The square room with white walls and cheaply veneered furniture could only be a hotel room. Why did they invariably decorate in crab-apple green? He shut his eyes again. Who was in the shower? A woman? He didn't remember. . . .

For several minutes he simply lay, nursing the pain in his head, the unpleasant pungency of his mouth, the odd soreness of his right-hand knuckles. Slowly, creaking like ungreased wheels, his mind began to probe. The one thing he wanted to forget was the one thing he clearly remembered.

The family conference.

Gathered like vultures to pick the flesh from his bones. If his stomach hadn't been heaving already, the memory would have been enough to turn it. His battering head resounded with the echo of his mother's cool, precise voice.

"Preston, darling," she had said, only slightly marring her alabaster brow with a frown, "you surely must understand that we need to present a united front."

A sense of helpless frustration had gripped him; he braced his shoulder against the stripes of the Queen Anne chair and forced himself to reply calmly. "I'm not trying to secede from the family, Mother. I just want to leave the business, find something of my own to do."

"Do? Do what? You've already admitted you don't know what you want," humphed his father. Jack Ridgeway never simply spoke. He huffed, he barked, he growled, and occasionally he even exhaled a hearty puff of pleasure, but he did not speak in the manner of lesser mortals. Now he aimed an admonishing finger at his youngest son and bellowed, "Damn it, Preston, whether you want to or not, you're going to have to start thinking of the family, of the name you bear, and the influence it carries."

Start thinking of the family? Preston wanted to laugh aloud. He'd thought of little else all his life. How could he possibly forget he was a Ridgeway? He wished to God he could. He let his eyes slide around the room, hating every inch of the inhuman formality. The stiff chairs, the elegant curved-leg cherrywood tables, the carefully selected porcelains set at artful angles atop them. It wasn't so much a room as a stage, a stage set for the actors surrounding him. He brought his gaze back to his father and said with impatience, "All I'm saying is I'd like to find my own way. What I do—or don't do—for Ridgeco doesn't have any real purpose—"

"Purpose!" interrupted his father in an explosive boom. He bounded back and forth behind the pearlescent satin sofa on which Felicia Ridgeway posed, his fists pounding the air as if striking his imposing desk in the boardroom

27

of Ridgeco Oil. "Do you think being a vice-president for Ridgeco is *nothing?*"

"We're only," put in Sterling smoothly, "asking you to keep the status quo for a few months, Preston. Once the election's over you can go your own way, if that's what you really want. Though, of course, we'd be pleased if you decided to continue in the company."

He'd spoken with perfect calm. Self-control was Sterling's strong suit. It made a perfect foil to his father's blustering temper and strengthened their position when manipulating in the worlds of oil, finance, and shipping. He leaned forward, employing his most soothing tone. "We're building the campaign around the issue of stability in government. Naturally we need to maintain stability in the family for the duration of the campaign."

Felicia meticulously smoothed the folds of her silk dress and said meaningfully, "For which reason we simply cannot accept any further public displays of your . . . social activities. Do think, darling, of the consequences to Gerard's campaign."

His earlier sense of helplessness now overwhelmed him. Preston knew it wasn't the unsuitability of the actress that disturbed them. It was the garish glare of publicity that had accompanied his rendezvous with her that raised their objections. He had agreed to be more discreet, then had offered to leave the company. They'd acted as if he'd offered to stop breathing.

He felt as if he were uselessly whacking his head into a wall. No matter what he said, he knew they wouldn't listen. They simply could not understand his need to be something more than a mere extension of the Ridgeway empire. He didn't fit in; he never had. His frustration with his inability to make them comprehend his needs came out in a cynical drawl. "Surely you don't need to bother yourselves with what I do, Mother. If all else fails, you can always buy Gerard his congressional seat."

"Preston! My God, how can you say such a thing?" Gerard gasped.

Glancing at his brother's face, Preston realized Gerard was truly shocked. His father suddenly roared that he'd better shape up, by God! His sister Angela disparagingly murmured something about such behavior ranking in the sphere of nursery rooms and Preston gave up trying to follow anything else they said. He'd heard it all before a hundred times, a thousand times.

His earliest memory was of being told to "act like a Ridgeway." And he had tried, God knows he'd tried. He'd gone to all the right schools, joined all the right clubs, dated all the right women, had even dutifully taken up his position in the company founded by his grandfather and great-uncle. His father, now nearing seventy, but still energetically active, had extended the family holdings from oil to shipping to banking and widespread subsidiaries that even included a chain of fast-stop shops. His eldest brother, Sterling, was a perfect successor to the throne of this kingdom. Gerard, too, fit in as the handsome prince, reaching into the political arena and thus spreading the family influence ever further. Princess Angela had added consequence by marrying Old World blue blood, never mind that her husband was a dull, dry stick fifteen years her elder.

Only he didn't belong. Only he wanted something more than to be a Ridgeway. The problem was, thought Preston with a wave of despair, he didn't know what the hell that something could be.

They conversed around him, as if he weren't there, which in a way, he wasn't. Abruptly he jerked to his feet. He had to get away from them before he lost the last of his temper and said things he didn't really mean. Snowy piles of carpeting cushioned his stride; it was several seconds before they even realized he was leaving.

"Where are you going? We're not through!" barked Jack.

Preston stood at the door, his hand clenching the knob as he slowly turned to face his father. "Aren't we? You told me to be more discreet and I told you I wanted to leave the company. I'd say that about covers it all."

Before his red-faced father could explode, his mother rose and said in her crystalline voice, "We'll leave the matter now, darling, for you to think over. Come have coffee with us tomorrow morning at ten, and we'll settle everything then."

Glancing from the rigid figure of his still handsome father to the regal bearing of his undeniably beautiful mother, Preston felt an oppressive weight settle over him. "Oh, hell, what's the use?" he muttered, pivoting.

He pulled the door closed behind him with a force enough to rattle the chandelier in the foyer. He crossed the marbled floor in three short strides, but was denied the satisfaction of slamming yet another door as it was held silently open for him by one of his parents' expressionless servants. What he'd wanted more than anything then was escape. Escape from thought.

Well, it appeared he'd gotten it.

Preston rolled to his other side. What was this damn pillow made of—cardboard? He punched it fiercely, then winced at the pain in his hand. He forced open his blurry eyes to examine his knuckles. They were bruised and slightly scraped. A fight. When did he get into a fight?

Staring at the lime green shag carpet, he willed it to cease undulating, then concentrated on where he'd gone after storming out of his parents' palatial Stone Canyon home. He'd thought about going to the club and getting politely inebriated, but instead drove aimlessly around, feeding the flames of his angry resentment. He remembered finding himself in the south end of the city, stopping at a godawful working-class bar, getting decisively blank. Preston rubbed a hand over his eyes.

There had been a barmaid with a pert little bottom in a tight red leotard.

The water was cut off. He heard a soft humming. He must have done well enough last night. Too bad he couldn't remember it. He closed his eyes and drifted drowsily, hoping to go back to sleep.

When he heard the bathroom door open, however, his curiosity overcame his desire to sleep. What did she look like, this hostess with the terrific—if he remembered correctly—curves? He raised his lids slightly and peered at her from beneath his long lashes. What he saw disappointed him.

Instead of the sexy, smoldering woman of the world he'd half-recalled, half-imagined, Preston saw a pleasant, but unremarkable young woman. Her hair was a short, wet clump of ordinary brown that hung raggedly over her ears. She stood before the mirror, fluffing it with her fingers, and he studied her reflection, mentally ticking off her defects. Her eyebrows were dark and thick and much too straight. Her eyes were nicely shaped, but nothing exceptional. He had a sinking feeling the color, too, would be common. Her nose was short and snubbed; her lips well shaped and enticingly full, but she'd done nothing to play them up. Her skin was neither fair nor tanned, but an indistinct in-between shade. Perhaps, he thought doubtfully, when she wore makeup, she'd look more appealing.

He lowered his gaze to her figure. What had seemed so terrific in a clinging leotard looked nice enough in blue jeans and lilac cotton top, but he saw nothing that would make him leap tall buildings. Maybe this wasn't the barmaid he'd admired after all. She whirled suddenly, catching him off-guard.

"Good morning," she said in a cheery voice. A sprightly smile enlivened the unexceptional face, imbuing her with a spirited sort of beauty. "Well, actually, it's afternoon, but the wish is the same."

He frowned. This certainly could not be the waitress from the bar. His taste had never run to impish pixies.

As his silence expanded, her smile faded. She gazed at him, then jerked her head in a brisk, conclusive nod. Turning back to the dresser, she picked up a voluminous bag of scruffed leather and shuffled through it, scattering combs, keys, and papers over the dresser's blond veneer top. Exclaiming triumphantly, she darted into the bathroom and returned with a glass of water.

"Here," she said, extending her hand to offer two tablets. "It's the best I can do, but it should help."

He struggled upright. The sheet fell to his waist and exposed his naked chest. He ran his hands through his hair, unconsciously flexing his muscles as he strove to orient himself. Finally he accepted the tablets from her hand and obediently swallowed. "Thanks for the aspirin," he said as he handed the glass back to her.

"Oh, I didn't have any aspirin. That was Pamprin." As he choked, she patted his back and said soothingly, "I'm sure it's better than nothing. It's supposed to relieve headaches as well as cramps, you know. I'll go get you some aspirin later."

He shoved her hand away and glared at her. Usually when he glared at someone they backed away. He knew the combination of his slanted eyebrows and his dark eyes made him look formidable. This woman, however, merely smiled and suggested that he make use of the bathroom while she go hunt up some coffee. She grabbed the leather bag, haphazardly stuffing the spilled articles back in, and headed for the door.

"Wait a minute," he said, forestalling her departure. "Who are you? Where are we? Are we anywhere near that bar?"

He'd read about faces crumpling, but he'd never before actually seen it happen. Her elfin face simply fell. She walked back toward the bed, then slid in one fluid motion to sit cross-legged on the floor. For several seconds she simply stared up at him, her face blank, her eyes searching his.

"You don't remember," she finally said in a flat tone.

A surprising desire to restore the animation to her voice came over him. He wanted to see once more the lively smile on her lips. Preston immediately decided it was worth a lie. "Of course I remember it, baby. You were great, really great. The best. It's just—" he broke off at the expressions crossing her face. First puzzlement, then disbelief, and lastly amusement. To his surprise, she began laughing. His gut reaction of anger couldn't be maintained in the force of her laughter. It sounded like the Christmas chimes he remembered from childhood—merry and tinkling and impossible to dislike.

"The best!" she gasped before ringing another chortling peal. "The best!"

Preston ruffled his already thoroughly disheveled hair with both hands. Gales of hysterical laughter was not the reaction he expected from a woman on the morning after. Annoyance began to return and he said roughly, "So I was wrong. You weren't the best."

Instead of looking offended, she shook her head, the drying curls flying in all directions. He glimpsed the flat glint of gold studding her ears and struggled to pull his sluggish mind away from the hypnotic gleam. What the hell was going on?

"I wasn't even g-g-good! I wasn't anything, not anything at all," she huffed on the tapering end of her laughter.

Comprehension forced its way past the battering ram walloping his head. "You didn't—we didn't—nothing happened," he muttered in a half-question.

"Nothing at all," she confirmed with another forceful shake of her short curls. She expelled a last giggle, caught his eye, and went on firmly. "I checked us into a single room only because it was cheaper. Even if that had been part of our bargain—which it most definitely was not—

33

you were too far gone to do anything. You passed out the instant I dumped you on the bed."

"Bargain?" God, his head was in no condition for this.

She sighed, then hauled her massive purse onto her lap and took out her billfold. "I knew it was too good to be true." She started to hand him a wad of bills, then paused and put one back into her purse. "For gas and my time. I deserve it," she said with a defiant tilt to her head.

He didn't take the money she was pushing toward him. "Look, I don't understand what you're talking about. I've got a pounding headache and I can't stand my own mouth. Why don't you go get that coffee while I clean up?"

Her thick eyebrows came together as she frowned. It didn't become her and Preston felt his irritation rising. She abruptly stood, laid the roll of bills on the nightstand, and left without a word. He wondered if she'd come back. Well, the hell with her if she didn't.

A quick hot shower cleared some of the mist from his brain. Bits and pieces of the evening before came together. The smoky, red-lit bar, the satisfying release of his anger in the swing of his fists. He had a vague image of an old, dark car, nothing like his sleek, canary yellow Lamborghini. He stepped from the shower hoping his hand-built Italian sports car hadn't been stolen or stripped down in that seedy south L.A. neighborhood.

Though unshaven, he felt nonetheless fresher and more able to deal with the confused whirl in which he'd awakened. As he donned his wrinkled slacks and shirt, he checked all the pockets and his wallet. So far as he could tell, nothing had been touched. She apparently wasn't a gold digger. He glanced at the money on the nightstand. If he hadn't paid for her body, what had he purchased from her? Would he ever find out? Would she return or not?

Should she return or not?

34

Chris stood before the vending machine in the lobby and pondered the situation she'd gotten herself into. *He* had the excuse of having been drunk. She had no excuse at all. He'd offered her a chance to escape and she'd grabbed it, without considering all the ramifications. Not once during the long night driving across the desert had she questioned the wisdom of her impulse. While he slept, hunched against a rip in the vinyl seat, she'd spent the hours planning her job-hunting campaign. Mile after mile had passed in pleasant fantasies of a new job, a new apartment, a new start in life. Even the shimmer of dawn greeting her when she'd stopped at the outer fringes of Las Vegas hadn't wakened her from such satisfying visions.

To discover that he hadn't meant to go to Vegas after all had brought her to reality with a crash.

In the prickly glare of the afternoon sun, Chris saw the grime sticking to the vending machine, saw the paint blistering away from the shabby motel and, with unwanted clarity, saw just how dilapidated her dreams were. Her visions of a brighter life were so well-worn they made this cheap, shoddy motel shine like a rainbow.

She clenched her fists, digging her nails into her palms. She must have been demented to have believed she could make a new beginning with five hundred bucks and a drive to Las Vegas. Listening to a drunk, of all things! What had she done, inhaled the alcohol fumes at the bar?

For one instant real anger surged through her. At herself for forgetting her cardinal rule never to get involved with a customer; at him, for disguising just how drunk he really was, for mesmerizing her with the dazzle of his smile and the desolation in his eyes. And like all drunks, this one hadn't meant a word he'd said. Perhaps he hadn't meant anything else he'd said either. Perhaps he was married after all.

That thought settled over her like a thick, chill fog. She refused to consider the notion that she'd actually gone along with this insane scheme because of the man and not

35

his money. But she remembered the shapely breadth of his shoulders and the soft curling mat of hair over his bared chest. She remembered how when she'd undressed him at dawn her hands had trembled. It had been a long time since a man had made her quiver like that.

She shook the image away. There was little sense in such visions. Even if he weren't married, Paul Richards was way out of Christine Casolaro's class. Chalk the night up to moonlight madness and let it go at that. The least she could do now was take the poor guy some coffee and tell him what he was doing in Vegas. She slid two coins into the slot, punched the proper selection, and returned to their room with two containers of coffee.

"I can't vouch for how decent this is going to be," she said as she entered. "Vending machine coffee is usually awful."

She was right. It was awful. But it gave them something to do while warily studying each other, something to cling to in the awkward constraint swirling around them. With an out-of-body feeling, Chris saw the humor in the situation and sympathized with Paul. Waking up in a strange motel with an unknown woman must be an unsettling experience even for the most hardened cynic. But her own emotions were no less disconcerting. Along with her amusement and sympathy she felt disappointed and distressed. She wanted nothing more than to get out of this ridiculous farce.

"Well, Paul," she sighed, "I guess you're as ready as you'll ever be to find out that you're not in L.A."

His brows slanted higher. Paul? It appeared he'd retained some sense last night. How could he find out what else he'd told her without revealing anything?

She took his reflective expression to be a question and continued. "You said you'd pay me five hundred dollars to drive you to Las Vegas. So here we are."

"Vegas?" He sounded stunned. He was. Oh, my God, had he *married* her? The last thing in the world he wanted

36

or needed was a wife. He had more than enough people ready to nag at him. But Vegas—why else would they come here? He dimly heard the barmaid speak and finally looked at her. Even the tip of her nose seemed to turn down in contrition.

"I am sorry," she repeated. "I should have known. You weren't in any condition—"

He cut into her stream of apologies. "Why Vegas?"

The hazel eyes he'd decided were common suddenly sparked with indefinable emotion. "I don't know. You said you were running away from home. My sister thought that meant you were running away from a wife, but you said you didn't have one."

Chris held her breath, releasing it slowly when he nodded. Reminding herself that it made no difference to her did little good. She felt absurdly relieved. She bent her head, hoping he hadn't read her reaction.

Preston saw the slight flush rise over her tawny skin and knew relief. They hadn't gotten married. Then what? A quickening of interest overcame his misgivings. "And you're . . . ?"

"Chris Casolaro. I work—worked—at The Scarlet Lady."

"Did you lose your job?"

That impish smile danced over her lips. "I didn't lose it. I threw it away. Walked right out on your arm."

"I'm sorry—"

"Don't be. I hated it." She shrugged. The loss of her job was the one thing about this mess Chris didn't regret. A little sigh escaped her lips. "I doubt if I'd have lasted there much longer. I guess that's why I agreed to drive you in the first place. I wanted out of The Scarlet Lady and there you were, waving your wad of money and offering it to me."

He empathized with her need for liberation. He wanted out too. But he didn't have her freedom; he couldn't throw his job away. Not unless the family went out with it. Did

37

she realize how fortunate she was? She could have left at any time.

"If you hated it," he asked after a moment, "why did you work there at all?"

She stared solemnly into the greasy swirls, then set her coffee aside. A slight resentment pricked her. She heard the unspoken message behind his query and forgot how unhappy she'd thought him. He'd obviously never had to do anything unpleasant in his life. Any feelings she'd had for him faded. She spoke with impatience. "There wasn't a lot of choice. Jobs are scarce and though Rosta paid minimum, the tips were good. By working nights I could take classes at Santa Monica during the day."

He sipped the muddy coffee, showing none of his mounting dismay. What had he done? If they'd thought him irresponsible before, it was nothing to what they'd think now. Running away with a college student! He imagined the shaking of heads, the resigned sighs when he'd failed to appear at his parents' this morning, and knew with a leaden regret that he'd have to go back and face their censure. Worse, that he'd have to go back to the pointless job, the empty social rounds.

Realizing she was staring at him, waiting for him to say something, he asked the first question that came into his aching head. "What name did you register us under?"

"Mr. and Mrs. Richards," she said slowly.

His brows rose, then fell. Registered as man and wife. But according to her they hadn't done anything. He slid his eyes over the curves discernible beneath the cotton and denim. At least, not yet.

Chris easily read the message passing through his assessing eyes. It was a message that disturbed her more than she cared to admit. Her gaze dropped, halting at the gold watch snugly circling her wrist. It was well past midday, well past time for her to leave. She slung her leather bag over her shoulder, dwarfing her curves with its gargantuan bulk. "Well, I'm going to head back to L.A.

You're more than welcome to come with me," she offered, certain he'd refuse. He was, after all, no longer drunk.

Her words flew meaninglessly past him. He gazed blankly at the portable television bolted onto a shelf. He was in Las Vegas. No, not he. *Paul Richards* was in Vegas. Paul Richards. He liked the sound of it. He liked the thought of it. He liked being Paul Richards. A feeling of freedom lapped slowly within him, spreading in wavelets, then crashing with tidal force at the same moment Chris said a quiet, "I guess this is good-bye," and took a step.

"Wait!" He wasn't about to let that freedom walk out the door. He dashed the coffee container into the waste-basket, then pulled out the most engaging smile he could muster. "I'm still at a bit of a loss. I admit I don't remember much about last night. Did anyone know we were coming here?"

She wavered by the doorway, suspicion in her eyes. Was he probing because he meant to do her harm? He saw her doubt and smiled harder. "What I told you last night was true. I am running away from home, but not because of a wife or anything that should cause your brows to clamp together like that."

The straight brows instantly unclamped. Thinking she needed to have her head examined, she went slowly back into the room. "The guys at the bar saw me leave with you but didn't know where we were going. I called my sister and told her, but I didn't know your name then, so she just knows I drove here with someone and intend to be home again tonight."

She tilted her head to the side and eyed him speculatively. There was an air of trust about her that led him to discard the lie that had been forming and tell her more of the truth than he'd ever intended.

"Yesterday I had an argument with my parents. Actually with my whole family. They tend to think I lack ambition, and I tend to resent their disapproval." He paused, not looking at her. He could feel the intensity of her gaze on him. Wondering why he was even telling her this, he continued, "I've got something of a temper and after listening to them dissect my work and social habits, I stormed out. I ended up drinking away my hostility."

So he was a hot-tempered playboy with disapproving parents. She supposed it was better than her earlier fear that he was a bank robber. *Poor little rich boy,* her mind mocked even while she felt drawn toward him.

"I didn't notice it disappearing as you drank," she said with mild sarcasm.

Sudden memory emerged with the image of another man's hand pawing the pert bottom he'd already mentally staked claim to. He smiled. "I'd have slid into pleasant oblivion if that jerk hadn't mauled you. That just stoked my resentment with the world."

"Not to mention your resentment with his face."

Her dry comment broadened his smile into a grin. "You should talk. You swing a mighty lethal tray, lady."

They laughed together, a tuneful blending that transformed strangers into friends. In a warm voice still ringing with amusement, Chris confessed. "For six months my dearest wish has been to smack one of those obnoxious louts with my tray, but I never dreamed I'd actually ever do it."

"Your gallant defense was much appreciated."

"As was yours, though it really wasn't necessary."

"No?" He sounded amused.

She let her smile linger, thinking how achingly handsome he was when he quirked his lips like that. How would that full mouth feel upon hers? She put a firm stop to such wayward thoughts. Shifting her tote, she glanced impatiently toward the door. "No. Where I grew up, you don't survive without learning how to take care of yourself. Look, I'll be happy to take you back to L.A. with me."

"I'm not going back to L.A."

She tried not to let her disappointment show as she

nodded and turned to leave. The thought that this was the last she'd ever see of Paul Richards left a thoroughly ridiculous void in the pit of her stomach.

"I don't want you to go either," he stated firmly to her retreating back. "I want you to stay with me."

Chris halted in her tracks. She slowly pivoted to see him eyeing her with a determined intent. His impression of her was clear, and fixed her somewhere between anger and disgust. Whatever she'd have done last night, in the clear light of day her response was clear. "Sorry, but flings like this"—she indicated the small, square room with a contemptuous wave of her hand—"really don't appeal to me."

"I'm not suggesting that. God, I need some decent coffee. Let's go somewhere where we can sit and talk."

"There is nothing to talk about," she said icily.

Her resistance piqued his ready temper; he flicked his eyes over her dismissively. "You're overrating your charms, lady. You can set your . . . maidenly . . . doubts to rest. I'm not asking you to go to bed with me, just talk to me over a cup of coffee."

Chris suspected she should fling out of the room, grandly slamming the door behind her, but her legs had stupidly turned to stone. She couldn't have moved if a three-alarm fire had blazed through the building.

He was in no mood to stand around debating with the barmaid. He needed that coffee. His head was throbbing incessantly. He pressed his fingers against his temple and rubbed. "Damn it all, I need some *good* coffee and some *real* aspirin."

She ignored the glare of irritation he sent her way. "I did the best I could under the circumstances. Even at that, it was more than you deserved."

His dark eyes snapped and his heavy brows drew together. "Do what you want. I'm going to find coffee I can drink." He strode past her, blatantly skirting the spot where she stood.

41

After a brief hesitation Chris started to follow him out. He stopped her. "Don't forget your money," he barked, sounding more like Jack Ridgeway than he cared to admit. Without looking back he strode down the narrow hallway toward the metal stairs leading to the parking lot.

She glanced back at the nightstand where the roll of bills still lay. She knew as she did so that this wasn't a man for her to get involved with. She knew as she did so that she should go directly to her car, get in, and drive back to Los Angeles without even stopping for gas.

The sharp clatter of his steps ringing on the stairs galvanized her. She dashed in, scooped the money into her purse, and raced back out behind him.

CHAPTER THREE

Within minutes they were seated on either side of a wobbling table the size of a postage stamp in the motel's dingy coffeeshop. Paul took no notice of Christine; his fingers tapped angrily on the Formica tabletop as his eyes searched impatiently for a waitress. When one at last appeared, he scalded her with a displeased frown. "Coffee now," he said imperatively. "Then we'll order."

The waitress cracked her gum and sauntered away. Paul looked thunderous. Chris suppressed a smile. This wasn't, she was certain, his usual treatment of a waitress. He didn't seem inclined to talk, so she silently read over the plastic menu and tried not to think about how stupid she had been for following him.

After five minutes Paul slapped his menu on the table. "What the hell is she doing, growing the beans?"

"Give the poor girl a break. You're not her only customer."

"All I asked for was a cup of coffee. What's so difficult about that?"

"You *demanded* coffee. You can't expect to be treated like a sheikh."

He opened his mouth, then shut it. Hadn't he said much the same thing countless times to his elder brothers? He wished his head would quit banging and, even more, he wished he hadn't snapped at Chris. He far preferred the

43

sprightly smile to the solemn disapproval. He was about to apologize when the waitress materialized with two steaming cups. Popping her gum, she held out her pad. "Whaddya want?"

Chris jumped in before he could bite the girl's head off, ordering a large glass of milk and a bowl of bananas in cream.

"That'll make you fat," he said.

Her head whipped up. Over the menu his dark eyes were twinkling. "Are you *teasing?*" she asked, her voice thick with incredulity.

"I don't know," he replied with a charmingly crooked smile. "With the state my head's in, it's hard to tell what's going on up there."

He was rewarded with the cheery smile. "I'll be kind and not say you deserved it."

"Oh, I admit I deserve it." He placed his order and as soon as the waitress withdrew on a resounding burst of bubble gum, he added, "And I admit I shouldn't take my aching head out on you. I'm sorry."

She hoped she covered her surprise. "No problem."

He sipped his coffee, then said casually, "Fill me in on last night."

"I thought I had," she retorted pertly.

"Remember you're dealing with someone who systematically destroyed countless brain cells last night," he said with a teasing smile that Chris was certain could easily have destroyed countless brain cells of hers.

"What do you want to know?" she asked.

"I can't make all the pieces fit. Like you. How did you end up in that bar?"

"I worked there."

"You're not the type. You said you hated it. I just can't understand why you took a job you hated."

Their brunch was delivered and for a few minutes they attended to the food. As she ate, Chris pondered what to tell him. Would he have a glimmer of comprehension what

44

her kind of life was like? She doubted it. Worse, she knew that when he didn't, she would feel absurdly let down. Yet she found herself shoving her bowl aside and blurting, "I told you. There aren't that many jobs that would allow me to go to school. I tried night school for a time, but that meant progressing at the rate of a single class, possibly two, a semester. I could see myself tottering up to get my degree at ninety-two and decided something had to be done. So at the beginning of the year I applied for day school and got the job at the Lady."

A white mustache curved over her upper lip. An urge to lick it away took Paul by surprise. He distracted himself with effort. "I am sorry about your job. Even if you weren't happy there, it's my fault you lost it. I'd like to make it up to you somehow."

"Don't worry about it. You didn't force me to walk out, and besides, the money you paid me is enough to tide me over while I look for another job. And," she concluded with a broad smile, "I enjoyed it. That was probably the grandest exit I'll ever make in my life. The look on Rosta's face alone was worth it."

She set her napkin over her lips and much to his regret wiped away the mustache. He mentally shook himself and got down to business. Leaning toward her, he said earnestly, "I meant what I said about not going back to L.A.; I need some time away from my family to think things through."

"Yes, but what's that got to do with me?"

"I have a home in New York and it's occurred to me that driving across the country would give me the space I need to get things into perspective."

She took another sip of coffee, waiting. She hoped her face didn't reveal the sudden tumult she was feeling.

"The problem is, my cash resources are somewhat limited," he went on.

The coffee burned its way to the pit of her stomach. Chris told herself that what she felt was pure relief and

45

nothing else. She set her cup down and began digging around in the depths of her tote. Finally she thrust the first bill toward him. It hung wretchedly in space for a split second, then slid to the scratched surface of the Formica.

He frowned, not taking it. "What the hell is that?" he demanded, his voice rough.

"Aren't you asking for the money back?"

"No. I'm asking you to drive me to New York."

The second bill crinkled as her fist closed over it. "What?"

"I'm suggesting that you drive me on to New York. I'll pay you when we get there—for time, gas, everything. What do you think would be a fair amount? Two thousand?"

One of a row of slot machines near the entrance paid off and the erratic clinking of coins against metal echoed the noisy click of her heart. No one, not even Paul, seemed to notice or care about the payoff. It was all too commonplace for them. Where she came from, the jangling of coin on coin would have caused pandemonium. Where she came from, money was not ignored. Chris stared at the crumpled bill in her hand, then raised her eyes. He didn't appear to be making a joke.

"You could rent a car," she said slowly, more to give herself time to think than to offer a solution.

"I told you, I haven't that much cash on hand. I'd like to be able to eat along the way," he mocked lightly. One talent he had cultivated over the years was charm. He made full use of it now, crooking his mouth into a lopsided smile guaranteed to melt any woman still capable of breathing. "Together, we could take turns driving, maybe even do a little sightseeing. I'd make it worth your while when we got to New York."

She didn't really believe a word her ears were hearing. Obviously the man was due to be certified crazy. And just as obviously Chris couldn't accept such an offer. She shook her head, her mop of flyaway brown curls swaying about her gold earrings. "Even if I thought you were sane—which believe me, I don't—it would be impossible."

"Why?"

"There's school for one thing."

"I'll pay all your expenses next semester, in addition to the two thousand."

Exasperation glanced over her features, then faded. "How rich are you anyway?"

"Rich enough to deliver what I promise."

"If you're that rich, you're rich enough to get home without my services."

What she said was perfectly true. He didn't even understand fully why he wanted this so badly, but he did. He'd never wanted anything so much in his life as he wanted her to agree. The idea of driving leisurely toward New York, freely as Paul Richards, was intoxicating. No matter where he'd gone, what he'd done, he'd had to live up to who he was, *what* he was. This was a chance to find out who he really was, what he really wanted. It was an opportunity to discover the direction his life should take and he had no intention of letting it slip by.

Again he looked into those hazel eyes. They were perfectly ordinary and yet they were unlike any eyes he'd ever seen. Clear, trusting, honest. He knew he couldn't lie to those eyes. Quickly sifting through what he could say without actually saying anything, he nodded. "That's true, but I don't have the money until I get to my bank in New York."

"Surely someone as wealthy as you claim to be could easily get credit," she pointed out calmly while wondering just how fast her pulse could pound before her blood vessels burst. She watched the fury flash through his eyes before he lowered his lashes and noted another item about him. He didn't like being opposed. She had to admit, though, that he covered it well.

"This is Sunday. I couldn't get credit today if I wanted it. But that's not the point anyway," he said with a friendly show of teeth. "The point is, I'd like to drive to New York, take the time to enjoy the sights. And I'd like your company—"

"What for?"

This time his smile was sincere. "Not for what you're so obviously thinking."

She flushed, wishing she could take back the sharp question. Of course he wasn't interested in her that way. He'd made that perfectly clear back in their room. She mumbled an incoherent disclaimer. She could see by the twisting of his mouth that he didn't buy it for a second.

"I told you, Chris, to help with the driving, to talk to, nothing more." He briefly considered offering her more money, then discarded the notion. Although he firmly believed everyone had a price—especially women—he had a gut feeling this one might be the exception. He couldn't chance insulting her. Instead, he leaned back and tried to look avuncular.

She should refuse firmly and leave; Christine knew that. After all, she really didn't know anything about him, and what she did know she wasn't certain she liked. On the other hand, the money *was* tempting. Her schooling next semester too. With silent mockery Chris asked herself whom she was kidding. Money had nothing to do with this rising excitement racing through her veins.

Calling forth a last attempt at rationality, she shook her head. "This is utterly absurd. What about clothes? Toothpaste?"

She was wavering. He switched on a smile of blinding charm. "We'll buy what we need today. It shouldn't be much."

"I'll need to call Theresa." She pursed her lips, then expelled her pent-up breath. Why fight it? She'd known the instant he made this insane suggestion, she'd accept. "All right."

He grinned triumphantly. He was really going to be

48

Paul Richards. For a week, maybe two, he was free of the restraints of being a Ridgeway. He was free to find himself.

"You should call your parents," she was saying, "and let them know where you're going. They'll be worried."

"I will." He covered his lie by standing and palming the check. He wasn't about to call them. He knew only too well the sort of pressure they'd put on him, all in the name of the family good, of course. He didn't want to be talked out of this. As he'd told her, he needed time to think, and for once in his life he meant to have it. "Come on, we have a lot to do with the rest of the day."

They paid, then Paul handed Chris a quarter from the change. "Want to try your luck?" he asked, tipping his head toward a vacant slot machine.

Her fingers curled over the coin. She was about to slide the quarter into the pocket of her jeans when she caught the challenge in his grin. Wrinkling her nose at him, she shoved it into the machine instead. A whirr, a few clicks, and it was all over. Her quarter had joined the others swallowed by the metal one-armed bandit. She stuck her tongue out first at it, then at him. "There. Are you happy? I lost."

"But if you'd won . . ."

"If!"

"If you'd won, you'd be hugging me in jubilation," he assured her with a cocky wink.

"Fat chance," she laughed, but with a quickening of her heartbeat. Walking out ahead of him, she warned herself to take care. He was danger with a capital D. His kind didn't mix with her kind and she couldn't allow herself to forget that.

Back in the room Chris reached for the phone, telling Paul he could call his family as soon as she'd spoken to Theresa. He swiftly shook his head, saying, "I'll call my parents from downstairs. That way you needn't feel rushed."

He slipped out before she could object. She wouldn't

have done so anyway. She was glad to be able to speak with Theresa openly. As it was, her older sister did not take the news well. It took Chris ten minutes of solid talking to convince Theresa she was neither crazy nor drugged. She did not explain about the payment nor about her arrangement with Paul, but made it sound as if she'd decided to drive cross-country with him for the fun of it. At last Theresa agreed Chris was old enough to make her own decisions, however irresponsible they may be, and the two said good-bye on Christine's promise to call as often as possible.

She hung up, wondering if she'd just made the biggest mistake of her life. Paul returned and she greeted him with a wavering smile. "Theresa thinks I've been drugged."

"My parents think I'm a disreputable ne'er-do-well." It wasn't a lie and it made her smile. He liked her smile. The upward curve of her mouth brought a beauty to her face that was lacking in her solemn moments. He opened the door and bowed with a flourish. "Shall we?"

She rose and crossed the room on shaky legs. He was only being friendly, she knew that, but the gleam in his eyes tingled over her like champagne bubbles. With effort she managed to get a grip on herself by the time they reached the parking lot.

Paul checked the car when she unlocked the door. "We drove from Los Angeles in *this?*" At her nod he slowly circled the vehicle, his face becoming blanker with each step. Coming back to her, he shook his head. "Are you aware," he asked dryly, "that this wreck on wheels has more rust than paint?"

"The Mav's never let me down yet," she replied with a saucy grin. "Just get in and hold your breath."

"The Mav?" He cocked a sardonic brow at her.

"Short for Maverick. Don't look so disparaging. It will get us where we want to go." She made a move toward the driver's seat, but he stepped in front of her and held out the flat of his hand. She frowned up at him.

50

He merely smiled. "I know Vegas and you don't."

Certain she was losing more and more of her marbles by the minute, Chris tossed him the keys and walked around to the passenger side. When she got in, she found Paul staring at her in something like shock. She glanced around the car, seeing it with his eyes, and wasn't sure whether she wanted to laugh or cry.

The Maverick had clearly led a rough life in its thirteen years. The dash was basic, no extras, not even a glove compartment. A long shelf ran under the dash, and a colorful twist of wires dangled where the radio had once been. The rearview mirror tilted crookedly and had to be held in position when looking in it; the horn had long ago been broken off the steering wheel. She supposed the interior had at one time been a bright blue, but now a thick, dark coat of grime was ground permanently into the vinyl. Cracks and tears buckled the length of both front and back seats, neither of which had seat belts, both of which had the disreputable shabbiness of neglected derelicts.

"You're sure we drove from L.A. in this?" he asked again.

Lifting her chin defiantly, she inquired in return, "Would you rather go back to L.A. and get your car?"

The image of his sleek low Lamborghini flashed in his mind. A fleeting regret was almost instantly discarded. He didn't want to be locked in the trappings of a Ridgeway. Wasn't that the whole point of this? "Forget it," he said.

"Forget it? Just forget a *whole* car?" She gaped at him in astonishment.

He smiled, shrugged, and pushed the seat back as far as it would go.

Chris didn't speak as he drove and she didn't permit herself to give in to the urge to watch him. His casual dismissal of his car brought new waves of doubt sweeping over her. The suffering she'd thought she'd seen etched into his features last night had been replaced by a sophisticated air of cynicism that disturbed her. *Everything* about him disturbed her! The way he tossed money around without a blink, the way he casually crumpled his expensive clothes, the way he oozed money and breeding from every pore. It disturbed her because it erected a barrier she knew she could never surmount.

Before reaching "The Strip," they stopped at a drugstore to purchase necessities from a list Chris had compiled on a paper napkin from the restaurant. As Paul wheeled a cart down the aisles, she ticked off each selected item. Soap, toothpaste, two toothbrushes, disposable razors, and blades were placed one by one in the basket. After Chris picked up a fourth bottle of shampoo, checked the price, and put it down, Paul heaved a sigh dripping weariness.

"Just pick one and let's get out of here."

She nibbled her fingertip. "Look. This one has a flyer coupon. Let's go back to the front of the store and see if they have extra flyers—"

"You're talking about all of a nickel," he cut in impatiently. He randomly plucked a bottle from the shelf and flung it in the cart. "Now let's go!"

Chris started to object, then pressed her lips tightly together. They made the rest of their selections in wordless hostility. At the checkout Paul scooped several bags of expensive smoked almonds from a display into their pile and Chris muttered a disparaging remark about being disgustingly easy with money.

"It's better than pinching every damn penny," he shot back.

He snatched up the sack and strode to the car. She trailed after him, already regretting having ignited his short-fused temper. They got in, she cautiously and he with a vicious slam of the door. What few threads had clung to the Maverick's balding tires were left behind on the pavement as he peeled out. In a city renowned for its reckless drivers, Paul hurtled through traffic with daredevil speed. They whizzed past an airport, whirled by the first of an endless chain of hotel casinos and wedding chapels. They were on Las Vegas Boulevard—The Strip. Unfortunately so were hundreds of other vehicles. Chris knew without doubt one of them must have her number written on his front bumper.

Too frightened to close her eyes, she clearly saw the light change to a demanding red and the blur of metallic blue rushing toward them. The shrill screech of brakes sounded simultaneously with the angry blare of a horn. She saw the missed-by-inches van pass out of view and decided that perhaps she ought to try to placate him.

"I think you should know," she stated in a voice vibrating with fright, "that I am developing a heart murmur."

He glanced at her and she ventured a mollifying smile. He looked away and took a corner at a speed Parnelli Jones wouldn't have used at the Indy.

"One more corner like that and I'm a definite candidate for open heart surgery," she said when she could pry open her lips. "Please, slow down."

The car instantly slowed. In fact, it crawled. Cars roared noisily past them. Pedestrians outdistanced them with ease. "That better?" he inquired on a sarcastic note.

"For my heart, yes. For getting anywhere, no."

He shot her another sharp look. Gradually the car resumed a normal speed and after a moment he said coolly, "I did warn you I had a temper."

"Well, yes," she conceded, "but you neglected to explain that it had a two-second fuse."

It was then that he realized he really liked this barmaid. He raised his brows. "Oh, surely more than two? Ten maybe."

"Five at the outside."

That brought a genuine smile to his mouth. "I seem to be making a habit of telling you I'm sorry."

She couldn't deny the power of his smile. It erased her irritation and distress in a single flash. It cloaked her with radiant warmth as her heartbeat hammered against her ribs. Glancing away from that blinding power, Chris silently repeated a message of warning. She must take care not to let his charm confuse her sense of caution.

"I'm making it a habit to accept your apologies," she said.

Again he glanced at her, then away. "I just couldn't see the reason for wasting all that time fussing over a few cents on a bottle of shampoo."

She tilted her head and studied him. His profile was finely chiseled, clearly revealing the strength and determination she already knew he possessed. Both jaw and chin were firm and thrust out—but that might as easily denote a stubborn implacability as a strength of will. Well, if they were to journey across the country together, things had better be clear from the start.

"You have to understand, Paul, that worrying over those few cents is as ingrained in me as tossing fifties out without a thought is in you. As much as I'd love to see New York, if you're going to get angry at me for it, we might as well give up on this idea of traveling together."

A muscle in his jaw jumped. His tone, however, remained neutral. "You've never been to New York?"

"I've never been out of Los Angeles."

He cast her a look of total disbelief. "Never?"

"Nope. Born and raised in the confines of L.A." She favored him with a sparkling smile and said lightly, "Traveling's another of those dreams of mine that you're making come true. Maybe you're really a genie in disguise or my guardian angel."

"Believe me, baby, I'm no angel."

"Oh, I believe you all right," she said dryly. "Angels with tempers like yours get their wings clipped."

He laughed, then paused. Abruptly he flashed that boyish grin at her. "Well, I'll just have to watch my temper. We can't give up on our trip—*your* trip, Chris. We're making your dream come true, remember?"

Once again the hypnotic force of his charm wouldn't be

denied. Knowing she was behaving irrationally, but feeling helplessly unable to do otherwise, she could only nod.

They parked near an elegant red brick building on Desert Inn Road. Chris was surprised when what appeared from the outside to be several expensive department stores, including Saks and Neiman-Marcus, turned out to be an open, well-lit, and well-kept shopping mall. In relative companionship they purchased the clothes Chris deemed necessary for the drive to New York. With what she assumed was rare restraint, Paul permitted her to check price tags and even to veto a couple of his more costly choices. He apparently meant to make good on his effort to compromise with her. It perversely made her want to let him have his way. Her common sense, however, overruled this insanity.

Soon they each had a new pair of jeans, two casual shirts, and a week's supply of underclothes. Chris ticked a mental list off on her fingers and murmured, "Let's see, I've got these joggers, but you'll need something other than dress shoes." She looked up to discover that Paul was no longer beside her. She rotated slowly, half-fearing to look, afraid she would not see him.

He stood before a window display, gazing at a mannequin draped in crimson silk crêpe de chine. Repositioning the set of her bulky purse on her shoulder, Chris marched forward purposefully to retrieve him. "What are you doing?" she demanded.

He glanced over his shoulder and smiled. Without answering her he grabbed her hand and hauled her into the classy boutique. Her protests were ignored. He didn't cease moving until he stood before a saleswoman as stiff as the mannequin in the window. Chris realized, however, that the woman was alive when her perfectly plucked eyebrows inched upward at the sight of them.

"We'd like the dress in the window," said Paul. "The red one. In size . . ."

He looked at Chris and without thinking she responded to the questioning lift of his brow, "Eight."

"Size eight," he finished.

The clerk wafted away and Chris turned to face Paul. "Are you crazy?" she asked, half-laughing. "I doubt if I can afford the hankies in this store much less—"

"That dress will look great on you."

"I'm sure it would, but—"

"I knew you'd like it," he cut in with satisfaction just as the saleswoman skimmed up with an armful of crimson silk crêpe de chine.

"Would you like to try it on?" inquired the clerk.

"No," said Chris.

"Yes," said Paul.

He took the dress and pressed it into Christine's unwilling hands before she could voice any further argument. The soft folds whispered over her arms. Long billowy sleeves were tucked at the shoulders and the skirt was full and draping. In the window it had seemed a deep blood red. Under the fluorescent glare the color was brighter, a brilliant flame of silken fabric. It was unlike any dress she'd ever seen and an aching to possess it welled up within her. Shifting her bag, Chris flipped up one of the sleeves to inspect the discreetly placed tag. She dropped the sleeve like a hot coal and thrust the garment back at the clerk. "I'm sorry, but this is much too expensive."

Paul intercepted the dress in mid-air and pushed it back at her. "Come on, babe. I keep thinking of you in that red thing you had on when I met you last night and I know this dress will make you look terrific."

Chris saw the clerk carefully averting her eyes and felt the heat climb up her neck to spill over her face. She refused to take the silk he was urging at her. "We're not talking nickels this time."

For a moment he simply stared. Then he dropped the dress into the salesclerk's hands. "I'll take it. And hose and a slip and whatever else is needed to go with it."

As the clerk floated to the cash register to ring up the sale, he held Chris by the elbow. "I don't need that dress," she said rigidly.

"It's my nickel and I'm buying it. Whether you accept my gift or not is up to you."

"Is it a gift—or a payoff for future services?"

He stepped back and narrowed his eyes as they slowly, coldly, assessed her from head to toe. His gaze went over her like an accountant totaling up a ledger and finding the sum insufficient. Chris felt the calculation of each curl and curve being added and subtracted and knew from the dismissal in his eyes that her debits far outnumbered her credits.

"Let me make it clear to you one last time, he said coolly, "you are quite safe with me. I'm perfectly capable of keeping my hormones under control around you."

"I did not mean—" she began stiffly.

"Didn't you?" he mocked. A seductive curve played over his lips as he drawled huskily, "If I wanted you, I wouldn't have to ravish you. If I wanted you, baby, you'd come to me."

The warm susurration wafted over the shell of her ear, misted the round dot of gold on the lobe. His breath grazed her skin, tingled her blood. She stared into the mesmerizing depths of his dark eyes and knew he was right. If he wanted her, she'd go to him without a blink. Wasn't that really why she was here? Wasn't that really why she'd walked off into the night with him? The knowledge filled her with self-disgust.

She dragged her gaze away from the drugging potency of his eyes and muttered, "Not conceited, are you?"

He laughed and sauntered off to pay the saleswoman. When he'd added the shopping bag to the mound of other sacks he was carrying, he walked into the mall, certain Chris would follow him. She did. She moved several paces behind him, feeling resentful and frowning in self-reproach. He glanced back, saw her frown, and stopped. She

57

obediently stopped too. She stood lopsided, balancing the weight of her enormous bag on one shoulder, and looking, he thought, ridiculously vulnerable.

A barrage of emotions ricocheted through Paul. He was nettled that she had argued with him about the dress, exasperated at her apparent unhappiness. He found himself wanting very much to make her smile. And immediately he wondered why. Why should he care if she didn't want the damn dress? Why should he care if she smiled or frowned? She was nothing more to him than a ride to New York. And yet, watching her struggle with the weight of that scuffed tote, he felt an unaccustomed surge of protectiveness. He didn't understand why. She wasn't beautiful. She certainly wasn't sexy. She was . . . ordinary.

With a sudden fatalistic shrug he decided reasons weren't important. Seeing her smile return was. He shuffled his load of paper sacks, reached out and flicked at the leather strap crossing her shoulder. "How do you manage to walk with that thing weighing you down?" His voice was deliberately teasing. "I've seen steamer trunks smaller than this so-called purse of yours."

She understood he was again apologizing. For a moment she considered refusing to accept it, but it was only a very brief moment. Chris wasn't the sort to hold grudges and she knew her real anger was self-directed. After all, it wasn't his fault she didn't appeal to him. So she summoned up a feeble smile and responded in kind. "We'd need a steamer if we bought everything you keep looking at."

"How about if we settle for a pair of dress sandals for you, sneakers for me, and a gym bag?"

They did just that, then finished the rest of their shopping in a whirl. Paul chided her for wasting money on a nightgown, saying sanctimoniously that he was saving them the cost of pajamas by sleeping in the buff. Even as she laughed, a slight dusky rose tinted her tawny skin, surprising him with a lightning flash of desire.

He caught himself up short. What the hell was he doing? He was behaving irresponsibly, he knew that. He couldn't really go through with this insane scheme to run away. But, he immediately rationalized, it was only for a few days, just long enough for him to get things into perspective.

The tide of her blush ebbed and he felt his desire wash away with it. A deprecatory half smile played over his mouth. He must still be slightly drunk. She wasn't his type of woman. He liked his women voluptuous and sophisticated, eager to romp and just as eager to move on to romp with someone else. She was the type to expect the emotional commitment he was incapable of giving. She was the type he generally viewed as strictly "hands off."

Looking at her now, he vowed to do just that. The last thing he wanted was to complicate the situation by getting involved with the barmaid. She was only the means to the end, nothing more.

CHAPTER FOUR

Under any other circumstances the flash and glitter of Las Vegas at night would have appalled Christine. To her eyes the flash was garish and the glitter was tarnished. The shrill laughter clashed with the incessant clatter of chips and the shuffle of cards. It all had a frantic pitch that sounded pathetic to her ears, but even at that it was hard not to join the feverish excitement surrounding her. She wondered how Paul was managing to resist.

Insisting that they have *some* fun while in the city that claimed to be the entertainment capital of the world, he'd thrust the bag from the boutique into her arms and ordered her to don the red dress. She hadn't even made a token protest. There was no sense in objecting, now that he had bought the thing. But when she had put it on, Chris caught her breath at the woman she saw reflected in the motel mirror. The crimson clung to her, outlining curves she hadn't suspected she possessed, promising a sensuality in her slightest movement. The sheer sleeves floated down her arms, the scalloped edge of the neckline hinted at the soft flesh hidden beneath the clinging silk. Gazing at this new vision of herself, Chris felt a small regret for neglecting to buy cosmetics or jewelry.

Paul didn't seem to notice the lack of either one. When she stepped out of the bathroom he was leaning negligently against the door, waiting. Catching sight of her, he slowly straightened. His gaze traveled from the careful disarray of her short brown curls to the tip of her new slim-strapped black heels. Finally Paul vented a low, wolfish whistle. "No doubt about it, baby," he said cheerfully. "Red is your color."

In truth, the cheerful tone had only been produced with effort. The sight of her in that dress stunned him. He'd known instinctively the color would suit her, but he had not expected the transformation from gamin to seductive siren. All the terrific curves he'd decided he had imagined on the barmaid were now displayed in a crimson cornucopia. It was all he could do not to partake of a handful of the plenty tempting him. But he knew she wasn't the sophisticate she so resembled. No matter how alluring, he wasn't about to get entangled with her. So he repressed the urge and led her away chatting amicably about Las Vegas nightlife.

The Strip was a dazzling carnival of neon sideshows that discomfited Chris. When Paul dragged her into the elegant red, black, and gold casino at Caesars Palace, she was grateful he had forced the expensive dress on her. It helped ease the discomfort she felt. At least she looked like she fit in. But she didn't and she knew it. The animated zeal, the inconstant illumination, the strained cacophony, all made her feel as if she were trapped in a distortion, a nightmare fun house. The intensity of those clustered at card tables, gathered around roulette wheels, or lined up in front of rows of slot machines disturbed her most of all. So much money and energy being wasted, in her view, on ridiculous games.

On the other hand, she suspected that life for Paul had been one enormous game. She had fully expected him to charge to the nearest table and fling cash onto the green felt. He once again surprised her by staying at her side, explaining various games with a lazy air of amusement. And though she'd learned at an early age not to rely on anyone but herself, she was thankful he hadn't left her on her own in this frenzied sphere.

Yet in a way she wished he had gone to one of the tables. His mere presence disturbed her even more than the constant furor. She kept visualizing the full-size replica of Michelangelo's "David" they had passed on the way in and wondering what a statue of Paul would look like. Would he look as firm and smooth and muscularly stunning as "David"? Beneath the creased slacks and shirt would his skin gleam over such well-shaped contours?

She tried to distract herself from such demented thoughts by listening to the music coming from a live band on Cleopatra's Barge, a small stage area surrounded by water. Over the music she heard the resonance of her thudding heartbeat. Next she tried focusing on the oddness of a tall, reedy woman in a nearly nonexistent but obviously expensive swatch of silvery crepe, placing a bet beside a short, barrellike man in tight slacks worn shiny with age. In place of the chicly gowned woman, an image rose of the woman she'd seen in her mirror, looking sleek and sophisticated and pressing tightly against Paul's sinewy length.

A jerk passed through her body, repudiating the image. Paul felt her tremor and glanced down at her with a slight frown. "Something wrong?"

"No." She sucked in her lower lip, then pushed it out. She realized Paul's gaze had fastened on her mouth and mistook it for a questioning demand. She hurried into speech. "I was just watching those two over there. What game is that they're playing?"

He continued to stare at her. She parted her lips to repeat the question and he looked away, toward the oddly matched couple. "Come on," he said abruptly. "I'll show you."

They pulled up to a horseshoe-shaped table where a card dealer faced six players. Paul took a seat and Chris stood behind him, happy to have something other than his

62

body to think about. The game was blackjack, a variation on the game she knew as twenty-one. She didn't try to follow the betting procedure, but simply watched the cards fall on the green baize. Several players lightly scraped the edge of their cards on the table and the dealer delivered another card. Paul kept his original two, sliding them under the chips he had placed on the table as a bet.

Dark hairs dusted the backs of his hands. Long fingers curled around the edge of the playing cards. Chris studied his hands and felt her heart begin to pound. They were patrician hands, hands of leisure, smooth and slender. How would those hands feel against her skin?

She could not have said how long her gaze remained fixed on those hands. She only knew that when Paul stood sometime later he was grinning. "Come along, lady luck, we've just paid for that dress of yours."

She followed him obediently, glad to be distracted from her dangerous fixation. He stopped at a crap table and once again she stood behind him while he played. He placed bets with an air of nonchalance, but after a time she could sense the tensing of his muscles as he got caught up in the excitement. She made no attempt to understand the game, disliking the exaggerated shouts, the continual murmuring of those gripping the rim of the table, the ardent attention focused on the rolling dice.

Eventually, feeling bored and neglected, Chris excused herself to Paul, saying she needed to powder her nose. His glossy hair undulated as he nodded, but she wondered whether he had even heard her.

In the ladies' room she sank onto a cushioned stool before a dimly lit mirror above a pink marble vanity. She eased her feet out of the pinching patent heels and flexed her toes. She waved away the aged attendant who started forward with a hand towel. Giving an affronted shake of her pink uniform, the old woman retreated to her corner stool, where she sat sourly eyeing those who dared trespass on her domain without leaving a tip. Chris watched her for a time through the mirror, but gradually her gaze was caught by her own reflection. She forgot the attendant and smiled ruefully at herself.

No doubt about it. Christine Casolaro should be carted away to a nice quiet padded cell. If she had a single grain of sanity left, she would bid Mr. Richards a fond farewell and race home to L.A. without looking back. Her smile slid into a frown. She dropped her gaze and saw the cloud of crimson.

Very slowly she brought her fingertip to the rim of red silk sketched against the swell of her breasts. She delicately traced the silken shell, her finger rising, then falling, then rising again. She closed her eyes and pictured one long, slender and smooth but very masculine finger teasing her skin. She shook with the force of the shiver that ran through her. Her eyes flew open and she stared at herself in derision.

This was the kind of nonsense giddy teenagers played at! She was certainly not a giddy teenager. She'd never had time to indulge in such antics and she wasn't about to start now. Thrusting her feet back into the shoes, Chris rose with determination. She was going back home and she was going now.

The restroom door swished shut behind her and a figure detached itself from the shadows to step in front of her. "What the hell were you doing in there?"

Her eyes widened at the sight of the anger mingling with relief in Paul's face. His shoulders were squared back, his hands jammed into the pockets of his slacks. Altogether, he looked like a belligerent husband. She put on a placating smile. "I told you, powdering my nose."

His scowl deepened. "For as long as you were gone, you could have powdered Mount Everest."

"I'm sorry," she said, trying to look contrite. "I didn't realize you'd be so impatient."

He stared her quivering lips as they vainly strove to hold back a grin and felt his antagonism seep away. "Of

64

course I was impatient. As soon as you left, lady luck, I started losing, so I cashed in my chips and came looking for you."

Concern glanced over her face. "Losing?"

He slid his gaze past her, then took her elbow and started to walk. "I almost began to think you'd skipped out on me."

Any thought of money fled from her mind. She heard the question behind the teasing statement and all her resolutions to go home flipped over on the same thud as her heart. "Skip out on my dream trip? Do you think I'm crazy?"

A sudden boyish grin charged over his mouth, erasing the sophistication, the cynicism, the hardness. The man she gazed at now turned her legs to rubber. She looked away, hoping he couldn't see the wild flutter of her pulse in her throat. He inquired if she'd like to play keno or try a slot machine. She shook her head. "I'd rather go," she managed to say.

He didn't demur, but led her through the crowds and out of Caesars. She did not look at the replica of "David" on the way out. Nor did she look at Paul.

They drove through the heart of The Strip, passing the postcard flash of the famous exteriors—the Sands, the Desert Inn, the Silver Slipper, and the Stardust. Chris exclaimed aloud at the absurd sight of a huge clown standing amid the mesmerizing neon, and the next thing she knew she was being led into Circus Circus, a tent-shaped casino with all the pandemonium of the three-ring Barnum and Bailey extravaganza. Trapeze stars and aerial dancers performed high above the floor to the accompaniment of a blaring brass band. A unicyclist wheeled dizzyingly. Children stuffed themselves with food from concessions on the observation gallery while below them parents placed bets at every game of chance to be found. Electronic zaps resounded from video games, adding to the din of the big-top show and the gamblers below. They wound their way through the dense pack of people, young and old alike, playing carney games on the gallery and purchased a couple of hot dogs.

"You still don't want to try your luck?" he asked.

She shook her head. "You go ahead if you want. I'll watch."

"You have mustard on your mouth," he said by way of answer. His eyes narrowed as he watched the tip of her tongue dart out to lick the mustard from the corner of her lip.

"Is it gone now?"

He pulled his gaze upward. Seeing the clear, honest hazel of her eyes, he wondered what the hell was the matter with him. When he'd stood waiting for her outside the ladies' room at Caesars, watching woman after woman come and go, he'd grown increasingly apprehensive. The rush of relief when she'd finally appeared had dizzied him. He didn't understand it. This wasn't some woman of the world eager to stoke the fires of his passions. This was just Christine.

He glanced down. It was all that damn dress. Why the hell had he been so insistent upon buying it? He crushed the hot dog wrapper into a ball and threw it away. "That hot dog whet my appetite. Why don't we treat ourselves to a steak dinner and a show?"

"Wouldn't you rather play another game?"

"No. I'd much rather share the evening with you." To his surprise, he meant it.

"Maybe we should go back to the motel instead."

"And maybe we shouldn't." He took her arm and turned her around, nudging her forward.

"Why not?" she asked pertly over her shoulder.

"Motels," he murmured lazily, "give me ideas."

She didn't have to inquire what ideas. Those ideas were made perfectly clear in that sensual drawl of his. They were made even more clear in the sudden warm tingling of her blood in her veins.

66

"I'm not sure I'm prepared for any more of an evening out," she offered in a feeble protest.

"Ah, but do you think you're prepared for an evening in?"

His dark eyes teased her, snapping with laughter. Chris felt her heart turn over. In a voice she feared was much too breathless, she agreed to dinner out.

They were unable to get into a big room show. Paul told her he could fix it, but didn't seem concerned when she shook her head. To her view, things worked out perfectly. Pleasing Chris with his thoughtfulness, Paul eschewed the lavish buffets in the casinos and took her instead to a small quiet restaurant off The Strip, where the only entertainment was a soft stream of drifting melodies from an unseen piano player. Over steak and king crab, they talked about impersonal things: the dry heat outside and near-freezing air conditioning in the casinos, the floundering economy, the summer's hit movie.

Paul ordered a drink in place of dessert and when Chris declined one, he tipped his head and studied her intently. His hand toyed with his knife, tapping it lightly against the rim of his plate. When he spoke his words were a cool counterpoint to the precise staccato of his knife.

"I'll bet when you were in school they called you Goody Two Shoes."

She darted her eyes from his face to his hand and back again. "And I'll bet that's not even close to what they called you."

Amusement curved his full lips. "Touché."

When he smiled like that she forgot how unreal this situation was. She forgot how dangerous it would be to let herself be taken in by his charm. She focused on the tablecloth and managed a credibly casual tone. "Actually I was called Scooter." Darting a quick glance at him, she explained. "I was small for my age and always getting in the big kids' way. They told me to scoot, and eventually I became Scooter."

67

His eyelids lowered as he ran his gaze over her. "Those kids obviously had no taste, no foresight. Couldn't they see the potential?"

Color blazed over her skin clear down to her toes. She felt ridiculously like an infatuated adolescent, tongue-tied and miserably self-conscious. She didn't know how to respond to the intimation in his look, his sensual drawl. The casual brush-offs she usually gave men on the make refused to come to her lips. At last she was rescued by the return of the waiter.

Over dessert she eyed him speculatively. Candle flames cast flickering shadows over the handsome planes of his face. He was undeniably attractive, she could certainly see that. She also knew him to be charming and quick-tempered and very handy with his fists. A warm smile touched her lips at the memory of the night before. The smile faded as she realized just how little she actually knew about him. She'd be with him for the next week, yet she had no idea what sort of man he was. She scooped up the last bit of whipped cream from her cherry cheesecake and purposefully set her fork aside.

"Why does your family object to your ambitions? What sort of ambitions are they?" she asked.

Those long fingers tightened around his whiskey glass. "Oh, it wasn't so much my ambitions as the lack of them," he replied flippantly.

"Do you lack ambition?" she persisted.

He shrugged. "They think so. I don't."

"Well, what are your goals?"

"Haven't you heard about the fatal effect of curiosity?"

"I'm not a cat," she rejoined tartly.

His sardonic brows slanted upward. For no discernible reason it disconcerted her. He smiled knowingly. "Finished? Or would you like some coffee?"

Afraid what her eyes might reveal, she examined the crumbs speckling her dessert plate as if she'd never seen a crumb before in her life. "Are you sure we can afford this?"

"If we can't, you can do the dishes," he teased.

"Did we come out ahead at the casino? Or did we lose money?"

He noted her use of the plural and wondered if it was deliberate. "Anyone who comes to Vegas expecting to win is a fool."

"So we lost," she said.

"Don't worry, Miss Penny-pincher, I still have enough to pay for a cup of coffee if you want it."

That brought her gaze up to meet his. She expected anger and found laughter in his eyes. Her pulse began to bump unsteadily. She could not speak, she could only nod. He raised a hand to summon the waiter and ordered coffee for them both, then paused and smiled at Chris. "And cream for the lady. The lady is quite partial to cream." When the waiter slipped away, Paul leaned toward her. "You did want cream, didn't you?"

"Yes," she said with a breathy sigh.

His eyes narrowed and the laughter vanished from them. The candlelight danced into the darkness of his gaze as he stared at her. She felt the imprint of his stare as his eyes moved slowly from her hair to her eyes, to her lips, then lowered to the red silk pressed against the fullness of her breasts.

"You're wrong, you know," he finally said. "You're very like a cat. Cute and cuddly one minute, sleek and solitary the next. And with a rough little tongue that likes to lick cream."

Chris wondered why her hair wasn't standing on end from the force of electricity bolting through her. The husk of his drawl shocked her, excited her, frightened her. What had happened? Last night they were strangers. This afternoon they were companions. And now? What were they now? What would they be tomorrow?

When the coffee came she poured in the cream and

watched it swirl, white through black gradually merging into a warm brown. Could other opposites merge together to form a lovelier whole? She pushed the thought away.

Paul fiddled with his whiskey glass, watching the liquid splash over the ice. She was quiet, waiting. After a time he began speaking in a slow, almost unwilling voice. "In one respect my parents are right. I don't have a defined goal. I just know I can't fit into the family mold. I've tried. I have to find myself before I can figure out what I want to do with my life. But they don't understand that. They just think I'm wasting my time."

"What is it that you do?"

"I don't really do anything, that's the point." He glanced past her, frowning. "Oh, I've a very important title and an impressive desk with a cushy chair, all of which mean exactly nothing. It doesn't make a bit of difference if I'm in that chair or not and I can't accept that. I want what I do with my life to make a difference."

Suddenly wondering why he was telling her all this anyway, he stopped. A closed, remote opacity came into his eyes, warning her not to probe further. He stood abruptly. "Let's go."

She mutely followed him out, as astonished as he at his sudden revelation. Once seated in the car, Paul propped his elbow on the steering wheel. "What do you suggest we do now?"

"We really should go back to the motel."

He slid his dark gaze over her. "And just what do you suggest we do at the motel?"

Knowing he was teasing, she laughed at his suggestive tone. "Oh, I propose a program of unrivaled excitement."

"Such as?"

"Such as removing tags from our new clothes and folding them into our new gym bag. For true kicks we can watch TV."

"If it works," he put in with light cynicism.

, ughed and concurred. "If it works. To top this
Shalleled thrill, we'll go to bed."

An abrupt tension swept away all humor. The car
seemed to overflow with it. Chris felt her smile sliding
away, but could do nothing to retrieve it. His eyes glinted
like polished onyx; she had the ridiculous notion that if
she did not look away, she would be forever lost in their
depths. She wrenched her gaze free, focusing on the colorful spectrum of lights beyond the window.

As the tinseled array of Las Vegas flashed past, Christine wondered again how she'd gotten herself into this. She
had not even noticed him for hours last night and when
she had the prickling premonition had warned her. From
the moment she'd first fallen into the dark intensity of his
gaze, she'd thrown caution and sense out the window. She
tried again to tell herself just how absurd she was being.
She couldn't really want him, could she?

He had baldly told her he was running away. She didn't
want the type of man who ran away from his problems.
She wanted the type of man who stood up to his problems,
a man who faced his responsibilities. She wanted a man
who earned his way, who asked rather than demanded.
She wanted a man she could respect.

And she wanted Paul.

When she remembered that *he* did not want *her*, it only
fanned her flaring anger at her own stupidity.

Her car door opened and she looked around dazedly.
They were parked before the shabby motel on the far
fringes of town and Paul was leaning on the open door, the
gleam of his smile shining down at her. "Your carriage has
brought you safely home, madam."

She got out and stood trembling. The warmth of his
hand on the small of her back prodded her forward. Her
heart pounded with each step. He pushed in front of her
to unlock the door and his arm brushed against hers. She
jerked back, then looked at him. He ran his eyes over her
knowingly and she felt furious with herself. When he held

71

open the door, she tipped up her chin and strode in with a false air of confidence.

The click of the closing door reverberated through the tiny room. She went immediately to the television and turned it on. A late night newscaster came fuzzily into view, with a wavering ghost beside him as he droned on. "They say two heads are better than one, but looking at this guy, I doubt it," she joked.

A muffled plop sounded behind her. Chris turned from looking at the double image on the television screen in time to see Paul's tie falling atop the careless heap of his jacket. "You should hang that up," she said without thinking.

He paid no attention to her, but began unbuttoning his shirt. As if hypnotized, she watched each small white button slide from each small hole, exposing tightly curled dark hair over his chest. So intent was she on the luster of skin beneath the feathery tufts, Chris neither heard the newscaster behind her nor saw the sudden tightening of Paul's expression. She saw only the sides of his shirt flare out away from the shapely sinews of his chest as he strode toward her. When he was a foot in front of her her breath caught and her heart ceased operation. He stretched out his arm. She swayed toward him and he reached over her head to turn the television off.

Disappointment, humiliation, and relief punched her in one mighty blow. Dismay hit her closely after. How could she have thought, how could she have hoped . . . ? It didn't bear thinking of! She felt the heat from his outstretched arm and bared chest and saw the smile in his eyes as he looked down at her. Afraid to touch him, she stepped to the side and summoned up a breath with which to issue a complaint. "I wanted to watch that."

"I thought we came here to go to bed," he murmured, following her with his eyes.

He was clearly amused and it annoyed Christine. "Among other things," she snapped in return.

72

Those expressive brows of his climbed, telling her just what things he thought she meant. "Oh?" he drawled.

She opened her mouth to make a retort, but shut it again as she realized he was enjoying getting her roused. She ground her teeth, but managed a pleasant tone. "Yes. We still have to prepare to leave in the morning."

The folds of her skirt whispered against her legs as she walked the narrow width of the room. She picked up the gym bag and swung it onto the bed. Silk rustled as she did so.

"Go get out of that dress," Paul abruptly ordered.

"In a minute," she replied absently. She started spreading their purchases out over the bed.

He swept up her nightgown and tossed it at her. "Now," he commanded.

She gaped at him in disbelief. "Who do you think you are—" she started hotly.

"For God's sake, don't argue with me! I'm only human. Now go change." He turned away from her and angrily stripped off his shirt, letting it drop to the floor. She stared a moment at the taut muscles straining over his back, then spun on her heel and retreated to the bathroom.

It only took her a few seconds to realize how foolishly she'd been behaving. She couldn't imagine what had been wrong with her all evening. She hadn't been herself at all. She looked down at the soft folds molded over her body. It was this damn dress. It was like nothing she'd ever worn before. Naturally she'd acted like someone else. She pulled it off in a flurry of red and yanked on the cotton nightgown.

Her own familiar face stared back at her in the mirror. But she saw something more. A difference in her eyes. She leaned closer to the glass. There was a heightened excitement glittering in the hazel depths. Seeing it, Chris muttered a soft curse.

I'm only human, he'd said. What did he think she was, a robot? If she had any sense she'd leave at once. But she knew she would not run away from the danger of Paul Richards. Run toward it more likely. A ghost of a laugh haunted her as she began to brush her teeth. By the time she finished she had regained her composure. She wouldn't waste time fruitlessly wringing her hands. She'd tackle problems as they arose.

They began rising rather more quickly than she anticipated.

Paul sat propped against the headboard of the bed, one long leg sprawled out over the cover, the other dangled to the floor. A pair of cobalt blue briefs was all that stood between him and candidacy for a nudist camp. Chris saw the length of his firmly toned body, saw the sinews that gave shape to his chest and legs, saw the fine dark hair that contrasted with the shadings of his skin, and felt her heart kick to an abrupt halt. For several seconds she was nonplussed, then she mentally shook herself. However much he affected her, she was safe. He had no interest in her as a woman.

She managed to pull her eyes away from him. Clutching the red dress tightly to her bodice, she sought an excuse, any excuse, to stifle the hunger gnawing at her. The gym bag stood beside her purse on the dresser.

"Did you finish the packing?" she inquired carefully.

"Where did you sleep last night?" he asked in reply.

All her self-command threatened to go AWOL. "I—oh, I—it was this morning really," she stammered. She called herself to order, straightened her spine, and gave him a firm answer. "The floor. I'd be happy to sleep there—"

"Then tonight," he broke in, "I'll take the floor."

Chris gave him a grateful smile in return. But within her gratitude ran a strong thread of disappointment.

He rose from the bed with a fluidity that endangered her fragile composure. This room was nothing but an oversize *box*! He was next to *naked*! But Paul seemed unaware of the tension gripping Chris. He simply yanked a blanket off the bed, grabbed one of the pillows, and settled himself on the far side of the floor. She didn't move until he asked her to turn off the light. She somehow managed to do so, then stumbled into the bed.

Darkness uneasily enveloped them. Chris heard the steadiness of Paul's breathing and resented it. How could he be so calm? She rolled onto her side, away from him, and listened to the echo of her erratically thumping heart. Then she angrily tossed herself onto her back and swore she'd insist on separate rooms from now on. She fell asleep cursing him for falling asleep so effortlessly.

When he was certain she'd at last gone to sleep, Paul punched his pillow and stretched restlessly over the worn carpet. The strain of the last hour had nearly driven him mad. He'd thought she'd never quit tormenting him with that dress. He stared at the ceiling and remembered the swish of silk against her legs, the crimson clinging tightly to her breasts, her buttocks. He remembered the silky warmth beneath his palm whenever he had touched her back. He remembered and began to fantasize that his hand had drifted downward to the pert curve of her bottom. He imagined the springy softness of it and only barely repressed a groan.

Damn that dress! He was aching like a schoolboy for the seductive sweetness embodied in that cloud of red silk. He'd thought his desire would wane when she changed, but even after she'd taken the dress off he'd hungered for her.

Thinking of her now, soft and vulnerable, sleeping in the thin, shapeless cotton gown, an arm's reach from him, his desire increased. He savagely struck his pillow and turned over, determined to put her out of his mind. He reminded himself she wasn't the sort of woman for him. One damn dress wouldn't make her the sort, not by a long shot. He sternly told himself physical involvement would be a mistake for both of them. He didn't want to hurt her and he was certain she would be hurt by any deepening of their relationship. Besides, he wasn't about to risk the consequences. He renewed his oath to keep his hands off her, certain the vow would erase the lascivious visions taunting him.

But when sleep finally, mercifully, assuaged him, he was still thinking of Chris. He was hoping she hadn't taken in what the newscaster had been reporting before he'd managed to turn off the set.

CHAPTER FIVE

Her first thought upon waking was the same as her last thought before sleeping. Paul.

She lay quite still, contemplating his contradictions. His sophistication and world-weariness. His kindness, his teasing, his devastating charm. The sadness in his eyes and the cynicism in his smile. The satanic slant to his dark brows. The sensitivity in the full curve of his mouth. She lingered over the image of his mouth and felt her heartbeat shift into high gear. The need to look at him swept over her. Slowly, cautiously, she opened her eyes.

On the floor the mustard-gold blanket was tangled over the white pillow. Chris stared, blinked, then stared again. He was gone.

She jerked upright. Her pulse rate escalated wildly. She tried to remain calm as she searched the room. He was lounging in the frame of the bathroom door, watching her. He wore the new jeans and a biscuit-brown knit shirt that defined the breadth of his shoulders, the slimness of his waist.

"Mornin', baby," he said softly.

Wasn't it odd, she thought dazedly, how he could make baby sound so endearing? She'd always hated it when Don Rosta called her that, but on his lips it had an altogether different effect. Her heartbeat gradually returned to normal and she croaked, "Good morning."

"I thought you meant to sleep the day away. Do you realize what's happened to our early start?"

"If you wanted to start early, you shouldn't have kept me up so late." She looked away from the potency of his smile. The strap of her gown had slipped off her shoulder. She nervously plucked it back into place, then wished she'd left it alone when she heard his mocking chuckle.

"I could have kept you up much, much later," he murmured.

A bubble of irritation swelled up within her. He'd told her plainly that he had no desire for her, so why did he keep making such provocative remarks? It made her angry because it fueled her growing desire for him. She suspected he knew it, that he was deliberately baiting her. She tossed her head back and eyed him disdainfully. "Do you really think so?" she asked coolly.

She saw the flash in his eyes, the tautening of his stance, and almost purred as she yawned and stretched. He watched the blankets slide away from her as she did so, then abruptly straightened. "I'll go gas up the car while you get dressed," he said brusquely. He left with an unnecessarily forceful closing of the door.

Leaping from the bed, Christine danced into the bathroom. Whatever did or did not happen between them, she was embarking on an adventure. The excitement that had ridden with her from Los Angeles rose up again. She was about to see things she'd never seen, go places she'd never dreamed of going. Though she'd teased Paul about being her genie, in a way it was true. He was making it possible for her to see the world beyond L.A., and she had to be thankful to him for that.

She brushed her teeth, then hummed merrily as she brushed the tangles from her hair. She was still humming by the time she'd donned new jeans and an embroidered apricot camisole that Paul had insisted she buy. Gazing in the mirror, she had to admit it looked good. He had good taste in women's clothing. Too good. In fact, it was an expert taste that must have taken a great deal of practice to acquire.

The song stilled on her lips. What kind of women did Paul usually buy clothing for? No one from her part of L.A., she was certain. That thought unreasonably depressed her and she packed her nightgown and red dress into the gym bag with a frown etched across her brow. When she had the last item securely within the bag, she checked to make certain her hundred-dollar bills were safely tucked inside her purse. Though she knew a maid was paid to take care of the room, she couldn't smother her ingrained habit of straightening the bed. Then she sat down to wait for Paul.

An hour later a new path was worn into the fraying carpet as she paced back and forth. She glanced at the round face of her watch once again and slowly sank to the edge of the bed. She couldn't believe it. Her mind, her entire being, felt numb. But one thought rang loud and clear.

He isn't coming back.

How could she have been so stupid? How could she have let him take off with her car? Why hadn't she insisted she go along to get the gas instead of letting him go off alone? Why hadn't she kept control of her keys? Now he'd stolen her car and stranded her in Vegas.

Bemoaning her stupidity wasn't going to get her anywhere. Feeling dejected and betrayed, Chris hauled herself back to her feet. She would have to find the bus station and get back home. She could already hear the I-told-you-so's snapping from Theresa's lips and see the derisive condemnation in Tony's eyes. And to think that she'd lain awake half the night aching to share the bed with Paul! She could only thank God she hadn't given in to *that* temptation.

It was cold comfort as she left the room, juggling her purse and the gym bag to close the door. The tote thumped against her hip as she strode angrily to the registration desk, bruising her side no less than her feelings. She paid for the room, depleting her slim supply of cash and rapidly diminishing store of temper, then inquired about the bus station. Naturally it was on The Strip. She thought about taking a taxi, but remembering that she no longer had a job and now had much less than her original five hundred, she resigned herself to the very long hike ahead of her.

She'd always thought herself a good judge of character. Obviously, however, she was less than astute. Certainly she'd worn blinders with regard to Paul Richards. She couldn't even sustain her anger at him. After all, she had gotten herself into this. She was the one to blame.

She crossed the parking lot and headed down the street, not really seeing anything around her. Immersed in thoughts of the classes she had missed today, of the possibility of begging Don to take her back at the Lady, she was only dimly aware of a blur of rusted steel blue on the opposite side of the road. She decided that even if Don would have her back, which given his last few remarks to her, she very much doubted, she would not want that job. If all of this was to have had some meaning, she had to take a new course in her life.

Though not happy, she at least wasn't despondent. In fact, as she thought about it, she decided she had a lot to be thankful for. Paul had been the impetus she'd needed to quit a job she detested but would in all probability have hung onto. Now she had no choice but to find that other job she'd been talking about for six months.

As for Paul himself, she could view herself only as lucky. She'd been tinkering with dynamite and could have been torn apart by the blast. She'd known from the first Paul Richards wasn't for her. If she ignored the emptiness squeezing at her, if she concentrated on her narrow escape, she was certain she felt relieved that things had worked out this way. Except for losing her car, of course.

She heard a shout and her step faltered. A sudden shriek of car brakes brought her to a stop altogether. Even as she turned toward the car that had slammed to the curb, her heart was vaulting in anticipation.

"What the hell are you doing? Where do you think you're going?" demanded Paul as he flung out of the car and toward her. A dark flush stained his face, which bore the distinct stamp of hostility. His fierce eyebrows clamped at a savage angle, his eyes shot furious sparks and his lips had thinned to an almost invisible line. Altogether he had the look of a man who would terrify any thinking person.

But Chris didn't take time to think. She simply reacted. The gym bag dropped to the pavement with a resounding plop, and her purse swung like a crazed pendulum as she lunged forward to cast herself into his arms. Tears began streaming down her cheeks, shocking her as much as it did him. She buried her head in his shoulder and gave herself up to the unexpected release of emotions she'd thought she'd successfully exorcised.

His arms closed about her, his palms pressed into her back. "Baby, baby, don't cry," he said roughly. "I'm sorry. I yelled. It's just I thought you ran out on me."

The raspy voice combined with the warmth of his embrace to make her tears flow harder. She tried to explain, but only a wracking sob came out, muffled against his shirt. The scent of soap mingling with aftershave was both comforting and stimulating. Chris shuddered as she inhaled it.

"Shh, shh," he murmured, half hoping she would go on crying so he could go on holding her. Beneath his palms he felt the crisp thin camisole and knew she was not wearing a bra. He pressed more tightly, feeling the softness of her breasts give way to the hardness of his chest. He continued to whisper into her ear as his hands drifted upward. His fingers played over the string straps knotted at each shoulder, then swirled lightly on the smooth, tawny skin between them. She felt velvety and warm, like a rose petal kissed by the sun.

81

A yearning to touch her every curve, every hollow rippled through him. His fingers shook as he lightly stroked her shoulder blades. She nuzzled closer. He could feel the heated wisp of her breath on his neck, the thump of her heart meeting his. The castaway tendrils of her hair gently brushed against his cheekbone. Paul felt desire stirring and waged an internal battle. He wanted to nuzzle his lips against the arch of her nape. He longed to curl his fingers over the full curve of her breast.

But he struggled to suppress his throbbing urges. To give in to them would mess up his plans. To give in to them would probably hurt Christine in the end. He did not want to hurt Christine. He tried to focus on her needs.

Given another minute he might have forgotten his plans, her needs, but he felt her tremble again and realized she had calmed. Reluctantly he let her go.

She sniffed and wiped her fingers over the tip of her nose. Her face was blotched with red and her lashes clumped into wet little spikes. Looking at her, his desire ebbed. He'd been acting like a boy touching his first woman and he couldn't understand why. As desire waned, irritation waxed. He wasn't used to denying himself; that he'd wasted his nobility on this decidedly unsexy woman with the splotched face annoyed him. His annoyance made his voice harsh as he demanded to know what was wrong with her.

"I don't know. I'm sorry. I didn't mean to—" She sucked in a deep breath. "I never cry. Honest. I'm sorry."

He watched as she swiped her hand across her cheek and felt his anger fade. He regretted that. He'd have liked to stay furious with her. It was far preferable to the sickening sensations he'd felt when he had seen her striding down the street and, if not preferable, at least safer than the need that pulsed within him when he'd held her. Sighing, he took a step back from her.

"What's wrong? Where were you going?" he asked, more gently.

"To the bus station. I thought—I thought you'd stolen the Mav," she replied on a final, frame-shuddering sniff.

First he looked stunned. Then he looked amused. Finally he threw back his head and laughed. "Baby, baby, who'd steal this wreck? There's not a soul alive who'd risk going to jail for this pile of junk."

"The Mav's not a wreck," she countered, but her denial lacked force. She felt like a fool. She wasn't acting like herself. She couldn't even remember the last time she'd been foolish enough to indulge in tears. Though her emotions were intense, she'd learned very young that crying was a waste of time and energy. That she would cry for such a small thing as having her car—and Paul—turn up had rattled her. It was damning evidence of her deranged mental state since meeting him. She wondered if she could be going senile at twenty-six.

"There's no horn, no radio, and the damn thing guzzles oil," he was saying with a shake of his head. "That's part of what took me so long. I also stopped and bought us a stack of maps and a guidebook. And some doughnuts. I didn't mean to be gone so long."

He collected the gym bag and swung it onto the back seat. Chris got in and inhaled the warm aroma of doughnuts wafting from the white box in the middle of the front seat. She lifted the lid. "Oh, honey-glazed! God, I'm famished." She picked one up and bestowed a blazing smile on him.

Paul sat with his hand on the ignition key. The ugly flush had faded, but shards of crystalline tears still glistened in her eyes and the dazzling radiance of her smile mesmerized him. As he stared her smile faltered. She lowered the doughnut. He couldn't stop staring at the quivering of her lips.

"I am sorry, Paul," she said quietly. "It was unforgivable of me to suspect you—"

"I wonder what it is about me," he broke in as he started the engine and pulled into the street. "First you

83

think I'm a runaway husband and now a car thief. God knows what else has gone on in that mind of yours."

She smiled sheepishly. "Well, I did think you might be a bank robber," she confessed.

"Good Lord." He shot her a teasing grin. "Tell me, do you think it's in my eyes?"

"No. Your eyebrows. They're positively fiendish, especially when you're bored or angry."

"Should I have them plucked?"

She laughed and shook her head, and knew in that moment that she could easily fall in love with him. She had insulted him by thinking the very worst of him and he was laughing it off, putting her at ease. She looked at the doughnut in her hand, then took a bite. Well, she wouldn't let it happen. Loving him would be fatal. He couldn't possibly return her feelings.

When she'd swallowed, she said in a serious tone, "All the same, I feel rotten about jumping to conclusions like that. I should have trusted you. I should have known—" She broke off and forced herself to look directly at him. "Paul, I really am sorry."

The sincerity, the self-reproach was clear in her eyes. He glanced away from her. This was not a conversation he was enjoying. With an impatient mutter he ran his hand down his thigh. "Damn. I hate new jeans. Could we stop at a Laundromat and run 'em through to wash out some of the stiffness?"

"It's almost noon—"

"Maybe tonight then," he interrupted. "I've mapped out today's route. I thought we'd go through Arizona."

"That sounds great."

He nodded and grabbed a doughnut. They didn't speak again until he'd negotiated out of the invariably tumultuous Vegas traffic and onto the southeastbound highway. Then he gestured toward the stack of maps he'd jammed onto the shelf under the dash. "We might as well check out some of the sights along the way. Why don't you look through those things and tell me what you want to stop and see?"

As she pulled out the guidebook and began to flip through it, he said, "By the way, I noticed your textbooks in the back. What's your major?"

"Business Administration. Boring, but practical."

"Why not something interesting as well as practical?"

"I didn't feel I had the leisure to look for something that was fun. In this economy it seemed safest to go with practical."

"Sensible," he said in a tone she wasn't sure was complimentary. "Have you ever thought what you might like to do?"

She kept her gaze fixed on the book opened on her lap. "Not really. I've never had any one talent to hone in on, no artistic flair, no deep love of literature, nothing to guide me."

"But what do you think you'd like?" he persisted.

"What is this? Twenty questions?" She half-scowled at him, then smiled when he cocked one of his brows at her. "Oh, very well. I like people. I'd like working with people, helping them."

"Is that why you came with me? The urge to take care of me?"

"Oh, of course," she assured him. "I always was the best baby-sitter on the block."

He glanced at her, then laughed, a warm note that stirred her blood. "Hmmm. Not only rough, but sharp too."

Puzzlement displaced the merriment in her eyes. "What?"

"Your tongue," he explained.

Goose bumps rose on her skin. Did he have any idea what the huskiness in his voice was doing to her? Fervently hoping not, she hastily turned her attention to the surrounding foothills. When she felt calm enough to turn the pages, she thumbed through the guidebook. She had difficulty believing she'd actually be seeing any of the vivid descriptions she read about. The Grand Canyon, the Painted Desert, the Petrified Forest, they all sounded unreal to her. They were places other people visited, not Chris Casolaro from Boyle Heights. This was an adventure such as she'd never dared to dream about. She cast a surreptitious glance toward Paul. Maybe he was her magic genie after all. . . .

When they'd reached the state line and the impressive sight of Hoover Dam, he looked at her. "Want to stop and tour it?"

Now that they'd started, Chris was anxious to keep traveling. She shook her head. They crossed into Arizona and she hummed softly under her breath.

"Happy?"

"More like thrilled," she replied. "Imagine, two days ago I'd never been out of L.A. Now I've been to Nevada and Arizona."

She sounded like a child exclaiming over a new toy. He reflected on all the trips to London, Paris, New York, taken without a thought, on how often he complained over having to go. She made him feel at once ashamed and pleased that he could make this small trip possible for her. He again glanced her way. She was such a surprising mixture; seductive, sensible, and sweet all in one. Could she really be genuine?

"How old are you?" he abruptly asked.

"Twenty-six."

He felt stupidly pleased. He'd thought her younger. Not that it made any difference one way or the other. They were strictly traveling companions, nothing else. "Never married?"

"Now I know you're playing twenty questions," she sighed. "No, I've never been married."

"Any lovers?"

The guidebook shut with a snap. Chris could not believe

her ears. "Not, I am sure, nearly as many as you," she said tartly.

"No," he admitted easily. "But, then, I don't breathe even a whisper of innocence."

"No, you don't," she agreed on a short bite.

"It was just a question."

"It was an insulting bit of prying."

"I didn't mean it like that. Look, ask me a question. I'll tell you anything you want to know," he offered.

"Oh, really?"

"Absolutely."

She wasn't able to maintain a shred of anger when he grinned at her like that and he probably knew it, the rat. She wrinkled her nose at him. He glanced at her and prompted, "Well?"

"I'm thinking, I'm thinking." She cast a look full of devilment his way. "Hmmm. I already know you sleep in the nude. . . . What's your sign? No—dumb question."

"Scorpio."

"That doesn't count. I didn't ask it. Give me time, I'll come up with a question to knock your socks off."

He chuckled and she turned her gaze to the view beyond the windshield, knowing all the while that she'd never get up the courage to ask about *his* lovers.

It was one of those days of startling clarity. The sun stood high in a vast sky of brilliant blue without a hint of a cloud to mar the radiant effect. Rabbit brush dotted ginger sand; occasionally the scraggly branches of a Joshua tree disrupted the unchanging terra cotta tableau. It seemed immutable, as timeless as the ages. Only the rush of other cars disturbed the stillness. Even the heated air didn't move, scarcely whisking through the open window to tangle Chris's curls. The Maverick, of course, had no air conditioning and if it had, it wouldn't have worked. Chris felt the sweat trickle down her nape, cling to the cleft between her breasts.

Without reason, a vision of Paul's tongue tracing the

trail of sweat down her spine and over her breasts arose in Chris's mind. Once implanted, she couldn't shake the image and each bead of sweat fell with tantalizing tenacity down her skin.

At length, she glanced sidelong at him. One strong hand controlled the steering wheel, and that rather lazily. His right hand lay upon his thigh, drumming a restless pattern on the deep blue of his jeans. Her gaze drifted upward to the line of his hip tightly hugged by the new denims. Her heart fluttered. She looked away. She cleared her throat and insanely said the first thing that popped into her mind.

"We'll have to buy you a belt."

Damn! What was she doing? She'd as much as told him she'd been watching him, studying him, wanting him!

He smiled knowingly. "And you."

"I don't like to wear belts." She could only hope her tone sounded normal. Her pulse certainly wasn't.

"Why not?"

"Too restrictive," she answered without thinking.

"Yes," he drawled. "I know what you mean. A belt can certainly get in the way when you're in a . . . hurry."

Catching the glint in his eye, she flushed furiously. Her response infuriated her. She hadn't blushed like this since she was ten! She deliberately turned her head, slid down on the seat, and closed her eyes. The hum of the engine and the constant motion gently swayed her to sleep. When the car stopped she woke abruptly and sat up. They were in a gas station. "Where are we?"

"Kingman," replied Paul. He smiled down at her and she forgot why she'd been annoyed. "Are you hungry?"

She nodded and after the car was filled they crossed the road to a small café where they slid into a booth with cracked red vinyl seats. After ordering a cheeseburger and a roast beef sandwich, Paul handed the menus to the plump, cheery waitress with a rakish smile that elicited a feminine giggle. Chris was astounded at the flash of animosity she felt. He switched on charm like a high-wattage light bulb and the effect was brilliant. But it was simulated, as easily switched off, and Chris knew she'd do well to remember it. She busied herself with drinking her water, admonishing herself with severe strictures not to forget it. When she dared to look up at him, Paul was yawning. For the first time that day she noted the purple shadows tinging his eyes and the small lines of fatigue etched into the corners.

"You're tired," she stated in quick concern. "Didn't you sleep well last night?"

He held back what was on the tip of his tongue—*No, I didn't sleep at all because I was too wound up with images of you in that damn dress*—but he managed to choke back the words. He shrugged and said instead that the floor was a bit hard.

"I am sorry," she began.

"Don't be. It was only fair, since you had the floor the night before. We'll just have to see what other arrangements we can work out tonight."

She slid her gaze away from him, looking toward the counter. A tall glass case held flaking pieces of pie and a roll that looked as if it could double as a hockey puck. She knew what "other arrangement" she'd opt for, given the chance. Not wanting to consider the implications of that, she said firmly, "I'll drive this afternoon and you can catnap."

With an extra swish to her walk the waitress delivered their meal. She didn't bother to look at Chris. She garnished Paul's sandwich with an inviting smile, then seemed to catch her breath. "Hey, you look like somebody."

He grinned in a way that made Chris long to dump ketchup on his lap. "The man of your dreams?" he asked hopefully.

The curvaceous blonde giggled. Chris attacked her French fries with vigor.

"But it's true. You look like somebody, you know? You a TV star or somethin'?"

"Or something," he replied. He picked up his sandwich and the waitress reluctantly departed. Chris somehow restrained herself from sinking her fork into the retreating rear end.

"Whew," said Paul on an exaggerated sigh. She glared at him over her hamburger. He cajoled her with a smile. "Remind me to stay on your good side. You just cut that waitress to shreds with one glance."

She mumbled something unintelligible about what she'd like to do to him with a single glance and took a bite. He chuckled and began eating. Chris chewed and swallowed and told herself she didn't care how attractive he was. So he could pick up girls like lint. She didn't give a darn. Not a single, solitary darn. The waitress could have him on a platter for all she cared.

When they got up to leave she determinedly held out her hand. With a brief look that threatened to destroy her shell of reserve, he dropped the keys into her palm. She resented that look, and, even more, she resented her response to it. As he sprawled at an angle over the passenger's side, his shoulder hunched against the door, she was pulsatingly aware of him. Her blood seemed to sing with the message of his proximity. It made her doubly angry with him, with herself. She listened to his even breathing as he dozed, and her resentment mounted.

Paul did doze, but not as deeply nor as easily as Chris supposed. He'd closed his eyes because the temptation to stare at her upthrust breasts beneath the thin camisole disturbed him. In profile, he'd seen the peaks pressing against the embroidered cotton, seen the damp shadow where perspiration had plastered the cloth to her skin. He'd seen and longed to touch what he had seen.

Before he drifted off to sleep he tried to puzzle out just why she affected him that way. He decided part of her appeal was in the fact that he knew whatever response he

90

received from Christine would be totally honest. She would not be responding to a name or a bank account. She'd be responding to *him*. That alone made her exciting. But there was something more, something elemental in the way heat burned in his loins at the sight of her well-defined hips and buttocks, at the agonizing thought of her without the jeans, without the camisole.

He had to remind himself how insane it would be to get involved with her. But, then, would it be any crazier than this whole escapade? He knew deep down that he was behaving like an irresponsible fool, but he also knew he wasn't about to turn around and head home. He might not find the self-awareness he was seeking, but he had to try. And getting mixed up with Christine would only complicate the search. He reaffirmed his decision to leave her alone and finally, thankfully, dozed.

From the arid desert surrounding Kingman they gradually ascended into wooded mountains. The blue spruce and tall ponderosa pine enchanted Chris. She had never seen the cloistered beauty of a forest. She forgot Paul; she forgot herself. It was all she could do to keep her mind on the road. When Paul awoke, the first thing he saw was a rosy flush of animation tinting Christine's cheeks. He stretched.

"Where are we?"

She glanced at him reluctantly, as if to remove her eyes from the view was a punishment. "We just passed through a town called Ash Fork. Isn't this stunning?"

"Why not turn off the interstate and drive into the forest?"

Her face lit up with excitement. She turned onto the next major road and drove into Kaibab National Forest. After a while she pulled to the shoulder and they got out to stroll beneath the whispering trees. Chris bent her head back and gazed in reverent awe at the pine, spruce, and fir stretching up toward the celestial infinity. Beneath them needles and pines crackled, echoing amidst the cathedral hush.

Abruptly, in mid-step, Chris slid down to her rump. Paul was beside her in an instant, concern darkening his eyes to a near-black. "Are you hurt?"

"No," she breathed on a happy sigh. "I'm content. I never really dreamed there was beauty like this. And to think this is Arizona. I expected Arizona to be all sand and desert and cacti, not"—she paused, struggling for words and not finding them—"not this," she said at last with another sigh.

He sank slowly to sit down beside her. He looked around, seeing it through her eyes. A clump of lavender wildflowers swayed in the breeze. Deep green fungus clutched the bark of a tree. A nest of leaves and grasses nestled in a hollowed log. He saw all this and felt humbled. With all the traveling he'd done, he'd never felt this uplifted. He had never before seen things as Christine saw them, with awestruck appreciation.

She fell back, spreading her arms out on the pine-strewn earth. She turned her head toward him and smiled. "Thank you."

"I should be thanking you," he said with real sincerity.

They sat quietly, listening to the wind rustle in the trees as the birds scolded the invaders of their territory and unseen creatures scurried frantically. After a while Chris stirred and Paul fought not to look at her. She sat up and leaves, needles, and dirt tumbled from her. He gave in and looked. Her flyaway curls were littered with a charming array of nature's ornaments. He clenched his fist to keep from ruffling his hand through them. He strove to recall all the reasons not to touch her.

She rose in a single, swift motion, not bothering to dust the bits of earth and grass from her jeans. She wandered away as he sat watching her. She bent and plucked an alpine blossom from a purple cluster, then gaily stuck it into the tangles above her ear. She whirled and danced back toward him. "I feel like a gypsy ready to cast a magic spell."

"You have," he murmured, his gaze moving from the lavender petals feathered beside needles in her hair down to the line of her cheek and finally to the full curve of her mouth. "You've cast a spell on me."

She stared a moment, her lips quivering, tempting him beyond reason. Then she pivoted, her arms outstretched as if to embrace the forest. "Don't you wish we had a camera? I'd love to have pictures of this to remind me that I was really and truly here."

He didn't trust himself to answer her. He came to his feet and brushed debris from his clothes. Before he realized her intent, Chris rushed to help him. She stood so close, he felt the imprint of her arm and leg against his. As her hands fluttered over his back he went utterly still, fighting the urge to pull her against him, to throw her back down to the earth's bed and blanket her in kisses.

She felt the sudden tension in him and looked up. "Oh, you've a smudge," she laughed. She set her fingertips to his cheek and gently stroked, liking the feel of hard muscle and bone beneath the slightly rough skin. Her thumb grazed his lip and Paul thrust out his hands.

He meant to push her away, to shove temptation aside. But he was neither a sacrificing man nor a patient one. With a low guttural groan, he jerked her toward him instead.

CHAPTER SIX

For a single heartbeat Chris stared with startled eyes at Paul. The stark desire on his face made her mouth go dry. Then she lowered her lids and let her body sway against his.

With the uncontrollable passion of a dam that has burst, he flooded her senses. She tasted the warm command of his lips, the urgent demand of his plunging tongue. The scent of pine still clung to him; the sunlight speckled his skin with patches of heat. Her hands were crushed against his chest, where the unsteady hammering of his heartbeat echoed into her palms. She moved restlessly, wanting to coil herself around him, but he mistook her action for resistance and his grip tightened, his hands forcing her supple curves to flatten against the hard line of his thighs, his hips, his chest.

Knowing instinctively what he needed, Chris melted within his uncompromising arms, surrendering herself completely. Gradually Paul realized she wasn't resisting, she was responding ardently with a fever that sent his temperature skyrocketing. His kiss softened. His tongue darted over her lips, coaxing rather than commanding. As he felt her acquiescence, he loosened his hold to glide his hands over her. His strokes were restless, hungry, and rousing. Tingles rose from her breasts to her hips and she unconsciously arched to meet his touch. With a heated groan Paul slid his hands under the cotton hem of her camisole and swept it up over her fine-textured skin. A low mew of desire tore from Chris when he circled the soft underside of her breast with his fingertips.

His body shook with the force of his need. He had not expected this. He had not expected to be overpowered by this gnawing, aching need to have her. But when he touched the puckered nipple, the last vestige of his control evaporated. He had to have her and to hell with the consequences.

He pulled his hands away, stilling her protests with a deep, predatory kiss, a kiss that locked them together as he folded her to the ground. Purple petals floated from her hair, gently perfuming the air as he laid her on her side, facing him. In one motion their legs tangled and their arms twined together.

In a saner moment Chris would have asked herself what she was doing, why she was doing it. But this was not a sane moment. With the same incredible, insensible but irresistible urge that had led her to drive away with him, she now gave herself to his impassioned seduction. At some level she knew she was being foolish, knew she could be hurt, but Chris didn't care. All she cared about was the fire he ignited in her blood with each exquisite touch, each intense kiss.

Sunlight filtered through the tall pines to twist with shadow over them. A cool mountain breeze drifted past, but brought no relief to the heat searing them. A pinecone dropped with a muffled thud, a bird shrilled, and two heartbeats pounded as one.

Paul eased back, wanting to see the wonder of her passion for him. With a sensual languor her lids fluttered open and drowsily questioned his sudden stillness. For several seconds he was utterly immobile, unable to pull away from the glittering capitulation he saw in her eyes. Then she brought her hand up to his cheek and he turned his lips to the center of her palm.

"Oh, Christine," he whispered huskily as he nuzzled her hand. "I want you. I'm burning up with wanting you."

She didn't deny him. She'd have bitten off her tongue before denying him. She raised her arms to him and he inched the camisole off, his fingers teasing her ribs, dancing lightly over her soft flesh. When a single shaft of sunlight gilded the tawny swell of her breasts, he paused, entranced. He gazed at the rosy buds centered in browned aurioles and thought his blood would burst from his vessels. His entire body trembled with the pleasurable torment of waiting, but he wanted to prolong this piercing excitement so unlike any other he'd known.

She quivered and he could wait no longer. He captured one stiff peak between his lips and murmured her name, his tongue humming against her breast.

Chris thought she would go mad with the delirium of it. She thrust her hands under his knit shirt and touched him feverishly, feeling the hard bone and firm muscles beneath the smooth skin. Feathery hair curled from his waist upward and she toyed with it. His stomach tightened in response and she was certain she would die if he did not take her.

"Paul, please," she begged softly. "Please."

He did not need to be asked. His hunger for her could no longer go unassuaged. Cradling her head with his palms, he drove his mouth against hers and rolled her onto her back, trapping her beneath the solid weight of his body.

She cried out and in his dazed state it was several seconds before he realized her cry was one of pain. He lifted his head and saw the grimace marring her features. She set her hands against his chest and pushed, then pushed again before he responded. As he shifted she sat up and a thick, red stream ran slowly down her upper arm.

"Chris! What is it?"

"I'm not sure, I think I landed on a rock." She looked

over her left shoulder and calmly pressed her right hand against the wet stain oozing from a jagged cut.

Paul uttered a vivid curse and yanked her hand away to examine her wound. The puncture looked about an inch long, but not terribly deep. It was, however, exuding blood steadily. He swore again. "Damn it, you're hurt!"

Despite her pain, she almost smiled. "Yes, I know."

He glanced at her and his frown deepened, altered from concern to anger. Her composure irritated him. He was still throbbing with frustrated desire, shocked from the abrupt halt, and she was looking at him as if nothing out of the ordinary had occurred. He turned his anger to the rock, an arrow-shaped projectile stuck upright in the ground. He loosened it with a vicious kick, then picked it up and hurled it into the clustered recesses of the forest.

"Do you think perhaps we should get back to the car?" Chris inquired in a faintly amused tone.

He whirled to find her standing unsteadily, her arm awkwardly bent as she held her hand against the wound. Her face had paled alarmingly. Without giving her a chance to stop him, he swooped her into his arms. "Do you have a first aid kit in the car? Have you had a tetanus shot? How badly do you hurt?" he fired at her as he carried her back the way they'd come.

"I hope you don't get blood on your new shirt," was all she said before closing her eyes and giving herself up to the pleasure of being held in his arms.

Thinking she'd fainted, Paul increased his stride, his concern for her now overriding his frustration. He wasn't used to considering other people's needs. The anxiety burdening him now was totally foreign. He did not like it. But he didn't stop to analyze his feelings; he simply knew that if something happened to her, he would not forgive himself.

When he set her carefully on the front seat, her eyes fluttered open. His relief was immense, but was almost instantly submerged as his anxiety pricked a vein of anger.

97

How could she frighten him like this? He pivoted away from her to impatiently begin rummaging through the gym bag.

"What are you doing?" asked Christine faintly.

He ignored her. He continued to ignore her queries as he extracted his white silk shirt. When he proceeded to rip it, however, her shriek of protest got his attention.

"Paul! Oh, how could you? Your shirt—"

"Shut up," he ordered. He staunched the flow of blood with the wad he'd torn from his shirt, then bound it in place with one of the sleeves knotted over her shoulder. He checked the map, then tossed it down with a muttered oath. With a speed that made Chris feel dizzy, he drove back to the interstate. She opened her mouth to ask where they were going, saw the tension in his jaw, and thought better of it. She kept her gaze fixed on the scenic view whizzing by and tried not to notice the pain in her shoulder. At the town of Williams he pulled off the interstate, but it wasn't until he'd parked in front of the Williams Emergency Center that she said anything at all. He bent to lift her from the car and she shoved his hands away.

"I can walk. Honestly, you'd think I'd been crippled. It's just a small nick in my shoulder."

He firmly thrust her flailing hands aside and picked her up to carry her, loudly voicing her objections every inch of the way, into the center. A little over an hour later she walked out beside a still silent Paul, her small wound having been doused with antiseptic and properly dressed. She had not needed stitches, but at Paul's demand she'd been given a tetanus shot. Her arm now ached more than her shoulder. He held open the door for her, then dropped the gauze pads and antiseptic he'd purchased onto her lap before getting in on his side. But he did not start the car.

After one long, strained minute stretched into another, Chris chanced a look at him. He was staring out over the wheel. As if he sensed her gaze upon him, he turned to look at her. Her breath caught at the dark emotion she saw reflected in the jet black of his eyes.

"That was sheer hell," he said through lips that barely moved.

She tried to lessen the tension thrumming between them. "*You* think it was hell? You should've had the shot!"

He did not even smile. He continued to look at her blankly, then he slowly stretched out a hand and patted the place beside him. "Come here," he said softly.

She looked down at the long, smooth hand thumping the seat, as if seeing a tarantula sidling over the vinyl. Amid the hustling reality of the emergency center she'd come to half-believe she had imagined the explosion of passion in the sun-dappled forest. It had all been conjured up out of her own throbbing desires, hadn't it?

He watched the conflicting expressions cross her face. He knew just how she felt. He'd wrangled against his desires for two days. A derisive curl touched his mouth. He was through fighting to be sensible. He was through being noble. Desire had won out in the forest. As irrational, as dangerous as it was, he meant to have her. She had not moved. He repeated more firmly, "Come here, Chris. I need you."

Feeling like a puppet whose strings were being shortened, she went to him. He took the pile from her lap and dumped it onto the shelf beside the maps. Then he turned to her and slowly brought his palms to her cheeks. His gaze searched hers. If he continued to look at her like that, Chris was certain she'd need to return to the fluorescent clatter of the emergency room for treatment on her heart.

"You'll stay with me tonight," he said thickly.

Her tongue felt weighted with lead. She managed to open her lips. His eyes dropped to them and they parted further on a short, thrilled gasp. "I—I have been—"

He kissed her once, a brief thrust of his lips against hers that spoke volumes of determination. He leaned back, his hands still framing her face. "You know what I mean. What happened between us isn't finished. We'll share more than a room tonight, Christine. We'll share a bed. We'll share each other."

Despite the emphatic statement, his eyes implied the question he refused to ask. She wondered what was in that shot she'd been given. Her heart and her pulse were leaping like spring lambs, but her mind and her tongue seemed mired in a slough of molasses. When he pressed his hands angrily against her bones and prompted, "Chris?" she somehow nodded. At once a long shudder rippled through him; she felt it in his fingertips as they eased from her cheeks.

"Then we'd better be on our way," he said with a wry smile.

The road to Flagstaff cut through the heart of two national forests. To Christine it was like being in Wonderland, the beauty of it so immense, so vastly different from anything she'd ever known. She wanted desperately not to miss a moment of it, but the emotional excitement of the day, the extremes from her despondency in the morning to her fiery desire in the afternoon, simply eroded her ability to stay alert. Even her initial tension of being pressed so closely to Paul failed to keep her awake. Her eyelids drifted down and she slept.

She woke with a shiver, caressed by a cooling breeze. The busy hum of a city surrounded them and a pink-hued twilight was just beginning to touch the streets. She looked around, dazed.

"Cold?" asked Paul in a voice that cloaked her in warmth.

"A little."

His right hand had been resting on her left thigh. He reached around her shoulders and pulled her tightly to his side. "Don't worry. We'll soon be inside."

She trembled violently at the husky intimation in his tone. "Th-this is Flagstaff?" she stammered.

"Yes." He glanced at her. Whatever he saw sent a fleeting frown over his face, but it was quickly smoothed away. He withdrew his arm and repeated, "Don't worry, baby."

He wasn't talking about the cold and she knew it. She fixed her gaze on the view and worried. What had she agreed to? He'd sleep with her all the way to New York, pleasuring himself, fulfilling his wants and needs, and then casually say good-bye. And if she let him pay her, she'd feel like a prostitute. But could she back out now? Did she even want to? She could feel the sexual tension rising from him like heat from a steambath.

Flagstaff was a mountain town, scented with pine and bustling with tourists. The dark green tower of Elden Mountain dominated the northeast end of the city; beyond that, the snow-capped San Francisco peaks rose into the pink-streaked sky. Lumbermen sauntered down the street; dusty, work-worn cowboys lounged next to battered pick-up trucks; Indian women strutted by in native costumes to catch the interest of the passing stream of tourists. According to the guidebook, winter crowds swarmed in to go skiing at the Snow Bowl just thirteen miles away; in summer they came for camping and sightseeing and trading for jewelry, blankets, ceramics, and baskets peddled by Hopi and Navajo Indians.

They stopped at a half dozen hotels and motels without finding a room. Paul's frustration mounted with each stop. He'd spent the short drive from Williams remembering the sight and taste and feel of Christine and anticipating the night to come. Finally Chris suggested they stop at a gas station and ask someone where they might find something. Paul somehow managed to rein in his rising anger to seek advice from a middle-aged, grease-daubed attendant. Chris watched through the windshield and knew whatever he was hearing wasn't pleasing him. His shoul-

101

ders tensed beneath the brown knit shirt; his hands angrily rode the hips of his jeans.

He came back to the car with ringing steps, got in, and sat silently for several seconds. "There isn't anything to be had," he said at last. "They're about to have some big powwow and the town's booked solid."

"Nothing at all?"

"He said there's a youth hostel that might be able to take us in," replied Paul flatly.

It was obvious there was something more. Having already learned a bit about Paul's temperament, Chris waited patiently. At length he glanced at her. "But it's dormitory-style, five people to a room, men and women separated."

Her eyes widened. Chris rapidly lowered her gaze to her lap so he could not see the amused relief, the agitated disappointment attacking her. Up to this very moment she'd never believed in fate, feeling intensely that people made their own destinies. Now, however, she began to realize only providence could have arranged such an ironic dénouement to this day.

He set his fingers under her chin and tipped her head up. "We could stay the night in the car."

"We'd freeze. It's chilly already, by midnight—"

"Don't tell me," he muttered, "the heater doesn't work."

"Only when it wants to," she admitted.

He cursed, then said, "Doesn't anything on this damn heap of scrap metal work?"

"The cigarette lighter," teased Chris.

For one second he looked as if he longed to hit her, then his face changed, softened. He stroked her cheek with his thumb. "I'd keep you warm, baby."

She shook her head. "It isn't practical and"—she set her fingers lightly against his lips to still his protest—"I'm too old to find the idea of sex in the back seat appealing."

The breath of his sigh warmed her fingertips, then he

102

gently nibbled on the pads. "I only hope," he said as he kissed each finger, "that this damn hostel has an ice-cold shower."

Laughing, she pulled her fingers back. She flicked her lashes at him. "Maybe we'll get lucky and they'll be full up."

"Another remark like that and we won't get to the hostel."

She laughed again and he at last started the car. It was a heady feeling, knowing she could excite a man of the world like Paul. She may not know much about him, but she was certain he had never been inclined to back-seat romance. It wasn't his style. His suggestion had implied a level of need that intoxicated her. She couldn't decide whether or not she hoped the hostel could accommodate them.

It could. Ignoring the wild west decor, they checked in and paid for the beds and rented sleeping sacks before sharing a meal at a natural-food café downstairs. Chris dug happily into a pita bread sandwich stuffed with bean sprouts while Paul stabbed at his broccoli quiche with an impatient air. Once he looked up and caught her smiling at him, laughter in her eyes.

"Just what do you find so amusing?" he asked belligerently.

"You. Yesterday morning you looked at me as if you wouldn't touch me with a ten-foot pole, and now you're making mash of your quiche because you can't."

A very leisurely smile replaced his scowl. "Which shows you how stupid I can be on Sunday mornings."

"Especially after Saturday nights," she teased.

"Especially after Saturday nights," he agreed with rueful self-reproach. He toyed with his food, then looked at her. "I knew then, you know."

"Knew what?"

"Knew I wanted you. I took a look at you in that tight

103

red thing and my hormones started jumping. Even drunk I knew I wasn't about to leave that dive without you."

Her own amusement faded. She stared down at her sandwich, focusing on a bright red wedge of tomato nestled into the lettuce and sprouts. So she had been just a pick-up after all.

"Oh," she said dully.

The clink of flatware, the chatter of other eaters filled the silence that divided them. She managed a bite of her sandwich and wondered how she got it down her constricted throat. Then Paul leaned forward. "It wasn't the same for you? Isn't that why you ran away with me?" he inquired quietly.

"No," she said, and knew she was lying. She could only hope he didn't know it. "No. I went with you for the money. And because I knew you were in no condition to drive yourself."

"The social worker instinct," he snapped.

"You should be glad. I got you to Las Vegas in one piece. And by the next morning—when you were sober— you didn't want me anyway. You made that very clear."

"The next morning I was too hung over to listen to my hormones."

"If what happened today was just your hormones talking, it's a darn good thing we have separate rooms tonight."

"It wasn't just *my* hormones, baby. Yours were pretty damn vocal—or don't you remember how you begged me to love you?"

They were suddenly glaring at each other, bristling with hostility. Chris sputtered with speechless hurt and rage. How dare he accuse her of begging him! She wouldn't ask him for a quarter to make a call. Sprouts sprayed over the table as she slapped her sandwich down on the plate and jumped up.

Paul lunged forward and grabbed her wrist to keep her from leaving. "Where do you think you're going?"

"Anywhere you're not."

He yanked on her wrist, jarring her up to her back teeth. "Sit down," he ordered.

"I am not a dog," she hissed. But she sat down.

"No," he concurred in a voice suddenly husky. "You're not."

His anger, which had been ignited by frustration and a bruised ego at the notion that she hadn't wanted him the way he had wanted her, began dissolving as soon as he touched her. He liked the silken feel of her. He wondered if she was that smooth and soft all over. Loosening his clasp, he kept his fingers curled about her wrist and began lazily rubbing his thumb over her skin. "You look like a gremlin when you're angry."

"I thought the line was 'you look beautiful when you're angry.'" He didn't say anything and her temper flared anew. "And don't you dare tell me I'm not beautiful!"

"I wouldn't dream of saying anything so ungallant," he murmured, but he felt a quiver of surprise as he looked at her. It was true. She wasn't beautiful. And yet he fervently wanted to leap over the table and take her then and there. He attempted to distract himself from the lewd direction of his thoughts.

"How's your shoulder?" he asked.

"Sore."

"And your arm?" he prodded with one of his switched-on smiles. His fingers crept upward.

Chris gazed at the smile, shivered at the touch, and allowed herself to be mollified. She couldn't be mad at him because she wasn't beautiful. And how could she be mad at him for wanting her on sight? She decided it would be much safer not to answer that one. She returned his smile and extracted herself from his hold. "There's a knot there the size of an orange. I'm beginning to think I'd rather have lockjaw."

His smile vanished. "Don't joke like that. I got the

fright of my life when I saw that stream of blood on your shoulder."

"You think I wasn't frightened?" He didn't respond to the teasing lilt in her tone, so she sighed and pointed out, "Hey, I was the one in pain, remember."

"I'm in pain too," he said. "I'm still aching with frustration. God, I want you."

Her stomach fluttered at the naked desire that set rigidly over his face. "I, um, I—shouldn't we go to bed?"

He thrust back his chair with a jerk that bordered on violent. "Damn rocks," he muttered under his breath.

She wisely kept silent as she followed him from the restaurant. She doubted she could have spoken anyway. She didn't have enough breath left for speech.

Upstairs, he paused outside her door. He leaned toward her, brushed his lips against her temple, and whispered, "Dream about me. Dream about us in a forest without rocks."

Then he spun around and strode down the hall toward his own quarters. She watched him go with a tingling mixture of regret and relief, then resolutely went into her own room.

The hostel had a ten o'clock curfew with lights out by eleven, so when she entered, her four roommates were already there. Two pretty blondes were playing a game with a ragged deck of cards while speaking in a lilting foreign language that she thought sounded Scandinavian. A third lay curled in her bed, tucked in a ball so tight, all that could be seen of her was a tumbling mane of sandy hair. The fourth occupant sat on the floor, her legs knotted like a pretzel with her hands on the knees, murmuring to herself as her long hair swayed over her shoulders. Chris cast them all a cautious smile and began spreading her sleeping bag out over a narrow bed that seemed to have more lumps than mattress springs.

She made her way to the bathroom down the hall and returned, feeling better for having washed and brushed her

106

teeth. As she entered, the yoga enthusiast unfurled and stood. Her hair was a mixture of dull red and brown that reminded Chris of the desert surrounding Kingman. Streams of it flicked the air as she glided toward Christine.

"Howdy," she said in a friendly way, but her eyes glinted with sharp assessment as they traveled over Chris. She was a tall string of a girl, with a long, thin face that had experience stamped over its youthful lines. An uneven fringe of bangs covered her brow, melting into her almost-invisible eyebrows. Her eyes had a wary half closed look, as if she viewed the world with a perpetual squint, and her wide mouth had a hard bite to it. A feeling of recognition crawled up Christine's spine as she studied the girl. That hardened, prematurely aged look covered half the faces she'd grown up with.

"I'm Jennifer." The girl waited and as Chris said nothing, went on. "You slumming?"

Chris looked at her with raised brows. "Come again?"

"I mean, well, you don't look like the type to stay in a hostel, you know."

"Don't I?"

Jennifer smiled a slow, easy smile that took the pinch out of her narrow face. "Not on a bet."

That much was true enough, thought Chris with a wry smile. She wasn't the hostel type. She glanced around, taking in the youth of her roommates, the austere accommodations, the narrow cot, the sleeping bag, and asked herself what she was doing there. "There wasn't any room anywhere else. How about you? Stay in hostels often?"

Shrugging, Jennifer leaned forward and whispered, "Take my advice and sleep with your money tucked in your pants."

"Thanks for the tip." Chris ran her eyes over the starveling, taking in the bagginess of the fraying jeans and the shapeless fit of the faded pink T-shirt, and wished she'd smuggled some food up from the café.

The girl straightened. "No problem. Where you traveling to? The Canyon?"

"No. We're on our way to New York."

"Super. Who's we?"

"My—uh—my friend and I. He's in a room down the hall."

Sliding to the middle of Christine's bed, Jennifer shook her head and sighed knowingly. "That's the trouble with hostels, you know? The price is right, but the rules are a drag. They make you feel like you're in school or something. I only stay in a hostel when I can't find somewhere else just as cheap."

Agreeing with a noncommittal nod, Chris tugged on her nightie and neatly folded her top and jeans. Watching her, Jennifer asked with a teasing, yet too worldly air, "How do you think your old man's getting on with the boys?"

"He's not my old man," Chris denied, too quickly.

A knowing, disbelieving look flicked across her gaunt features as Jennifer said, "Oh, yeah?"

It was stupid, utterly ridiculous, the way that look upset her. Chris told herself it was just a kid's smart-aleck remark. She tried to shrug it off, but only partially succeeded.

The lights flicked off and on twice, signaling the five-minute warning to lights out. Jennifer muttered something about adolescent rules, which brought an unwilling smile to Christine's lips. Talk about adolescents! Chris gently nudged her bony shoulder and the girl flashed a broad grin as she scooted away to scramble into the next bed. The card players reluctantly gathered up the deck and crawled into their beds across the room. The lights went out. Night shadows scurried over the bare floor to hide in corners.

Amid the hushed whispers and bedsqueaks and the clash of breathing from the others, Chris lay on her side and tried not to listen to the echo of Jennifer's worldly wise "Oh, yeah?" as it bounded within her mind. He wasn't her old man. He wasn't her anything. Not yet.

Slumming. The word jumped out of the darkness. Chris shivered within the sleeping bag. The kid didn't know it, but she'd been right on target with that one. Only it was Paul who was slumming, not she. She'd known at first glance she wasn't his type. He was just amusing himself for the duration of the trip.

She flipped onto her back. The bed groaned in protest. Her sore shoulder landed on a lump with the resiliency of a brick. She stifled a moan, but couldn't smother a sudden wave of misery. What was she doing here?

Had Theresa been right all along? Had she been drugged? Yes, she thought, she'd been drugged all right, drugged by the potency of dark eyes and the charm of quirking lips. *Fool!* she called herself and again rolled to her side.

With a stubborn resolution she enumerated all the reasons why she should not allow him to seduce her. She was far too attracted to him, for one thing. While he plainly admitted his desire for her was purely physical—just hormones!—Chris feared her attraction went far deeper. She found herself reacting to all the worst things about him, to his short temper, to his melancholy eyes, to his impatience and, most of all, to his obvious hunger for her. The fact that he could also be utterly charming and tender frightened her. It confused the issue, blinding her to the basic fact that for him this was another sexual interlude.

If she ignored all that and took a chance on heartbreak by giving in to her own desires, if she allowed herself to become his lover, Chris knew she could not accept payment for this trip. She couldn't become a paid companion. Such a notion was repugnant to her. But if she didn't take the money, she would be mired in a financial mess. No job, no school, no way to pay her rent.

She counted objections until she was certain she'd be counting them in her sleep. Instead, she fell asleep to dream about sunlight and shadow twining together in a forest without rocks.

110

The door creaked as she cracked it open, causing her to wince and hold her breath. All four of her roommates slept on, apparently undisturbed. Chris slid through the narrow gap into the hall. A shadow wavered and she jumped, only barely repressing a shriek.

"Dream about me?" queried Paul with a smile that should have carried a warning label for the weak-hearted.

Her mouth still hung open; Chris could not move. His black hair was endearingly sleep-tousled, the harsh lines normally in his face were for once smoothed away. A very pale powder blue shirt was tucked negligently into his jeans, the sleeves rolled haphazardly to his elbows and half the buttons undone. Looking at him, all her desires and fears swept over her in a crashing wave.

"You scared me to death!" she whispered furiously.

"Well, I've said you're like a cat. Actually you're more of a kitten, but that still leaves you eight lives to go." He was grinning, but his smile tilted lopsidedly as he looked at her. The nightgown she wore was very thin. He could see the dark aureoles of her breasts beneath the fabric. Seeing them, he remembered how she had looked with only sunlight and the shadow of his body covering her, and his throat went dry.

Chris saw the direction of his fixed stare, realized what she was—and wasn't—wearing and huddled back against the door. He caught hold of her arm, impeding her retreat. "I've been waiting nearly an hour for you to get up. Checkout time's at nine thirty. How long till you think you'll be ready to leave?"

"I'll meet you downstairs in ten minutes," she said quickly. He nodded, bent to kiss the top of her tumbled hair, and left. She called herself a fool every step of the way to the bathroom. Once again the clear light of day threw the picture into sharp perspective. She was going to put a stop to this before she did something thoroughly demented. The last thing she needed was to fall for him. Once they would reach New York, he'd forget about her and she'd be left trying to piece her heart back together. In no way was she going to set herself up for that sort of fall. She wasn't going to become his playmate of the trip and she'd make that crystal clear to him as soon as she got downstairs.

After washing and changing the gauze on her shoulder, she returned to her room and pulled on her jeans and her other new top, a cream blouse splashed with violet pansies. The sleeves were short and puffed; the wide collar dipped into a gentle V. It was light and cool and buoyed her with false confidence as she sped down to confront Paul.

He was waiting at the foot of the stairs. She felt his eyes upon her each step of the way. Her pulse accelerated alarmingly.

As she reached the last step he grabbed her by the waist and whirled her into his arms, bumping her purse wildly against the gym bag in her hand. She gasped and suddenly her lips were branded by his.

The impact was hot, hard, and hungry. The feverish pull of his mouth against hers was better than any of her dreams. Mewing, she opened her lips to the caress of his tongue; she wove her free hand into the thick, soft layers of his hair. Her veins seemed to run with molten blood, burning her to her very core. She forgot her new resolu-

112

tions. She forgot the ache in her shoulder, the knot in her arm. She forgot where she was, why she was, who she was. She surrendered totally to this searing fantasy.

Gradually he eased her feet to the floor and nibbled gently at her lower lip. Still nestling her to fit the mold of his body, he teased her with light kisses over her cheek, then flicked his tongue over the shell of her ear. "Now, that's what I call the way to start the morning," he drawled in a voice of smoke. "You pack more punch than Wheaties."

"So," she sighed breathlessly, "do you."

His hands grabbed her hips, then he forced himself to lessen his grip. He rubbed his jaw in her disheveled curls. "Did you miss me last night?"

She could feel the ripple of his muscles as he spoke. The effect was intoxicating, like a mind-altering drug. She tipped back her head and drowsily met his gaze. "Not at all," she murmured, and half-lowered her lashes at the sudden darkening of his eyes. "You were right there in my dreams all night long."

With an incoherent mutter he crushed her lips once more to his, letting her feel the depth of his need in one mighty thrust of his tongue. When he drew back he was trembling, out of breath, flushed. Paul brought his hands to her hair, the tenderness of his touch as he brushed the curls back from her face at odds with the force of his heavy-lidded gaze.

"I missed you last night. For all the sleep I got, we might as well have driven on through. Next time, baby, we'll take our chances in the car."

The mention of the car brought Chris back to reality. She shivered, but whether from her lingering exhilaration or from fear she couldn't have said. Wiggling out of his clasp, she fortified herself with a deep breath and said firmly, "Paul, I've thought this out all night long—"

"So have I," he interrupted huskily. He reached for her, but she eluded his hands.

113

"I'm serious. We can't continue this way."

Paul's reaction was far from encouraging. The warmth went out of his face, his brows clamped together. "What do you mean?" he asked on a growl.

"I mean this." She gestured helplessly and struggled to explain herself. "The deal was strictly traveling companions, nothing more."

"That was before."

"It's now too," she insisted. Her chin tilted upward. She couldn't allow herself to forget again, as she just had, that he was talking strictly hormones.

His expression softened a little as he watched hers harden. He spoke in a cajoling caress, "Chris, sweetheart, surely you want me as much as I want you?"

"You only want me because I'm here. Once we're in New York you'll forget I ever existed." She spoke with the steeliness of cold conviction. Yet a hope that he would deny it fluttered in her breast.

"Contrary to what you seem to believe, I do not lust after every female within ten paces," he said with gentle sarcasm.

She drew a long breath, trying vainly not to be disappointed. "I'm not your type and you know it. You're just slumming. Why would you want someone like me?"

He had no answer for that. She was right, she wasn't his type. He didn't know himself why he wanted her. He tried out one of his smiles on her. This time, however, she wasn't buying. She took his silence for concurrence and turned away. "Damn it, Chris," he began.

"We'd better get on the road," she cut in coolly.

He yanked the gym bag from her hand and eyed her with hostility. She met his glare directly. After a tense moment he spun away from her and stamped outside. Sighing, knowing she'd done the best thing but unable to suppress her regret over it, she followed him out. She had done the right thing. She had. Yet the explosive pleasure

114

of Paul's kiss tingled on her lips to tantalize her with doubts.

Scowling, Paul got into the driver's seat and waited with barely restrained impatience. She got in and handed him the keys. Before leaving town, they stopped at a convenience store and purchased a cooler, ice, beer, and sodas as well as some stale pastries and coffee. Until they were well past the lush meadows and mountain glades of Flagstaff, conversation in the Maverick was limited to "Like another roll?" and "Thanks" or "No thanks."

But as they came out of the mountains and into the desert, Paul felt he had to speak out. He knew she was being sensible. But he didn't want to be sensible. He wanted Christine, he wanted to be loving her senseless. He shook free of the images that flooded his mind and said in what he hoped was a voice of reason, "Look, I don't know where you got the crazy idea that I'm slumming with you, but that's not how I feel at all."

She dragged her eyes from the vast nothingness stretching out around them. "Oh, come on, I'm from the wrong side of town and you know it."

"What's that got to do with anything?"

"It's got everything to do with everything." There was a nasty ring to her tone that she couldn't erase any more than she could eliminate the hope that he would somehow convince her she was mistaken. She was certain he couldn't have any lasting interest in her, but she wanted desperately to be shown that he could.

He clenched his jaw. He wasn't used to rejection of this type and he had no clear idea how to deal with it. "That's a copout. Tell me what happened between last night and this morning to make you change your mind about me."

"Nothing changed my mind. I just came to my senses, that's all. From the moment I met you I knew you were out of my class." She glanced nervously at him, caught the glare he shot her way, and quickly turned her gaze to the window. "Look, can you deny that you're upper class?"

115

"Upper class? What the hell do you mean, upper class? We don't have a class system in America."

That brought her eyes back to him in a hurry. "Don't have a class system? Where have you been living? On a desert island? Oh, we don't have a peerage, I'll grant you that, but we certainly have an aristocracy, a privileged class based on wealth."

"I repeat, what has that got to do with us?"

"We don't mix. It'd be like putting gravel in with diamonds and expecting no one to notice all the stones didn't gleam. Maybe you get your jollies dabbling with the lower class, but I'm not up for dabbling."

His grip tightened about the steering wheel. The car picked up speed. After ten strained seconds he said harshly, "You're a snob, you know that?"

Her brows came together in just the way he most disliked, emphasizing how straight and thick they were. "*I'm* a snob?"

"Yes. You. You've got anyone not on the poverty line marked down as a bastard."

"It's a fact of life that the rich are too rich and the poor are too poor."

"And that automatically condemns the rich in your eyes."

"Yes, it does," she snapped. It wasn't true, but she was angry with him for making her defend herself, for making her explain why she didn't want to get involved with him. She wasn't about to admit the simple truth that she was afraid, afraid of being hurt.

Another surge of speed sent the car flying over the interstate. The engine seemed to snarl and the flash of white lines dizzied Chris. She couldn't see the speedometer in its recessed oval, but she knew the indicator was well past fifty-five. She wanted very much to ask Paul to slow down. The hard set of his jaw, however, warned her not to say a word. Swallowing back any criticism, she turned

116

her gaze to the sere beauty sprawling endlessly around them.

A shroud of silence settled heavily between them.

The sun had not yet reached its zenith when they pulled off at a scenic stop overlooking the Painted Desert. The view was breathtaking. Clay slopes were nature's canvas for a vibrant display of colors, from rosy pink to geranium red, delicate lavender to deepest purple. Hills rose and fell in a stunning spectrum, constantly shifting hues as cloud shadows passed over them. It cast a hypnotic spell; Chris momentarily forgot her worries.

Paul stood behind her, trying to convince himself to let well enough alone. He should be grateful that she didn't want to make a mess of the situation by becoming his lover. Unfortunately gratitude didn't come close to what he was feeling. He looked at her as she stared raptly at the distant mesas.

Perspiration had dampened the back of her blouse and he could clearly see the ridge of her spine. As he gazed at the thin cloth clinging so tightly to her back, he remembered how she felt, her scent, her taste. Her short dark curls clumped together on her nape, forming a lovelock that settled it. His indecision was over. He was going to have her and any consequences be damned.

He set his hand on the small of her back. "Like it?" he asked in a carefully friendly voice.

Tipping her head to the side, she murmured her assent. The heat of his palm seemed to burn through her blouse. Oddly it made her feel like shivering. With credible composure she asked, "Don't you?"

Looking straight at her, he replied, "I find the view . . . mesmerizing."

Her pulse catapulted. She licked her lips. They still felt dry. "Paul—"

"Don't say it, Chris. Don't shut me out because of what you think I am. Wait until you know."

Doors slammed as another car stopped and a family of

four joined them at the site. She looked down at the canvas toes of her jogging shoes. What could she say? Could she tell him it wasn't he that she feared, but herself? She didn't give love easily, but when she did it went deep. She feared the depth her feelings might plummet; she feared the heartache she would suffer.

The strident voice of a woman telling her children to stand still brought her back to reality. She lifted her head and said evenly, "Let's go back to the car. We can talk on the way."

He nodded and they returned to the Maverick in a silence so palpable Chris thought she could reach out and grab it. She wiped her brow, shoving her sweat-sodden bangs back, as if by doing so she could sweep away the confusion clogging her mind. Once in the car, they sat, tensely immobile. Finally Paul swiveled to face her. "Well?" he prompted.

"I—you're—we're rushing," she stammered. "It's been only three days. You can't expect me to know what I feel, what I want after just three days."

"I know what I want."

"Oh, I know what you want too. You've made that perfectly clear," she bit back with more than a shade of scorn. "It took you all of three minutes to want that."

Shouting, the two children ran up to the car beside them, followed by their scolding mother and camera-laden father. Muttering under his breath, Paul started the car and turned back onto the highway. Once on the way, he inquired coolly, "So what do you think you want?"

"I'd like to stick to the bargain we made," she answered promptly, wishing it were the total truth. "And I think it would be better if we didn't share a room."

"Afraid I'll attack in the night?" he said in a nasty tone.

She was more afraid she would, but she couldn't tell him that. She waited a few seconds, then said slowly, "You asked me not to shut you out. Well, I'm willing to

118

do that. But you have to be willing not to press me too much, too fast. Give me that chance to know you, Paul.''

He didn't say anything and Chris slumped in her corner with a sense of defeat. If he really wanted her, surely he'd argue more strenuously. But, of course, she was relieved that he hadn't. Wasn't she? Wasn't she pleased to have gotten her way so easily?

He knew he should be pleased that she was willing to get to know him. But that was the problem. She wanted to get to know Paul. Paul, not Preston. With a sinking feeling in his gut, he imagined her reaction to Preston Ridgeway. It wasn't a pretty image. Given her emphatic views, the Ridgeway name wouldn't be likely to thrill her. He briefly wished he'd told her the truth from the beginning, but he knew it was too late now. It was too late for the chance he so badly wanted.

Shrugging off the nagging feeling that he was making the wrong decision, he commented on the continual spectacle of rockhounds working with picks at the roadside. She murmured noncommittally. He tried again, asking her what she thought of the desert. She replied tonelessly that it was a lot of empty space. Though he felt like shaking her, he let her lack of response go by. He was determined to be patient. He waited a while, then nudged her and pointed out the sight of a golden eagle floating like a cork on a spiraling thermal current.

Chris effused over the beauty of it, mentally congratulating herself on a fine performance. At the moment she felt as effervescent as a wrung-out washrag. Despite the bright colors of the sandstone, shale, and clay, she had decided the desert was oppressively uniform. There was little vegetation beyond the scrub brush and cactus clinging tenaciously to the baked earth. Tumbleweeds sometimes drifted across the road, but failed to disturb the unrelenting dullness engulfing them. The air was stifling; the sun was sweltering. Perspiration saturated the back of her blouse, dripped down the front of her brow. She thought if Paul asked her one more time what she thought of the view, she would throw up.

Suddenly a wave of nausea hit her and she knew she was going to do just that.

"Please . . . stop," she gasped, then doubled over and stuck her head between her knees.

One glance at her and Paul pulled to a halt. He slammed out of the car and raced to the other side. He yanked open the door and reached for Chris, who frantically pushed his hands aside. He grabbed both of her hands in one of his and swiveled her sideways, facing out the door. It was not a moment too soon. Miserable, embarrassed, Christine lost her breakfast on the shoulder of the interstate.

Her head still hung between her knees. She didn't think she could lift it up. She wasn't sure she wanted to. She heard a string of curses coming from the back as Paul wrenched the cooler out of the car. Eventually a cool, damp cloth touched the back of her neck and she moaned.

"Why didn't you tell me you weren't feeling well, baby?" asked Paul. He laid a palm against her cheek. "You're burning up. You should have said something," he chided gently.

"I didn't know . . . I'd no idea . . . I was going to . . ."

He shushed her and, using another remnant of his silk shirt, continued to sponge her neck and face, wiping away the traces of her sickness. He raised her head and dampened her throat, then her arms and hands. She sat limply and allowed him to minister to her without objection until he began unbuttoning her blouse. Then she feebly swatted at his hands.

"What are you doing?" she grumbled.

"Not attacking you, if that's what you're thinking," he said with amusement thickening his tones. "Now be a good girl and let me take care of you."

She didn't have the strength to fight him. She felt like a gigantic rag doll as she let him turn her this way and that

120

while he undid the bottom half of her blouse, rolled it up to just beneath her breasts and tied the ends in a jaunty center knot. When he unzipped her jeans, she muttered vaguely, but didn't stop him from removing them.

"Damn, we weren't using our heads back in Vegas at all. We needed shorts, not jeans." He eyed the pair in his hands with disfavor and tried not to notice how sheer her underpants were. "If I could rip these damn things . . ."

"I've got a pocketknife," she mumbled without thinking.

The shadow of a smile played over his lips as he reached around her to where her purse sat on the floor. He lifted it out onto the ground and dug through it, ultimately coming up with a three-inch folded knife. "Is there anything you don't have in that thing?" he asked with a tender chuckle.

Too weak to respond to his teasing, she raised her head in time to see him set the blade against the denim. "No, don't," she sputtered. "They're brand new."

He paused. He gazed at her flushed face and felt his pulse slow to normal. There was, it seemed, a reward for suffering all this anxiety for someone else. The relief afterward tasted incredibly sweet. "Well, at least I know you're going to live. You're alert enough to worry about the jeans."

"If you have to cut, cut up my old pair," she pleaded on a faint wail. "These haven't even been washed yet."

With a heavy sigh he left her. After rummaging in the gym bag, he came up with the jeans she'd worn from L.A. It took some doing, but eventually he sawed through the denim with the pocket knife and slid the ragged results onto Chris. Though she insisted she felt much better, he refused to start off again until she'd downed one of the cold sodas. The rippling of her throat as she swallowed did things to his blood the most impassioned kiss from his last woman had never accomplished.

121

"What happened, Chris? Was it the heat? An effect of that shot you had yesterday?"

She shook her head and kept her eyes on the can in her hand. Rivulets of condensation ran down the aluminum. The metal felt cold, wet, real—sharply accentuating the hot, dry, illusory sensations clouding her mind. Her head tried to tell her that the incessant sun, the stultifying air, the constant jiggling motion of the car, perhaps the shot, had combined to make her sick, but her heart seemed to insist it had been the battle with her own desires. She sat mutely hoping her misery would fade.

After fussing over her like a mother hen with a particularly troublesome chick, Paul decided to go straight on to the next town and find something to feed her. Chris didn't argue; she had the notion he wouldn't listen to a protest that she wasn't the least bit hungry. So she let him stuff her back into the car and not quite an hour later they entered a valley bordered by fantastic red cliffs over which sleepily sprawled Gallup, New Mexico.

During the drive there, Paul paid no attention to the scenic plateaus. In between constant side glances at Chris, he engaged in mental combat. In the end, he came to a new decision. He had to tell her who and what he was. For reasons he had no wish to examine, he didn't want her to decide she wanted Paul Richards. He wanted her to want him, as he was, with all his faults. He had to be honest with her.

They ate in an air-conditioned truck stop café, where Chris, self-conscious in her raveled cutoffs and tucked-up blouse, had to be nudged into a booth by Paul's firm hand at her back. He watched every bite of her bland cheese sandwich go down and was solicitous to the point of being obnoxious. She accepted his attentions meekly, certain his behavior stemmed from an innate kindness rather than any special concern for her well-being.

"You're looking better," he said after studying her face

122

for a time. "Your color's back to normal. How are you feeling?"

"Fine. I'm really sorry about that back there. I don't know what came over me, I never get sick." She fiddled with the straw in her cola, refusing to meet his eyes. As it was, the intensity of his stare made it impossible for her to enjoy her meal.

"Chris . . ." He hesitated, searching for the right words. She glanced up at him curiously and he said, "I don't agree."

Puzzlement crossed over her features. "Don't agree to what?"

"That we don't mix."

She looked at her sandwich, then set it down. "Are you going to bring that up again?"

"Damn right," he replied easily. "I'm going to keep bringing it up until you understand that the size of my bank account has nothing to do with our relationship."

"It has though," she protested. "Somebody like you hasn't got a hope of understanding someone like me. You silver-spoon types just don't know what it means to struggle for a living, to go without. You probably take for granted things I wouldn't even dream of having."

"That doesn't matter—"

"Of course it matters. I know it's not like you're a Rockefeller or anything, but it still matters." Her eyes widened at the oddly blank look that crossed Paul's face, and after a short pause, she added, "I'm not the kind of sophisticated female you're probably used to. I'm not used to indulging in casual affairs one week, then forgetting about them the next. You should stick to your own kind and I'll stick to mine."

"That way you won't be sullied by the decadent rich, is that it?" he demanded, no longer making the least effort to restrain his temper.

The way in which he bit out each word made her head throb. She pressed her fingers into her temple and sighed.

123

"Please, Paul, don't let's argue. I'm sorry if my views offend you, but I'm not up to defending myself just now."

He didn't look placated. His jaw was thrust forward; his eyes were snapping with an anger she didn't understand. He was furious with her. It was obvious to him she wouldn't welcome the truth. He wanted to be straightforward with her, but he didn't want to see the contempt for him in her eyes. He couldn't tell her and because he couldn't, he felt resentful toward her. He palmed the check and stood, saying curtly, "Coming?"

Outside the adobe café, her stomach clenched over her lunch as Chris followed behind Paul's stormy stride. She cursed herself. He had tried to discuss the matter in an open, friendly way and she had turned it into an argument. He had been kind and caring when she'd gotten sick and she hadn't even thanked him. By now he was probably realizing what a narrow escape he'd had; he was probably congratulating himself on having nothing to do with her. And *what*, her mind shrieked, did she care anyway?

At the car she hesitated. "Um, Paul—?"

His glare sizzled over the sidewalk. "What?"

Still Chris wavered. "Maybe . . . maybe I should drive?"

"Shut up and get in," he commanded, yanking open the door.

She obediently got in on the passenger side. Her ears rang as he banged the door shut. When he got in she closed her eyes and kept them squeezed tight as they started through town. After a while the urge to look at Paul was irresistible. The pale blue of his shirt had turned to a deep royal where sweat gathered on his back, under his arms. His hair was ruffled from the wind blowing through the open windows. His skin looked sticky with heat. She was certain she'd never seen anyone more handsome.

He glanced at her, catching her eyes upon him. Before he could look away, she blurted out, "Thank you!"

Looking back at the highway, he muttered, "For what?"

124

"For everything. For yesterday, for today." She looked away from him, nervous, but determined to give him the thanks he deserved. "You knew just what to do. I've been arguing with you all day, when I should be thanking you. I'm grateful you were there when I needed you."

All his pent-up tension evaporated like so much steam in the sun. Stretching his arm across the seat, he captured her hand. He tugged forcefully on it until she scooted to his side. Once she was there, her body a hairbreadth from his, he flashed a tender smile.

"Taking care of you could become a habit, baby." And as she smiled up at him, he knew it was the absolute truth.

Chris tried to ignore the happiness that frothed through her, threatening to deluge her common sense. She knew she shouldn't permit herself to feel this way about him. She knew she was setting herself up for a big, bad fall. She knew, but she didn't care. At this moment the happiness seemed worth the risk.

Paul gently stroked her skin just above her right knee and asked her how she felt. Trying not to reveal just how wildly her pulse was reacting to his touch, she replied casually that she was much better, then asked him when he'd last checked the oil. They conversed softly, almost as if they were being observed, and wanting to preserve the companionable atmosphere, they kept to neutral topics. The sticky heat, the stunning plateaus in the distance, the simple beauty of the Indian country. To their mutual pleasure they discovered they saw beauty in much the same places.

Late in the afternoon they pulled into a rest area and Chris stumbled out of the car, her muscles feeling cramped from the long hours of unaccustomed confinement. She retreated to the ladies' room where she refreshed herself by dampening paper towels and pressing them against her hot cheeks. As she did so she wondered just how much of that flush she saw in the mirror was due to the heat and how much to her driver.

Plunging her hand into the depths of her tote, she emerged with a plastic comb and brush. She divided her attention between picking tangles out of her windblown curls and issuing a lecture to her reflection on the follies of mistaking an infatuation for something more substantial. Especially when the object of said infatuation was a man who'd most likely discard her like a used tissue on the streets of New York. As insane as she'd been to take up with him in the first place, she assured herself she wasn't that monumentally stupid. She decided she had to have it out with him before driving so much as a single mile farther. Taking a deep breath, she left the sanctuary of the restroom.

Paul was standing in front of the Maverick, hood up, pouring oil into a funnel. He grinned as she drew near. "I'm glad you mentioned checking the oil. This damn car was practically empty again. I bought three cans in Vegas, but I probably should've gotten twice that many."

"What about the rooms tonight?" she asked, getting directly to the point before her courage ran out.

He shook the can, removed the funnel, replaced the cap, all with an irritating slowness. He wiped his hands on his jeans, then finally looked at her. "I thought you'd already made your decision on that."

"I have. But it's just, it's just—"

The hood of the car slammed down. "Just what?"

Her eyes flew to meet his. Hers were wary, revealing her nervousness and confusion. His echoed his disappointment, resignation.

"Just that I wanted to be sure you understood," she said lamely. She knew it wasn't that at all. She wanted to hear what he intended to do about it. A ridiculous half hope that he wasn't going to pay the least attention to her demands still wavered somewhere within her. But when he spoke it wasn't at all what she expected.

"Don't worry, it doesn't really matter."

Surprise and chagrin warred with her pride. Pride lost.

126

"Aren't you—don't you want to—" she stammered, unable to believe his mild acceptance.

He leaned forward so swiftly, she didn't have time to back up. He kissed her briefly but firmly, then drew back to smile crookedly at her. "Don't get the crazy idea that I'm giving up. I'm not, not by a long shot. But do you think I haven't already figured out that when you set your mind to something, it's set? Armed with a nuclear warhead, I couldn't make you stay with me if you didn't want to. You need more time and I . . ."

She waited, not daring to take a single breath.

His voice dropped to a husky caress. "And I want you to come to me out of your own desire, ready and willing. Especially willing, sweetheart. I want you very willing."

The echo of that raspy murmur ricocheted through her mind for the rest of the day.

CHAPTER EIGHT

His eyes were open, blankly staring, and his lips were spread in an eternal smile that stood out starkly on his mime-white face. The horned ends of the tricolored hat atop his pageboy haircut were tipped with straw. He carried a bright green-and-red watermelon, one slice raised as if about to be devoured.

A smile lingered on Christine's lips as she examined the kachina doll, wondering which god of the mountain this watermelon-lover could possibly represent. Her eyes wandered over several other wooden figurines in the case, but kept coming back to the watermelon man. From the tassels of straw to the toe of his bright red boots, he amused her.

"Like it?" asked Paul, coming up behind her.

Without taking her eyes from the display of Hopi handicrafts, Chris told him yes in a breathy voice of wonder. For the better part of the afternoon, they'd been window-shopping in the Bien Mur Indian Market Center on the Sandia Indian Reservation just beyond Albuquerque. For every minute of it, Christine had been entranced by the solid beauty of the massive silver and turquoise squash blossom necklaces and the tiny stone bird fetish necklaces of the Zuñis, the intricately patterned woven rugs and superb sandcast silver jewelry of the Navajos, the tightly woven baskets and beautifully tinted pottery as well as the charming kachina dolls of the Hopis.

Paul tugged on her arm. "If you can tear yourself away from the watermelon man for a moment, I want to show you something."

She nodded and turned with a sigh. "Don't you wonder, though, just what he represents? He looks so mysterious and yet so content."

"How can any man be content wearing only a loin-cloth?" he asked her in teasing indignation. "And starving too. God knows how long that poor guy's been trying to take a bite out of that melon."

Laughing, she leaned toward him and abruptly the pair of them were held immobile, suspended for a fraction of a heartbeat by a bolt of excitement. His eyes darkened as hers widened; not a breath stirred between them. Unspoken desire clamored, reverberating from heart to heart. A pudgy woman beneath an impossibly large sombrero crashed into them, tipped the fringed edge up, and giggled an apology. The spell was broken. The sombrero tottered on and they pulled away to resume walking.

The kachina doll was forgotten in the wild rocketing of the blood through Christine's veins. It had been this way ever since yesterday, when he'd told her he wanted her, ready and willing, that he would wait for her to come to him. She could scarcely remember the drive into Albuquerque; she could remember nothing at all of the Mexican meal they'd shared before checking into separate motel rooms. Though she'd tried to convince herself it was the aftereffects of her sunsickness, Chris had remained restless even after parting from him, vividly conscious of the room on the other side of the adjoining door. She'd tossed much of the night in a battle with her frustrations. Yet, oddly enough, from the moment she'd leaped from the bed, she'd felt alive, alert, ready for anything and everything.

Which was, she reflected with inner amusement, a darn

129

good thing. Over bacon and eggs Paul had declared they were going to spend the day playing tourist. They'd whiled away the morning by viewing the outside of San Felipe Church, Albuquerque's oldest building, then wandering through the galleries of the city's famed Old Town, enjoying the blistery bright sunshine and each other. After a light lunch at a restaurant in an old family hacienda, they'd driven to the Bien Mur Market where they'd happily examined the wares.

Paul now drew Chris to a case of exquisitely crafted jewelry. He tapped a finger on the glass, pointing out a silver necklace studded with bright red coral beads.

"It's perfect for you," he said. He looked at her expectantly, rather like a parent presenting a toy to a child and waiting for an excited reaction.

Chris glanced at the necklace, then over the other pieces in the case. "Ummm, lovely," she murmured. She glanced up to find a pair of accusatory eyes on her.

"Don't you like it?"

"Of course I do," she assured him, somehow managing to stifle her desire to laugh. "It's a stunning piece."

"It has pierced earrings to match."

Despite Paul's emphatic tone, Christine didn't hear him. She'd caught sight of an item that thrilled her. Hoping she showed nothing more than casual interest, she inched closer to the glass case and pretended to inspect the coral necklace. Actually she couldn't take her eyes off a finely etched silver belt buckle inlaid with turquoise. Excitement was leaping through her, but she didn't want Paul to see it. When she felt her expression was sufficiently schooled, she turned and smiled. "What else is there? Have we seen everything?"

Sighing, he led her away. They meandered on, and all the while Chris was busily making and discarding schemes to get back to that jewelry counter alone. She received a solution from an unexpected source. Paul halted and lightly tapped her cheek with one fingertip. "Why don't you go

130

back and look at that necklace alone, without any helpful hints from me?"

She couldn't believe her luck. She nodded and bolted past a cluster of chattering senior citizens before he could decide to come with her after all. Darting nervous glances over her shoulder, she asked a woman with thick black braids and a gaping smile how much the buckle was. The price staggered her and she started to turn away. On impulse she checked and declared firmly, "I'll take it."

With the buckle hidden in the vast depths of her purse, and with two of her precious hundred dollar bills now lodged in the cash register, she made her way back to the Hopi doll display. Paul was there waiting.

"The necklace is lovely," she said quickly, "but I don't really want it."

He accepted this with a philosophical shrug and they left the center. All the way across the parking lot Chris suffered agonies of doubt. Had she gone mad? So much money for a belt buckle! And why had she felt so compelled to buy it? To have something to give Paul when they parted in New York? Something to remember her by? Her heart plummeted. Who was she kidding? Once he was in New York he wouldn't remember Christine Casolaro if he had a ton of belt buckles. She simply wasn't the type of woman a man like Paul would remember. It depressed her to think about all that. She thrust the unwanted future away and concentrated on enjoying the here and now.

"I'd have thought you'd have come to your senses by now."

Chris listened to the disapproval crackling in her sister's voice and grimaced. "Don't worry, Theresa, I'm fine. Really," she added after a stretch of indignant silence.

"Well, you're old enough to do what you want," huffed Theresa, making it sound like she thought Christine's behavior ranked on the level of her three-year-old daughter.

131

The door behind her opened and Chris said hurriedly, "That's right, sis, I am." Her eyes met Paul's and she signaled for him to be quiet. He let the door slip out of his hand with a bang.

"What's that?" demanded Theresa instantly.

Directing a glare toward the door, she said soothingly, "Nothing. I'm—I'm calling from a public phone, that's all. Anyway, quit worrying about me, okay? I'll be in touch again in a few days."

"Look, Chris, I've had a talk with Tony and—"

With one of his most rakish grins, Paul came up to where she sat perched on the edge of the bed.

"—he's willing to let you—"

The bed sagged as he slid into place beside her. Chris shook her head at him.

"—have more freedom, more say in what—"

His lips whispered against the side of her throat. She involuntarily yipped.

"Chris? Is something wrong?"

"N-no, of course not," she squeaked while swatting her free hand at Paul. "I—I just stubbed my toe."

"Oh. Well, anyway, Tony's ready to admit that you should be treated to more respect around here. You don't have to run off to find independence, Chris."

"I haven't . . . run off . . ." The warmth of Paul's mouth tracing the arch of her neck was interfering with her ability to concentrate.

"Is it the rent money?"

His hands slipped under the hem of her camisole. She jammed her palm against the receiver and hissed, "Stop it! I'm talking to my sister!"

"Ummm," he murmured, his lips finding the curve of her shoulder as his hands inched upward.

"Christine! Are you listening? What's going on there? Are you all right?"

"No—I mean—yes," she said breathlessly. "B-but it's

132

crowded in here and I can't hear you too well, Theresa. I'll call again in a few days. 'Bye.''

Theresa's protesting squawk was cut off as Chris dropped the receiver into the cradle. Before she could give Paul the reprimand he so richly deserved, she found herself sinking into the mattress, the weight of his thigh pressed against hers, the hardness of his chest flattening her breasts. His breath nuzzled her quivering mouth and she lifted her lips to meet his.

His kiss was warm and gentle, exploratory rather than explosive. Yet its effect on her was the same as the scorching desire in his earlier kisses. He nibbled lightly; his tongue deftly danced with hers, but softly, slowly. Christine felt branded by it. He was stamping his imprint on her soul and there was nothing she could do to stop it. Not that she wanted to stop it.

He drew away from her and she half-opened her eyes, bemused with passion. He was smiling, his slanted brows tilting above his glittering gaze. How could she have thought those brows devilish, she wondered dazedly. They were almost . . . well, impish. Certainly they were endearing. He chuckled, the sound of the laughter humming down the length of his body, down the length of hers. She looked at his lips. She looked and she longed to possess them once again.

"So now you're a runaway too," he said in soft amusement.

"Hmmm?" She wasn't listening. She was watching the way the lines beside his mouth shifted as he spoke. It made her tingle deliciously, dangerously.

"You told your sister you hadn't run off, so she obviously thinks you have." Leaning forward to tease his tongue over the curve of her cheek, he laughed. "Face it, baby, it's you and me—the runaways."

She turned her head into the pillow; his mouth traveled up to her earlobe. Her breath quickened as his tongue

133

straight, unending stretch of gray pocked with black holes, broken only by pale clumps of ghostly grass along the shoulders. She squinted in vain for a road sign. There was nothing to be seen but the inky curtain of night. No buildings, no lights, scarcely any trees. Her palms gripped the steering wheel so tightly, she was certain her fingers would have to be pried free with a crowbar.

For once in her life Chris would willingly have broken the law and exceeded the speed limit by as far as her floored gas pedal would allow, but the Maverick responded only fitfully to her heavy foot, picking up briefly then gradually slowing to a snail's pace. Her unreasoning fear mounted. She tried to fight against it, telling herself that she hadn't felt afraid when she drove through the dark desolation of the desert. But then she'd been on a known highway with a known destination. Not only did she have no idea where she was, she had no idea where she was going.

A jackrabbit shot across the road and Christine nearly jumped out of her skin. Her resolution not to waken Paul wavered. She shook her right hand loose from the steering wheel. Not taking her eyes from the never-ending flash of white lines over black, she reached toward Paul. As if she'd hit another stretch of graveled road, the car suddenly jolted, then vibrated uncontrollably. She grabbed the wheel with both hands and held on.

"What the hell?" queried Paul sleepily as his head hit the window and he jerked upright.

The car shimmied, skittering from one lane to the other, then, with a last gasping shake, stopped.

CHAPTER NINE

"What the hell!" repeated Paul. He stared at Chris. She stared back, still clenching the steering wheel. "What's wrong?"

"I don't know," she answered, finding comfort in the sound of her voice. She released the wheel and wiped her damp palms on the sides of her cutoffs. "The car wasn't picking up. I'd accelerate and nothing much would happen, then it just started wobbling, skidded, and stopped."

"Try the ignition."

She turned the key. The engine whirred to life. Left in drive, the car lurched forward. Grinning, Chris stepped on the gas pedal. They rolled, stopped, stood still. Without the least vestige of a grin, she repeated the process. The results were the same. Paul sat up, rubbed his hands over his eyes, sleepily ruffled his hair, and yawned. "Where are we?"

The look she threw him spoke volumes of resentment. How could he be so calm? Didn't he care if they were out in the middle of nowhere in the dead of night? "I don't know."

"Don't tell me you got us lost."

Even in the dim light cast up from the headlights she could see his mouth twitch. "I wouldn't dream of telling you anything of the sort," she muttered.

His chuckle carried softly on the night breeze. She ignored it. He bent over the back of the seat, fished around, and eventually tossed her purse into her lap.

"What's this for?" she inquired, sounding as put out as she was feeling.

"With as much junk as you manage to cram into that thing, I naturally assumed that you've got whatever's needed to repair this wreck." He was clearly teasing; the gleam of his smile flashed at her.

"I'm so glad you find this situation so àmusing," she said in what she hoped was a tone to depress his ill-placed humor. Between her earlier fright and the annoyance of being stalled, her own sense of humor seemed to have taken a momentary leave of absence. She began wrestling with the contents of her tote and, after much cursing, she extracted a pencil-slim pocket flashlight. She thrust it at him.

"That's it?" he murmured on a sigh of laughter as he got out to aim it into the bowels of the engine. The thin beam, however, was woefully inadequate against the opaque shadows permeating the night. She joined him, shivering a little at the unfamiliar noises droning out of the darkness surrounding them. Paul jiggled cables and checked wires, then straightened with a shrug. "I think we'll have to stay here for the time being."

"Stay? Here?"

She sounded shrilly disbelieving; his enjoyment of the situation dimmed. Seeing her without her usual reasonable sangfroid had both amused and affected him. A sense of protectiveness he'd never suspected he possessed rose up within him.

"I only meant until daylight, baby," he said in his most soothing voice.

"But that's not for hours!"

"Well, yes, it usually takes several hours between nightfall and daylight."

She couldn't see his smile, but she heard it clearly

147

enough. "Don't be patronizing," she muttered, feeling like a fool. "Can't you do something to get us out of here?"

"That toy you called a flashlight isn't worth a damn and I can't mess around with an engine I can't see. We'll just get back into the Maverick and wait for another car—"

"I haven't seen another car go by," she said petulantly.

"Then we'll sack out and get some rest until the sun comes up. There's no sense in getting worked up over something we can't change. You're the clear-headed one, Chris; you know that."

His moderate tone, his reassuring hand at her back, his sensible attitude, did, in fact, calm her. Now that she'd had time to overcome her ridiculous fears, her usual equanimity reasserted itself. "You're right of course. I'm embarrassed to admit it, but driving out here, all these noises and nothing to be seen—well, I got scared. I started thinking about every grade-B sci-fi flick I'd ever seen and every time a cloud passed over the moon, I half-expected to hear a werewolf howl."

He didn't laugh, which pleased her. "All those noises," he said as he nudged her toward the passenger side of the car, "are just cicadas and crickets and other little creatures that go bump in the night. We're bigger than they are."

"But they outnumber us," she returned with a teasing smile as she slid onto the seat. Her smile faded when, instead of going around to the other side, he slipped into place beside her, forcing her over. Her smile actually became a frown when, as she started to move away, he caught hold of her shoulders and pulled her against him.

"Shhh," he whispered before she could protest. "Let me hold you." The scent, the warmth, the sheer maleness of him anesthetized her. Feeling like a rag doll too limp to resist, she allowed him to settle her body against his. He sat propped against the door, legs stretched over the seat, with his arms cradling her lightly beneath the rise of her breasts.

With her back pressed into him, she could feel the

148

thump of his heart, the rise and fall of his chest. Her buttocks were flattened against his firm hips; her legs entwined with the muscled length of his. When he told her to just relax and go to sleep, she almost laughed in his face. Sleep! As if she possibly could with her every nerve jumping frantically wherever his skin, his clothes, his breath, touched her.

But she didn't laugh. If she laughed, her breasts would graze the arms encircling her. If she laughed, her entire length would quiver against the entire length of him. No, she did not dare laugh.

His breath caressed her cheek, stirring the tangled curls tumbling over her ears. The heat of it set fire to her blood. She was certain the tips of his fingers would be scorched simply from touching her. She was about to combust.

"What are you thinking?" he whispered, stirring a great deal more than just her hair. After a lengthy pause he tightened his hold on her and repeated, "What are you thinking?"

"I—how warm I was," she replied breathlessly.

"How," he murmured, "warm is that?"

"Uh, very."

The tip of his tongue touched the tip of her ear. "Like boiling?" he prompted huskily.

"Uh, more like—" She couldn't concentrate on words. Her thoughts were centered on the lazy flick of his tongue as it traced the shell of her ear, the arch of her neck.

"Yes?"

"More like, like—"

His mouth nuzzled the top of her bare shoulder. His hands slid over the leotard to cup her breasts, his fingers curling possessively up over the nipples.

"Like burning up," she gasped.

She twisted her head to find his mouth waiting hungrily to take hers. She opened her lips to him with an ardor that astounded her. There had been other men, other kisses in her life, but no one, nothing like this. Nothing like this soul-searing need to take and be taken, to give and be given.

The taut restraint that had contained him while holding her shattered. With a ragged breath he plunged his tongue between her parted lips and drank in her sweetness. He skimmed his hands over as much of her as he could touch, over the surface of her stomach, down the silken thigh, up over the curve of her hips, past the slick fabric covering her ribs, to the soft roundness of her breasts. He felt as if he'd waited years to touch her, to kiss her, to know her.

He didn't question his unusual gut-wrenching need. He simply knew that each time he'd touched her, his desire to do so again spiraled. He simply knew that each time he'd kissed her, his passion intensified. He simply knew that he had to sate this hunger tormenting him before he went mad. He had to have her.

Pressing her against the back of the seat, he eased out from beneath her, one hand unsnapping her cutoffs in the process. Drugged by the potency of his lips, his hands, his swirling fingertips, she made no protest. She raised her hips as he yanked the denim downward and silently cursed the fact that her leotard clung tenaciously to her skin. She wanted nothing but Paul clinging to her skin.

She slipped her hands beneath his shirt. The heat of his skin raised her own temperature several degrees. She twirled her fingers through the soft hair matting his chest and exulted in his groan. She reached for his jeans; he squirmed to accommodate her and banged his knee against the steering wheel.

He swore and she giggled. He jerked up to glare at her and bumped his head on the roof. She giggled harder. Suddenly she saw just how ridiculous this entire situation was. They were behaving like a couple of groping adolescents. Worse, like bumbling adolescents.

"Maybe," she choked between increasing laughter, "this isn't such a good idea."

Bracing his arms on either side of her head, he gazed

down at her and felt his moment of anger dissipate. He ached with wanting. "You got a better one?" he asked in a thickened voice.

She saw the unveiled yearning in his set expression and stopped laughing. "Paul, this isn't the right time . . . or place."

"Back seat?" The sharp query carried a note of demand. She wordlessly shook her head.

A shaft of moonlight veered in through the windshield. It cast an eerie glow over his profile and glossed his dark hair with a bluish sheen. He sat utterly motionless, a sculpture of the night. Then abruptly he jerked away from her. Yanking the keys from the ignition, he got out of the car. He was at the trunk before Chris fully assimilated he had gone. She got out and came up behind him.

"What are you doing?" she asked, casting nervous glances to every side of her.

He pulled out the faded green blanket she kept in the trunk and walked to the roadside. She scampered after him, swallowing back the impulse to leap into the car and lock all the doors. She'd have sooner walked through her old neighborhood alone at midnight than be so vulnerably exposed in the midst of this vast unknown field.

"What are you doing?" she croaked again.

He bent to spread the blanket over the grass. "I'm doing what I should have done back in Flagstaff."

The clamoring of her heart drowned out the mysterious discord sounding from the shadows. "W-what?" she whispered.

Slowly straightening, he turned to her. He didn't touch her. He didn't have to. The tension in his stance was enough to immobilize her.

"Let me love you, Christine," he said, and she thought she might burst with the sudden, overwhelming need that filled her every pore.

There was a moment, a single flicker of time, in which he hesitated. Then with an impatient growl he swept her

151

to him. He lifted her and her mouth moistened the column of his neck. He lowered her to the blanket and her breath misted his jaw. He pressed down upon her and her body molded to his.

His weight settled upon her and Christine knew she would make no further objections. This had been inevitable from the first moment she'd noticed him in The Scarlet Lady. This had been inevitable since the beginning of time. When he brought his lips to hers in a kiss of questioning exploration, she yielded to him with an eagerness that told him there would be no denials. She was as he'd wanted her to be—very willing.

He felt as if his heart might pound right out of his chest. He teased his fingers over her, from shoulder to breast to hip and back again, and knew no woman had ever felt so warm, so soft, so delightful. He could not get enough of her.

She marveled in his feel; the smooth skin, the hard bone and solid sinews beneath, the downy hair atop. Wherever she touched, her fingertips tingled. The excitement was almost unbearable. Her blood rocketed through her veins and her entire being throbbed with the need of him.

His fingers danced over her back, seeking a zipper. They raced over the straps, searching for buttons. They slid over the flat plane of her stomach, then upward. Cupping his palm over her breast, feeling the nipple thrust against the slick material, he leaned away from her.

"Is this what's known as tamperproof packaging?" he inquired on a husky chuckle. "How in hell do I get you out of this thing?"

"Oh, I'm sure," she said between light, tantalizing kisses, "you'll think of a way."

He did. His own clothes were quickly flung off and he again lay beside her. He burrowed his face into her neck, nuzzling his mouth against the frantic beat of her pulse. And then, at long last, he touched her.

Her breasts were full and exquisitely soft. Her nipples

were firm buds delightfully responsive to his caress, his kiss. Her belly radiated a tantalizing heat beneath his fingertips. Her thighs were supple, smooth, satiny.

She had ached to know what he would feel like. Now at long last she knew. He felt like heaven. He moved with control over her. His hands were smooth, yet strong and sure. His lips were moist and warm and hungry. His arms, legs, belly, were firmly muscled. His chest was a solid mantle over her, feathered with soft, tickling curls. His buttocks flexed as he poised, hard and hot, before finally, he fused with her.

There was a breeze. It did not cool the bonfire of sensations that blazed between them. The delicate texture of her skin beneath his palm. The taste of his sweat upon her tongue. The intensity of the ecstasy he saw imprinted upon her face. The unsteady clanging of his heart as it thumped against her.

Above his shoulder Chris could see the radiant spangle of stars across the sky, the opalescent face of the moon, the gossamer streaks that drifted past it, and this time she appreciated the startling beauty she saw. The whole world had taken on a new look. It was the look of love.

So this is love, she thought, and shook with the thrill of it. This feeling of wanting to give all, to take all, to be all with another being. It was wondrously new. She could not contain the passionate elation bursting through her. Sizzling with love and need, she arched toward him, taking him deeper within her.

His body went taut. He was incredibly sensitive to her lightest caress. She touched him and he felt special. She kissed him and he felt gloriously privileged. It was new, this sense of gratification that went beyond the physical. It increased his excitement tenfold, until he felt shell-shocked from the blast.

Control shattered in a delirious explosion. Their bodies tightened together. Cries of fulfillment floated away on the breeze, leaving behind the clash of rasping breaths, the

153

clatter of racing heartbeats. They lay entwined, sated, and spent. Gradually mingled breaths eased; shared heartbeats slowed.

Unwillingly Chris became aware of the itch of the grass as it poked through the thin blanket and the chill of the air skimming over her naked skin. She heaved a sigh. "We'd better get back to the car and try to get some sleep."

He slowly raised his head and gazed down at her. She couldn't see his expression, but she felt the rumble of his chuckle and the moist warmth of his words. "You know something, baby? Sometimes you carry practicality too far."

"But it itches. And the breeze is chilly."

"And I want to hold you in my arms."

How could she fight such logic?

A single band of light struck Christine's eyelids, prying them open. She saw dark eyes glitter brightly beneath quirking brows and a full mouth curve crookedly beneath a broad, straight nose. Tousled layers of thick black hair and even, white teeth. She was still dreaming. She closed her eyes.

"Oh, no, you don't, sleepyhead," said a low, masculine voice. A hand shook her shoulder. "I've waited long enough for you to wake up."

She raised her lids and saw Paul trying to scowl at her, but laughing instead. No dream, after all, but a beautifully real morning. She stretched, her body lazily snaking over the rumpled blanket. His hand skated down from her shoulder to take hold of her breast. She drew in her breath and he smiled knowingly. The caress, the smile, the very gleam in his eyes displayed a new air of possessiveness. Her pulse instantly began misbehaving.

He set his mouth tenderly to her breast. Her heart achieved a record high vault. "H-how late is it?" she asked, not caring in the least.

154

"Mmmm," he replied, and his lips hummed over her taut nipple.

"D-don't you think we—we ought to get up? Somebody might—might drive by."

He flicked his tongue just once, but it was more than enough. When he did that she didn't care if the whole world drove up to watch them make love. When he pulled away and abruptly stood, she wanted to cry out in protest, but the sight of him stole away her breath. Sunlight glinted over bone and sinews, highlighting the solidity of his shape. It gleamed over the dark hair tangled on his chest, emphasizing the musculature beneath. In the moonlight her fingers had traced the path the sunlight now took. In the moonlight she'd known the texture and taste of him. If he had not walked away, she was quite certain she'd have gone on staring at him forever. Telling herself not to be any more foolish than she'd already been, she hastily drew on her leotard.

When he returned he bowed with a gallant flourish. "Your turn, my dear. The conditions are somewhat primitive, but on the other hand there's plenty of space."

She saw at a glance that he was right. They were surrounded by space and nothing but. The highway stretched out straight ahead, into a seeming infinity. Flat fields of golden grain expanded outward on either side of the road, unbroken by the least sign of habitation. To the right, in the far distance, a ring of trees stood in a lonely quartet.

As she walked to the back of the car she tried to reassure herself. Even if the Maverick still didn't run, another car would pass by sooner or later. Otherwise there wouldn't be a road here, right? She heard Paul start the motor, saw him turn on the lights. He was just getting back out when she came around the side. She knew a fleeting regret that he'd gotten dressed.

"The engine works fine, the electrical system is unaffected, but the damn thing won't go. Step on the gas pedal and nothing, zilch."

"Any idea what it might be?" she asked, trying to keep her worry out of her voice.

She failed. Paul caught the note of anxiety she was trying to hide. He grinned confidently and said, "Probably in the carburetor. Let's have a look."

He strode to the front of the car and lifted the hood. She followed him. They peered inside. Glancing at her, Paul said, "If you have any tools, get them for me."

Grease spread from his hands to his shirt to his brow. He talked as he probed, occasionally raising his head to grin encouragingly at her. Chris hung at his elbow while he regaled her with a convoluted but unrevealing tale of a boyish prank, a time when he had emptied his guppy population into a champagne punch being served at one of his parents' parties. She laughed and he inquired lightly, "Was that your stomach growling or mine?"

"Both, I think. I'm famished. Are you making any headway?" She shielded her eyes with her hand and peered up and down the highway. "If we wait to be rescued, we're sure to starve. I can't understand why they built a road nobody uses."

He wiped one grimy hand on the back of his jeans and the other on his shirt. "To trap unsuspecting and hungry travelers, of course."

While he continued puttering, she queried him about his eyestrain of the day before. He mumbled an unintelligible reply and submerged his head farther beneath the hood. The sun inched upward. Chris folded the blanket and returned it to the trunk. She came back to watch and wait and eventually she reached over to tap him on the shoulder. He raised his head.

She leaned against the right headlight, seemingly obsessed with the sight of her jogging shoes. "You don't have the foggiest idea what you're doing, do you?" she inquired pleasantly.

"Nope," he confessed cheerfully.

"Then what have you been doing all this time?"

156

"Nothing. Fiddling with the battery cables mostly."

"But why?"

Swiping his hands over his jeans, he stepped away from the car. "To keep you from getting too concerned. You looked worried and when you worry, your eyebrows come together."

She paid no attention to this incomprehensible speech and pointed out that all he'd really done was waste time. "I knew I should have signed up for that auto mechanics course. I thought all men were practically born fixing pistons and plugs."

"Don't be sexist."

"Do genies have sex?" she asked on a teasing note.

"You ought to know," he pointed out with a look that increased her pulse rate alarmingly.

"The next genie I employ will be mechanically minded," she said airily.

"There isn't another genie who'd take on the job. The pay is lousy, the hours are irregular, and the benefits—well, come to think of it, the benefits *are* highly gratifying . . ."

She ignored his playful leer. "Don't you think you could do something more constructive than soothe my supposed fears?"

A totally charming, masculine grin played over his mouth. "Absolutely."

Chris heard the intimation in that one word and felt her happiness wilt. Though the noon sun lacquered her skin with a fine glaze of perspiration, it was the remembered heat of the night that enervated her now. She'd given herself to him and with her body had gone her love. She knew by doing so she'd doubled, tripled the amount of pain she'd eventually suffer.

"We could start walking," she said impassively. "This road must go someplace."

A frown replaced his smile. The hint of rejection in her cool words annoyed him. Once again the realization that

157

he was behaving like a crazy fool piqued him. He needed to have his head examined, running off like this. What had he hoped to prove? How could he hope to find himself on some godforsaken road in Kansas? He wished to God he'd never gotten drunk, never met her, never left Los Angeles. He spun away from her. "Then you'd better put a shirt on over that leotard. You could get a sunburn."

He grabbed the gym bag from the car, and with a short, jerky movement tossed jeans and a lilac top at her. He tugged off his brown knit and drew on his blue shirt. As he rolled the sleeves up to his elbows, he surreptitiously watched Chris zip up her jeans. His blood began pounding. He forgot his fervent wish never to have met her. He forgot his regrets, his self-reproach. He forgot everything but how he'd delighted in every splendid inch of that body.

"It's a gorgeous day for a walk," said Chris brightly when she straightened and declared herself ready to go.

"Couldn't be better," he agreed.

Carefully not touching, they began walking. They spoke of the wonderfully sunny morning and thought about the long hours of the previous night. Just as Paul was remarking for the third time at the expansiveness of the sky over the horizon, a low rumble chugged into the air. They looked at each other, then up and down the road. Even as they stared, the grumbling resounded louder, defining itself as the throb of an engine as an ancient pickup truck rolled into view.

For one stunned moment neither moved. Then they were waving and calling out for the vehicle to stop. It kept rolling. It passed them by in a blur of begrimed yellow. Chris thought she would scream in pure frustration, when suddenly the grating noise was spliced into silence. The truck perched on the pavement, waiting. As if afraid the mirage would disappear, they broke into a run. As they reached the truck, the door of the cab swung open and a man leaped nimbly out.

His face was hidden by the visor of a dusty olive cap

emblazoned with a beer company logo, but his neck was etched with deep creases and the hands he set on the baggy hips of his dirt-covered denims were veined and lined like a map marking years of hard labor. His voice, when he spoke, creaked, as if protesting being used at all. "Something you folks need?"

"You may have seen our car left down the road," said Paul as he held out his hand. "I'm Paul Richards and the fact of the matter is that we got lost during the night. Our car broke down and we abandoned it to seek help."

The weathered lips cracked in a brief smile. "Floyd Kilmer. I saw the car," he said. He shook Paul's hand. "And I wondered just which fool'd lost it."

"I'm the fool."

The creaky voice groaned with what Chris supposed was a laugh. He removed his cap and ran a hand through a mat of peppery hair. "Well, I'll tell you what. I'll take you on into town and we'll see if young Huber can't get out here and fix your car."

"We'd appreciate that," said Paul, and once inside the old truck Chris voiced her own gratitude, saying with a pretty smile, "We really do thank you, Mr. Kilmer."

"Just Floyd'll do."

"Where exactly are we, Floyd?"

"'Bout three miles out of Oscar." He glanced at her and his mouth quirked. "That's Oscar, Kansas."

She firmly suppressed the urge to tell him she was perfectly aware of being in Kansas—what other state would be so relentlessly flat and empty? Instead, she focused on the road ahead. A smattering of trees abruptly erupted out of nowhere. Above the treetops, faded lettering on a globular gray watertower faintly proclaimed they were entering the town of Oscar. Chris leaned forward eagerly.

If Ashland had seemed a small dot of humanity to her, Oscar was a mere speck of dust on the roadside. The main street stretched for all of three blocks, distinguished only by a tall grain elevator at the far end. Like opponents in

159

a boxing ring, two white-spired frame churches poised on opposite corners at opposite ends of the street. Worn metal signs advertising Nehi and seed corn decorated the false fronts of a hardware store, a grocery, and a café. A rusting tractor sat like a gigantic ornament in front of a boxlike ice cream stand.

A horn trumpeted. Floyd hollered a greeting out the window, then turned into a gas station perched beside railroad tracks. Peeling paint on a glass front zigzagged with masking tape read HUBER'S. Two once-bright red gas pumps stood idle, but the yawning doors of a garage revealed a pair of legs in stained overalls extending from beneath the body of a two-toned sedan. Chris rather hoped they would be attached to a body.

They were. Even as the trio scrambled out of the truck, the legs slid forward and a young man materialized. He sat up and layers of blackened blond hair fell over his brow. "'Lo, Floyd," he said cheerily. "What can I do you for?"

"These folks broke down the road a ways," answered Floyd, gesturing toward Paul and Chris with a tilt of his head. "You so busy, Kenny boy, you can't run out and take a look at their car?" He tipped his head back and let out a grating of laughter.

"Oh, I suppose I could make the time," the young man joked. Brushing his hair back with a grimy hand, further darkening the once-fair strands, he openly sized them up. He let his gaze linger appreciatively over Chris, pausing at all the obvious places before coming to his feet with a grin that shone brightly in his grease-smeared face. He must be, mused Chris, quite good looking when the mask of dirt was scrubbed off. He had an aura of masculine confidence that signaled success with the female population of Oscar. He set down a wrench and held out his hand, then drew it back to wipe it on his overalls and again gave them that gorgeously gleaming grin.

160

"Ken Huber, at your service. What make of car? Any idea what's wrong with it?"

Though he spoke ostensibly to Paul, he steadily eyed Chris. She smiled and answered him warmly, "It's a 1970 Maverick and we're fairly certain it's *not* the battery cables."

The smile she shot toward Paul was impish. The look she received in return was not. The satanic slant of his brows was very much in evidence and when he spoke, he conjured up all the warmth of a hanging judge pronouncing sentence. "I'd like you to take a look at the car—if you can peel your eyes off my wife, that is."

Much later Chris would wonder why she didn't object loudly to this blatant lie. At the time she simply gaped at Paul, soaking in the steely tension of his rigid jaw, the dark flush of fury staining his face.

The mechanic's confident grin faltered, then revived with a hint of sheepishness. "Well, let's go have a look. At the car," he hastily added.

Paul immediately became all sunshine and smiles. He held out his hand. "My apologies. We should've introduced ourselves. I'm Paul Richards and this is my wife, Christine."

His gaze dared her to deny it. She didn't. Why she didn't, she hadn't a clue. Instead, she stood placidly permitting him to change her marital status to all and sundry without so much as a raised eyebrow. Perhaps, she decided later, she'd been catatonic from the shock.

Floyd accepted their thanks with the shriveled split of his lips that passed for a smile and for the second time that morning Chris and Paul got into a pickup, this one Ken's dented tow truck. The cab was crowded, and Chris was squeezed in the middle. Being so close to Paul was doing frightening things to her blood pressure; what he'd said was slowly sinking in. *My wife,* he'd called her. She cast a cautious, sidelong glance his way.

Why had he said such a thing? Could it be that last

161

night had meant more to him than a mere satisfying of his physical needs? Could there be the least chance that he, too, had felt that burst of love as they joined together? Her blood seemed to roar in her ears; her palms were suddenly clammy. She must not deceive herself with such hopes. She'd tackle him about the lie and until then she would not think about last night.

And into her mind came an image of a white-hot touch and burning kisses. . . .

She was mercifully jolted from her unsettling reflections by their arrival at the car. After describing in detail what had occurred the night before, Chris stood back to let Ken examine the engine. She refused to allow herself to so much as glance at Paul. They'd have to have it out as soon as they could snatch a minute alone, and she wasn't looking forward to it.

In the end they hitched the car up and towed it back to the garage. There, the privacy she dreaded was granted in full as Ken left them in a silence that could have sunk the *Titanic*. The setting was hardly conducive to a confrontation. Sunlight fingered its way past layers of grime coating the windows to pick out blankets of dust covering boxes of stale candy and stacks of oil cans. The smell of gas permeated the air, overpowering even the acrid odor wafting from the restroom. Skating her eyes past the dirt and dust, Chris took a deep breath and faced him.

"Why did you tell him I was your wife?" The words came out so fast, they were nearly mashed together as one.

"To stop him from eyeing you as if he were one step away from crawling atop you. And to stop you from flirting with him."

"I was not—"

"You damn well were," he cut in fiercely. "You think I couldn't see the message in the smiles you were giving him? You might as well put out a neon sign advertising a body for hire."

162

His lips had barely moved. His jaw was clenched to the breaking point. He was jealous! She realized it with stunned disbelief. A high-voltage thrill charged through her veins. His emotions must be involved more deeply than she'd suspected. He must think of her as something more than a warm body. Her heart raced as she tried to gather her jumbled wits together.

Her silence seemed to him to be a rebuff. He thought of the way she'd looked at the mechanic and his blood pressure skyrocketed. He didn't give a damn what she wanted. After last night he wasn't about to let her go waltzing off with somebody else. He'd make her understand that soon enough. He reached for her.

A nervous cough heralded Ken's return. For two frantic heartbeats Chris thought he was going to grab her anyway. On the third he slowly pivoted. "Yes?"

"Well, uh, I can't fix your car, Mr. Richards," said Ken. He swept his hand through his hair and the greased layers stood up like a cock's tufted crest. "The U-joint's missing from the drive train and I'd have to order the part to fix it. Might take weeks to get it here, being as it's such an old car."

"Weeks!" exclaimed Chris, all else abruptly forgotten.

"What about a rental car?" Paul asked slowly.

"Here? In Oscar?" The crest toppled as Ken shook his head at the absurdity of such a notion. Then he grinned. "Old Wilma Admires has a car for sale. It's been up for sale since about the end of the war. You'd be doing the town a service if you bought it, keep her off the streets. She's about a hundred if she's a day, can't see, can't hear, and when she's out driving—"

"What about the car?" interrupted Paul impatiently.

"It's an old Pontiac, not in much better shape than that heap of yours, but it runs. It should get you out of town."

"How much?"

"Dunno. Few hundred."

Paul frowned. "I don't have that much."

It was Christine's turn to shake her head in disbelief. She'd come to look upon Paul's wallet as a never-ceasing flow of funds, rather like the milk jug in fairy tales that never ran empty. "Of course you do! Don't you?" she asked.

He glanced at her and his frown tilted into a crooked smile. "No. I've spent it. Lost some in Vegas too. But you've still got that five hundred—"

"No, I haven't!" she cut in on a near wail. "I—I paid for the room in Las Vegas, remember, and—and I spent some . . ."

Her words trailed into nothingness. She looked help-lessly at Paul. He looked searchingly at her. They both looked quizzically at Ken Huber. He skated his eyes past them and shrugged.

"Kinda looks to me like you're stuck here."

CHAPTER TEN

"Stuck!" Paul and Christine harmonized like the chorus in a Greek tragedy.

"Bus comes through once a week and that's on Thursdays. That was yesterday. So unless you find another way out, you're here for at least another week."

"But what about my car?" asked Chris, still trying to assimilate the loss, in one blow, of both her car and that previously unlimited supply of money.

Ken slouched against the counter and fiddled with the credit card imprinter. "It'd cost several hundred to repair it. And like I said, it could take weeks to get the part. You'd be better off junking it."

"No. We can't do that," she said firmly. She laid her hand on Paul's arm. "What are we going to do about the car?"

Paul, however, didn't give a damn about the car. He had things of more importance on his mind. "Where can we get a room for the night?"

"Well, my folks might be willing to put you up—"

"I meant a motel."

"Mister, there's no motels in Oscar. People don't come here to stay—they drive right on through and don't even blink as they go by."

Chris had been nibbling her lip, trying to pull herself together. Now she thrust up her chin with the stubborn will that her sister Theresa knew so well. "Is there anyone who might be willing to take in boarders for a week or so? Paying boarders?"

A slow smile lit up Ken's face to its usual cheery glow. "Well, Mary Sullivan might be very willing. Her husband was killed in a huntin' accident last fall and things have been rough on her ever since. Real rough. I could give her a call."

She stopped him from picking up the phone on the counter. "Thank you. But could you tell us if there's any chance of finding a job here? Somewhere we could work until our car was fixed?"

"Chris, are you crazy? Stay here?"

Her chin went up higher. "You can do what you want, but I'm not leaving here without the Mav."

"The Mav?" queried Ken, looking from one to the other as if considering inching out the door before they turned violent.

"My car," she replied absently. "You go ahead and order that U-joint or whatever it is. I'll get the money to pay for it somehow. I'm not afraid of hard work."

"This isn't my idea of a honeymoon spot," said Paul through his teeth.

"Honeymoon? You mean you two are newlyweds? Oh, well now, no wonder you're so on edge. Look, let me call Mary and see what I can do about gettin' you fixed up with a place to stay. We'll see about jobs later."

Chris didn't attempt to alter his misconception of their nonexistent marriage. While he called his friend, she listened to Paul's arguments with a stony face. Following a long stream in which he'd mainly said she wasn't being rational, she said with force, "Maybe not. But the Mav's the only possession I've got—"

"It's just a car and a wreck of a one at that," he interrupted harshly.

"I had to work like hell to get that car, used and falling apart as it is. You might not be able to comprehend what

166

that means to me. But you can understand this: I'm not leaving this town without my car. If you want to leave, I'll give you back your money—"

"Don't be insulting. If you throw that money up at me one more time, I'll ram it down your throat."

Paul slammed his hands into his pockets and glowered at her. The tilt of her chin remained firmly upthrust. Those damn thick brows of hers were looming over her eyes. He promptly decided he'd been suffering from an overactive libido. He didn't desire her in the least. She was too assertive, highly aggravating, and not particularly attractive. One phone call and he'd be on his way. His frown deepened.

"If you're staying," he said with a hint of belligerence, "then I'm staying too."

Her relief was immense. For all her bravado in telling him to go, it had been the last thing she wanted. But not for the world would she have him know his emphatic tone had thrilled her right down to her socks. "Suit yourself," she said with as casual a shrug as she could manage.

He felt like shaking her senseless. Where was the gratitude he'd expected? The relief? But, then, Christine never did what he expected of a woman, of anyone. He decided what he really wanted was to kiss her till her bones rattled.

"That's not"—he leaned forward to whisper—"a very bridelike attitude, sweetheart."

"Sorry, but I don't know much about a bride's attitudes."

"You'll learn."

Her lips parted on a gaspy breath. Paul couldn't resist the invitation. He leaned closer still and kissed her, a smacking kiss that resounded through the glassed-in station and brought Ken's eyes sweeping over them. The attendant rapidly averted his gaze. After a moment he hung up the phone and announced loudly, "I'll lock up and drive you on over to Mary's," before turning around to grin knowingly at them.

167

They returned his smile, Paul with an inordinate amount of satisfaction and Chris with a strange shyness that brought a soft glowing blush to her cheeks that was, had she but known it, distinctly bridal.

Ken soon ushered them into the front room of a two-story beige frame house nestled within a spattering of lushly leafed elms. To Chris, who'd grown up in over-crowded city slums, the large meticulously groomed yard seemed as expansive as a corner park. Like all the homes they'd passed in the short drive, a bright rainbow of flowers adorned the neat lawn and a full garden plot could be seen beyond a porch at the left side of the house. She heard birds singing as they mounted the steps of the front porch. Crossing the threshold, she felt a pang of envy. How lucky the people were who lived here.

Mary Sullivan greeted them with a wavering smile. "How do you do?" She paused, as if uncertain what to say or do next, and nervously plaited her fingers.

Without meaning to, Chris stared at the woman. Her cascading mane of hair would have held anyone's attention. It was the shiny bright copper of a newly minted penny, rippling past her shoulders in bountiful waves. But it wasn't the stunning red hair that caught Christine's eye. It was the gaunt youth of the woman. For some unknown reason, she'd expected her to be much older. In fact, Mary was much her own age, and would have been a beautiful woman had it not been for the shrunken figure within the navy slacks and plain white blouse. Her cheeks were rounded, but sunken in; her curves suggested at a ripeness stripped away.

Chris noticed the twisting fingers and she realized how rude she'd been. She glanced around, took in the sparse but comfortable furnishings, the plaid couch with a striped afghan tossed over the back, the brown vinyl re-cliner, the plump armchair, and addressed Mary with a smile. "It's a lovely home. I hope we're not putting you to any trouble."

"Oh, no," denied Mary quickly. "I'm glad to have you for as long as you need to stay. The rent will be very welcome, but I'll do my best to make you welcome too."

Chris held out her hand. "Christine Caso—I mean, Richards," she amended, shooting a resentfully embarrassed glare at Paul. She'd never be able to do this! Deception simply wasn't part of her nature.

Mary, however, laughed and the tension evaporated in the merry sound. She shook hands. "It's hard to get used to, isn't it? Ken told me you were newlyweds."

"As of Sunday," answered Paul before Chris could say a word.

"Less than a week!" Mary cried. She cast a startled look at Paul. She narrowed her green eyes at him, then seemed to catch herself up short. "I'm sorry, I didn't mean to stare. It's just that you look familiar, like someone I've seen recently, but I can't place who."

"I have that kind of face." He set her at ease with a smile. "I'm always being mistaken for guys on TV or in the news."

Chris glanced at him in some surprise, thinking his looks quite distinctive. Certainly there couldn't be two men in the world with those brows! But there had been that waitress in Kingman. . . .

"Well, let me show you the rooms," said Mary, "and then we'll talk over supper. Ken, why don't you get cleaned up while I take them upstairs?"

"Is that an invite to supper?" he asked, grinning.

"Only if your hands are clean," she retorted with a saucy shake of her coppery hair.

Chuckling, Ken ambled from the living room to the dining room and on back into what Chris deduced must be the kitchen. Mary led them through the dining room, but turned to the left where an open door faced a short hall and yet another door. The second door led outside, Mary

169

explained. To the left of the hall was a small closet, to the right a staircase.

"You'll have privacy, you see. We'll shut the door to the dining room and you'll have your own entrance and all."

Upstairs they discovered a very spacious bedroom, two smaller rooms, and a good-size bathroom all opening off an airy rectangular hall. One of the smaller rooms had a sofa, a chair, a coffee table, an endtable and a wall of bookshelves. The other was bare. Peeking into the bedroom, all Chris really saw was the double bed. The sight interfered with her ability to breathe. Memories of last night flashed through her mind, only to be crowded out by visions of the night to come.

She turned swiftly to Mary. "But if we take these rooms, where will you sleep?"

"My bedroom is downstairs. I haven't slept up here since—well, not in near a year. The kids have their rooms in the basement. We bought this monster of a house, planning to have a large family, but, well, it didn't turn out that way."

"You've children?" asked Chris.

"Only two, though at times they seem like a dozen. Eric's ten and Deirdre's almost seven. They're at their grandparents' farm for the weekend, so you're spared the holy terrors for a couple days."

They settled on a price, to be paid weekly, and arranged that Chris and Paul would care for their own rooms while sharing the kitchen downstairs with Mary and her family. When they returned to the living room, Ken was sprawled over the recliner, watching the evening news on a portable television. He glanced at them and Chris felt her mouth drop open. She'd suspected he'd be goodlooking, but she'd had no idea he would be an Adonis under all that dirt. He'd obviously taken a shower, and his hair fell in damp wisps of burnished gold over his brow. Without the smudges of oil and grease to distort them, his features were clearly classical—straight and strong and utterly breathtaking.

"Stop staring," demanded Paul on a low growl as he prodded her back with an ungentle hand.

She didn't bother to deny that she'd been staring. She simply sank to the couch and informed Ken outright that he was the most handsome man she'd ever seen. While Paul frowned heavily, Mary briskly chided her, "Don't go giving him a big head. It's plenty big already. The way the girls round here chase this boy!"

"Just 'cuz I'm not tottering into senility, she thinks of me as a boy," he muttered, not entirely without acerbity.

"Oh, you!" Mary answered. "I'm just trying to salvage my pride. If I admit how old you are, I have to admit to my own age—and believe me, that's much worse than thinking of you as a boy."

"I hardly think, Mary, girl, that your five years advantage on me qualifies you for senior citizenship." But he was grinning again, that dazzling gleam that had first hinted to Chris of his masculine beauty.

With a good-natured ruffle of his hair, Mary sauntered off to the kitchen, refusing all offers by Chris to help. "Tonight's my treat," she insisted.

"This is the most cheerful I've seen Mary in near a year," Ken told them in an undertone as soon as she had disappeared. "Since Tim died she's been just barely scraping by, and with the two kids it's been real tough on her."

There was a warmth in his voice that told them more than he was saying, but neither remarked upon it. Instead, they discussed the possibilities of finding employment. It looked grim, Ken informed them. "Oscar's a dying town. You can see that for yourself. Farms are foldin' all around us and there's no stimulus to the economy here. Most of my generation got out soon as they were old enough to take a hike. Hell, I've got the only gas station for miles around, and I'm just barely gettin' by. When my dad

171

retired I thought I was fixed for life, ownin' my own station and all, but now, who knows?"

He saw the frown on Paul's face, the worry in Christine's, and immediately switched to a more optimistic tone. "I'll make a few calls after we eat and see what I can turn up. There's still plenty of folks around here willin' to lend a helping hand."

Over a hamburger and broccoli casserole, Ken and Mary dissected possibilities. Chris told them she'd prefer an office or clerical job, but that she had waitressing experience and would be willing to do manual labor if she had to. When asked, Paul shrugged, then saw the challenge in Christine's eyes and said he would do whatever they could find him to do.

"You could ride into Pratt with me," suggested Mary. "I work part-time in a bank there and drive near fifty miles there and back four days a week. If you did get jobs, I'd be happy to let you have my car for the fifth day."

"That would be kind, but only if you'd let us share gas costs," said Chris. She drummed her fingers on the tabletop and was about to remark that Paul could wire to New York for money when she heard Mary mumble something about a wedding ring. She gawked across the table at her. "What?"

With a flush that clashed vividly with her hair, Mary stammered, "Oh, I noticed that you—you don't have a ring, that's all. I just wondered."

Chris stared at her left hand as if she'd never seen it before. The bare fingers seemed to shriek at her. A ring! They hadn't thought about a ring! She slowly raised her eyes to meet Paul's. Hers were accusing. His, she noted with rising anger, were amused.

"I'm afraid, Mary, that our courtship was somewhat . . . rushed. We met in Vegas and got married the next day."

"The next day!"

He presented her with his charming smile, the one that

could make a woman forget her own name. Chris saw it and longed to kick him under the table. "I was so intent on capturing this lovely lady, I couldn't think about rings." He turned the charm on her with a liquid gaze that could only be termed mooning. Christine's desire to kick him sharpened drastically.

Ken tactfully changed the subject and Chris never did get around to asking Paul about his New York money. She was too busy being angry at him for putting her in the position of deceiving people as kind as Mary and Ken.

Directly after dessert Ken got on the kitchen phone while Mary washed up, again refusing to permit her guests to help her. "Enjoy it," she said with a smile, "you'll have kitchen duty soon enough, so let tonight be my present. For your honeymoon."

They could do nothing but concede and retired to the living room, where Chris immediately rounded on him with a furious hiss. "How could you do this to me?"

"Do what?" Paul eased himself into the recliner, stretching his long legs out with apparent comfort.

"Force me to lie to these people! They're being so kind —I feel like a rat." She raged up and down the oval braided rug spread over the hardwood floor, her short brown hair whisking over her ears in flyaway curls. "I'm no good at lying. I'll make a million mistakes. They'll know I'm lying and hate me for it."

Paul lifted his arms. "Come here, baby."

She glared at him. She dug her toes into the variegated braids of the rug. But her ears rang with the soft, endearing *baby,* the one that made her tummy flip. With a sigh of resignation she went to him. He enfolded her in his arms, tugging her onto his lap. It was, oddly enough, not the usual sexually tense contact they shared, but a comforting embrace.

"I'm sorry, Chris. I didn't mean to get you into this mess. It just happened. I had to say something to stop the looks you two were exchanging."

173

"We weren't—"

"Even so, I can't very well tell them the truth now. We're in too deep, baby." His hand lazily stroked her leg. He smiled down at her, tenderly, possessively. "Think of it as a white lie—one of the good lies told to benefit another."

"Oh? And who would that be?" she asked in a pert, breathy way that started his heart hammering.

"Ken," he replied brusquely. He dropped his gaze to where his fingers were feathering her thigh. "I wanted to smash his pretty face in when you were ogling him. Do you really go for that golden beach-boy look?"

There were crescent shadows where the light angled over his long eyelashes and a shaded crevice that widened from the bridge to the tip of his nose. It was ridiculous, this desire welling up in her to trace the outlines of those shadows with her lips, her tongue. She lowered her gaze, saw his fingers whirling lightly over her blue jeans, and swallowed tightly.

"I think he's very handsome, yes," she forced out. The arm circling her back clenched and she quickly added, "But that doesn't mean I have any designs on him. Besides, a half-wit could see he's in love with Mary."

His hold slowly loosened. "Maybe so, but I still don't want him getting any ideas about you."

There was a definite warning in that soft whisper. Hearing it, Chris felt a wild surge of hope that he was coming to love her. She smiled at him coyly. "Oh? And why not?"

"Because I don't intend to share," he said on a hard bite.

Disappointment stabbed at her. "You don't own me, you know."

The harshness left his face. He smiled provocatively. "No? Not even after last night?"

She envisaged the pink flowered quilt tucked over the bed upstairs and saw just what the outcome of their relationship would be. Already the pain of it was pricking her and, fearing what was to come, she shivered.

"Cold, baby?"

"Uh-uh." The comfort of his touch had been chased out by a rush of warmth she had difficulty ignoring. She didn't want to be feeling these things for him. He did not, could not, love her. She lay her hand over his, stilling the rousing motion of his fingers teasing her thigh. Seeking a distraction, she seized hold of an earlier thought and said unsteadily, "Why don't you just wire your bank in New York to send money? Your parents have had time enough to cool down—"

He slipped his hand up under her top. His fingers felt warm and smooth on her skin. "I haven't, though," he murmured huskily.

"Y-you haven't w-what?"

"Cooled down. In fact, I'm heating up."

She shoved his hand away and straightened in his lap. She glanced at him and wished she hadn't. His eyes were heavy-lidded with desire. She tried to stand, but he clamped her to him. "Paul, I'm serious. Just because I'm staying doesn't mean you have to. It's stupid for you to be stranded here when help's only a phone call away."

"I'm serious too."

Skepticism ran through her eyes and her chin went up. He recognized the stubborn intent in that thrust and a sudden doubt shook him. She was being damned persistent about his leaving. An ugly suspicion wormed its way into his brain. She said she wasn't attracted to Ken Huber. But she'd also said he was the most handsome man she'd ever seen. . . .

More, he realized that Ken didn't have the impediments of his wealth and privileged background. She'd made her opinion of the Ridgeways of the world unmistakably clear. Though she didn't as yet suspect he was quite in that class, she had told him more than once that they did not mix. Anger and disappointment assailed him in equal parts.

After last night, how could she think that? The weight of her in his arms felt so right, how could she think it wrong?

He heard her say again that he had no reason to stay. He came to a decision.

"Okay, I'll have to confess," he said, heaving a sigh. "I lied about the bank in New York."

For several seconds she did nothing more than stare at him blankly. Then she was off his lap with a leap that equaled an Olympic broad jump. "You what? Do you mean—"

"I mean, I conned you into giving me a free ride. I lied about the money, my parents, everything."

She looked so astounded, so hurt, that for a minute he regretted these new lies. But memories of the passion they'd shared the night before overrode any scruples. After last night he wasn't about to hand her over to Ken Huber. He was determined not to leave her and he was fully prepared to perjure his soul in order to stay.

"You mean you weren't going to fix me up next semester? You weren't going to pay me for driving you all over kingdom come? You actually let me drop out of school and abandon my job all for *nothing?*"

"The point is, I can't leave here until you do," he said in a voice meant to soothe. It didn't.

"How many other lies have you told me? Are you married after all? Was Theresa right about you? Why you—you—"

She was visibly trembling, but only half the reason was righteous anger. The other half was an odd relief. Relief to know that instead of the wealthy playboy she'd feared so far out of her class, Paul was a con man, a man living hand-to-mouth, a man within her sphere, after all.

He rose slowly from the recliner. Though at a disadvantage, she threw back her head to shake her fist in his face. "You rat, you," she finished somewhat lamely.

"I could say I'm sorry, but that would be another lie." He caught hold of her shaking fist and set his lips warmly against the knuckles. "I'm not sorry, baby," he whispered. "I'm damn glad you're with me. I want you with me. I want you."

Was this sinking feeling, this fluttering from head to toe, was this what they meant by the term *weak-kneed?* She thought she'd melt right to the floor in a puddle of excitement. All her unnamed fears of sophisticated ladies from the big city vanished. The barriers of wealth and social position had been demolished. He was as reachable as the length of her arms. She shook with the urge to embrace him and, even more, to kiss him madly.

She would have, too, if Ken and Mary hadn't walked in just then. Paul retained hold of her fist long enough to place another tender kiss on it, an act which simultaneously exhilarated and embarrassed her. The tingle of his mouth lingered on her skin, distracting her at first from what Ken was saying.

"I'll talk with Floyd in the morning, see if he can't take you on temporarily, maybe until after harvest," he told Paul. "He couldn't pay much, mind you, not with the way his farm expenses have skyrocketed while prices have dropped, but with his arthritis he could use the help."

"And while I'm at work tomorrow," put in Mary, "I'll see if the bank needs any help. Or anything else around town."

Paul and Chris tried to thank the pair of them, but both refused to hear it. "Hey, you don't know how glad we are to have somebody new to talk to," Ken insisted with one of his easy smiles. "I could give you a tooth count, complete with number of fillings on everybody in this town. Actually you're doing us a favor. Oscar needs new blood."

They all laughed and he headed for the door, telling them he'd place the order on that part first thing in the morning and get back with them as soon as he could. "Walk me to the truck?" he then asked Mary with studied nonchalance.

She agreed, and on her way out explained that she'd set

out fresh towels upstairs, that the sheets were clean, that if they needed anything, "just holler."

"You going to come or yak all night, Mary, girl?" demanded Ken, grinning. She went out with a tsk and a laugh. The front door closed behind them.

Silence swelled like some vast empty tidal wave. Christine's breath was washed away in the deluge. She knotted her hands together and felt as nervous as a girl on her first date. Considering all that she and Paul had been through the past six days, her breathless agitation at being alone with him was the height of absurdity. It ranked right up there with having run off with him in the first place.

"Baby—"

Breaking in with an overly bright cheeriness, she gushed, "I think we've found our mechanically minded genie after all. Two of them."

"You're not allowed more than one genie."

"They're guardian angels then. Honestly, can you believe it? What do they know about us? We could be criminals on the run for all they know. Really, I've got to talk to Mary. She's too trusting!"

"Funny, I've thought the same thing about you," he said.

"Yes, and see where it got me," she rejoined, stabbing a condemning finger in his direction. "You weren't to be trusted!"

He reached for her, but she eluded him, swiftly skating into the dining room. She couldn't think when he was too close, and she needed to think clearly now. A barrage of second thoughts had descended to add to her confusion and she intended to sweep them away before entangling herself any further with him.

Paul followed her, forcing her to back up until the wood of the table gouged into her buttocks. When she bumped to a halt he smiled. It was a slow, provocative smile, the sort of smile that melted bones indiscriminately.

"You never answered me," she said, taking the offensive. "Are you married?"

"No." He stepped closer.

"How do I know you're not lying? You lie like a rug."

"Trust me."

"Trust you?" She almost choked in her astonishment. "How can you ask that of me? You've spun me one big yarn after the other and you expect me to *trust* you?"

"This hasn't been a lie," said Paul as he pressed himself against her. "My wanting you is real and true."

He bent to kiss her. She swiveled her head. He buried his lips in the side of her neck. She vainly pushed at him; he refused to release her, grinding his hard frame ever more intimately into her softness.

"It-it's not the s-same," she objected breathlessly. "You know it's not. I—being lied to—it's made me feel—vulnerable."

He could feel her heart beating beneath his. He could feel her breasts flattened against his chest. He could feel the heat of her breath. Flames of desire licked through his blood. For one agonized moment he wished he could go back and start all over with her. He wished he could court her with champagne and flowers, deck her in diamonds, take her without all the lies.

"Baby, I won't tell you any other lies, I swear it," was what he finally whispered in a thickened voice.

She studied those deep, dark eyes of his, wanting desperately to believe him, yet fearing to. His muscles were tensed, held rigid down the length of her. The heat of his body radiated through his clothing and hers to set fire to her skin.

"Cross your heart and hope to die?" She felt foolish, reverting to the childish oath, but she needed reassurance; she needed something to hang her fragile trust on to.

"I'd rather . . ." He pulled her away from the table. "Much rather . . ." He lifted her into his arms. "Cross your heart."

179

"Promise," she pleaded.

Carrying her across to the stairway, he murmured huskily, "I'll cross my heart, but I won't die. Not yet. Not until you've let me love you again."

It wouldn't matter whether he kept his promise or not. She wouldn't live to know about it. Her heart had stopped.

At the top of the stairs he paused. Her lashes fluttered, then lifted. He'd meant to dash into the bedroom and plunge himself into her. Instead, he heard himself say softly, "There is no lie in the way I respond to you. There is no deception in what I surrender to you."

Her arms tightened around his neck and her mouth moistened the column of his neck. Feeling the acquiescence in her, he strode into the bedroom without bothering to turn on the light and toppled gently onto the bed, still cradling her in his arms. Even as the mattress sagged beneath their weight, he planted impatient kisses amid her curls and sought her softness with fevered hands.

He had not thought tonight could be as special; he had not thought she would be as wondrous. He had thought wrong.

Tendrils of her hair tickled his nose, enchanting him. The supple flexing of her body as his hands raced restlessly upward fascinated him. The firm uplift of her breasts tempted him to splay his fingers over the peaks. Through the cotton of her top, he could feel her nipples harden and he marveled all over again at the wonder of her. Once again the incredible sensuality that surpassed the physical filled him.

Christine felt his lips in her hair, felt the band of his arms ease from around her, felt his hands begin to explore the ridge of her spine, the curve of her hip, the swell of her breasts. Her body shook with hunger—and with the urgent need to make him love her.

With a little moan she thrust wildly against his chest, pushing him into the quilt-covered bed. Her mouth sought and found his. Her hands clung to his shoulders. Her body writhed over his, raising an ardor in him that threatened his control.

Her aggression surprised him. But as her tongue probed the depths of his mouth and her breasts rubbed against his chest, he gave himself up to the delight of receiving what Christine had to give.

Unbuttoning his shirt, she feathered her fingertips over his chest and found she was the one tantalized. Burrowing into the column of his neck, she pressed hot, fierce kisses into his skin and found she was the one roused. Skimming her mouth over his shoulder blade, she teased him with her tongue and found she was the one delighted. She had meant to bind him to her and found the bonds shackling her ever more tightly instead.

"Whoa, slow down," he begged on a raspy breath. "We've got all night."

She tensed above him. "Just tonight?"

With a single fluid motion he reversed their positions. He smiled down at her. "And the next and the next and the next."

His smile gleamed in the darkness above her. Reaching up, she lightly placed her fingertips on the sensual curve of his mouth. There was so much she wanted to say. She wanted to tell him she loved him; she wanted to beg him not to hurt her; she wanted to ask him how long it would be until he tired of her. Instead, she swallowed her fear of the future and murmured, "And the next after that."

A shudder rippled through him. He knew then he would not be able to count the number of nights he would want to be with her. He swore to treasure the few he would have. He swore to return to her the indescribable fulfillment she gave to him. Slowly, softly, he brought his lips to hers. His kiss was a gentle avowal.

He undressed her piece by piece, taking time to seek and savor the silken treasures of her body. He touched. He tasted. He throbbed with the pleasure of it. When he thought he would pass out from the strain of holding back, he rose, dumped his clothes onto the floor, then sank into the upraised arms waiting for him.

The mattress rocked with the cadence of their loving. Her brown tangles crushed into the down of the pillow as she arched, lifting her hips to him. His black locks brushed against the planes of her cheek as he bent his head to take what she offered. As he plunged deeper, deeper within her, he devoured her with lips that savored the special taste of her mouth, her neck, her breasts. Her fingers curled into his back, feeling the rhythmic shift of his muscles as he worked. His fingers dug into the quilt, feeling the rumpled sheets as she shifted with him. Their breaths labored together, becoming louder, harder, as they reached for the summit.

A sharp, short cry tore from Christine. A low, guttural groan sounded from Paul. They lay twined together, bodies damp with exertion, souls spent with satisfaction. When he could breathe steadily, he lifted his head to look at her. Her lashes flickered against cheeks still flushed. Her breath came from lips still swollen and parted with passion. He looked at her in wonderment. How had he missed seeing how beautiful she was? How had he been so blind?

As he stared, her lids lifted. Her parted lips curved upward. "Was that a properly bridal attitude for you?"

He sucked in a breath. He released it as he bent to nibble on the edge of her mouth. "Ummm. But you know what they say."

"What's that?"

"Practice makes perfect."

"I don't know if I can be a perfect bride," she murmured on a sleepy yawn. "I'm not even a bride, you know."

"Close enough in my book." He rolled to the side, pulling her with him. He fluffed her short curls with his fingers and decided that if he died now, he'd go out a happy man. It was a new feeling for him. He decided he liked it.

Wrapped in the cocoon of his warmth, she ignored the tiny sting of his comment. She wasn't going to let anything mar her joy. She felt complete, whole, total. She didn't need anything else, not a single thing. She had Paul; she had this time with him. She was bursting with happiness.

They drifted to sleep, each sweetly enveloped in a new-found peace, each sweetly dreaming of the other.

CHAPTER ELEVEN

The arrival of Mr. and Mrs. Richards did not go by unnoticed. Though Mary had gone to Pratt for her half day at the bank, a steady stream of neighbors came to the house throughout the following morning. Mrs. Gellhaus stopped by "to leave a recipe Mary's been asking for." Leah Holdhusen "just had to have the latest copy of *Good Housekeeping*" and couldn't find hers to save her soul. When neither Paul nor Chris could find the issue, Leah dismissed it with a shrug and said it didn't matter, but stayed twenty minutes more, ostensibly looking for it herself while making thinly veiled inquiries into their circumstances.

Nadine Dixon didn't bother with such guile. She greeted them with "So you're the new wonders" and proceeded to tell them how the town hadn't been buzzing like this since Tillie Arnold gave birth to triplets.

"Well, yes, that must have been exciting," said Christine, shooting a look toward Paul that warned him not to dare laugh. He intently studied his fingernails and kept silent.

"Oh, that was nothing," said Nadine. A twinkle shone in her blue eyes, but her mien remained perfectly serious. "What made it all so very interesting, you see, was that on the same day Tillie's husband ran off with the Cowens' youngest girl."

184

Paul was seized by a fit of coughing. Chris cleared her throat and said uncertainly, "How—how unfortunate."

"Yes, wasn't it?" she agreed placidly. She pushed back her short gray hair with a bony hand and asked, "Any idea how long you intend to stay?"

"Uh, no," replied Chris. "Our car—"

"At young Huber's. Used to be old Huber's, you know, until his father retired. Had to. Hernia." Nadine stood abruptly. She was a thin, straight line of a woman who would have been easily overlooked had it not been for her large, luminous eyes. They enlivened her face, smiling when her mouth remained solemn. "I daresay you'll want to go on over and talk to Ken. Mary'll be home round 'bout one thirty, same as usual."

She left them and, after one stunned second of silence, they looked at each other and burst into laughter.

"Grab that suitcase of yours and let's get out of here," said Paul. "I'm beginning to understand what it feels like to be the monkey at the zoo."

"I liked Nadine though. She wasn't just nosy."

"No, she at least was entertaining."

"I thought for sure you were going to embarrass me by laughing out loud," said Chris as she slung her purse over her shoulder. "Although I rather think Nadine wouldn't have minded a bit if you had."

They walked the few blocks to Ken's gas station, ambling beneath the canopy of trees lining the street. Beyond the cottonwoods and elms sat a succession of two-story frame houses painted white and peach and beige, with large yards and flower gardens. The chatter of birds clashed with the clack of roller skates and the clamor of lawn mowers. The sweet scent of fresh cut grass wafted on the air. A man glanced up from hosing his car and waved.

"I thought this sort of town existed only on television," said Chris, lifting a hand in return.

"So did I." Paul glanced down. Yearning clouded her face; he knew a sharp desire to erase it. As always since meeting her, his reaction surprised him. He didn't see himself as a protector.

"Life must be so"–she paused, seeking the right word— "so content here, don't you think? Simple and quiet and calm. Imagine growing up here."

He thought of the estates, the travel, the private schools of his own boyhood. No, he couldn't imagine growing up here. He smiled crookedly, a little sadly. "Don't you think it would also be dull? Look at the people this morning. Their biggest entertainment is trying to discover who the strangers in town are."

She wrinkled her nose at him. "It's natural that they'd be interested in us. I think Oscar is perfectly lovely."

He swooped and kissed the tip of her nose. "And I think anywhere you are is perfectly lovely."

Chris was still quite breathless when they arrived at the gas station. Was that the sort of thing he said to every woman? Or dared she hope she was special? She caught herself at that. If she dared to think such things, she would only end up falling farther and landing harder.

Ken was at the desk in the front of the station, writing in a ledger. The instant they came in he slapped the book shut and shoved it aside. "Thank god you've come. I've been hoping I'd be rescued." At their obvious puzzlement, he grinned and waved a hand toward the ledger. "Book work. I hate it."

He jumped up and swept a pile of papers from a metal folding chair. Gesturing Chris into it, he went on. "I sent in the order on the U-joint this morning, but don't get too excited. Delivery runs six to eight weeks."

"Which means eight to ten, right?" said Chris, sighing.

Neither noticed the dismay that flicked over Paul's face. There was simply no way he could stay in Oscar that length of time. He slid his gaze over Chris. Well, when the time came, he'd just have to convince her to leave that damn car here. He realized Ken was addressing him and forced himself to pay attention.

186

"The good news is I spoke to Floyd and he agreed to give you a try out on his farm," the younger man was saying. "His son Vern does most of the actual farming these days, but it's really more than he can handle alone. Floyd said he'd talk to you about it after church tomorrow."

"Does he understand I don't know anything about farming?" asked Paul.

"Well, you could kinda say that," drawled Ken. "To quote Floyd, 'That city boy probably wouldn't know a field from a road,' but he thought you'd be trainable."

Chris tried to stifle a giggle and failed. Her giggle escalated by degrees to a guffaw as she took in Paul's arrested expression. But within seconds his astonishment transformed into amusement and he laughed with her.

"I've been called a lot of things, but that's the first time I've been called trainable," he said, wishing his father could have heard it. "Well, if he's willing to give me a try, I'm willing to give farming a try."

Chris fiddled with the leather strap of her purse. "Do you think Mary will turn up anything for me?"

"I've got something up my sleeve if she doesn't." Like the Cheshire cat, he was all smiles. "I had a real stroke of genius, if I do say so myself. I called my mom."

They gaped at him blankly. Finally Paul prompted, "And?"

"She told me Peggy Lenge's getting married to Garland Vandiver over in Coldwater."

Chris looked quizzically at Paul, who lifted his shoulders in a mute echo of her bewilderment. "Oh?" she said.

"Peggy's the day waitress at Dieble's Café." Seeing their continued incomprehension, he explained, "She's going to quit as soon as she's married and help Garland run his farm. With your experience, Chris, you'd be bound to get the job at the café. I thought we could catch Bernie, Bernice Iverson, that is—she's the owner of Dieble's—at church tomorrow and introduce you."

She smiled gratefully. "How can we ever thank you?"

One of his gorgeously engaging grins lit his face. "Try convincing Mary I'm the greatest thing since sliced bread. Now, I'd better get to work or I'll be lookin' for a job myself."

They left him and strolled up the main street. The sidewalks were cracked and sunken in patches; the storefronts were faded and peeling. The windows in the church weren't stained glass, but simply a colored plastic pressed over the panes. A hand-lettered sign outside the library announced it was open on Wednesdays and Saturdays. At the far end they turned and started down the other side of the street.

Paul asked her, "Do you still think Oscar perfectly lovely?"

With a tilt of the chin that he recognized, she stoutly declared it was. "It's quaint."

"More like antiquated. I wonder if we fell through a time warp and landed back in 1954?"

She responded to this with a sniff of disdainful indignation. Pausing by the ice cream stand, he offered to make it up to her by treating. "What do you think a Twisty is?"

"Let's get one and find out," she said.

It was a tall cone, half chocolate, half vanilla twisted together. Chris ate hers with relish. Watching her tongue dart out to lick the ice cream prevented Paul from totally enjoying his. Memories of the pleasurable sensations he'd derived from that tongue warmed him. He began to think staying a few weeks in Oscar wouldn't be such a bad idea after all.

Wandering on, they peered into the window of a clothing store and tried not to giggle at the display of small print house-dresses and bib overalls. Paul bent his head and whispered in her ear. "Yup. Nineteen fifty-four it is."

She somehow suppressed the urge to explode with laughter in full view of the store clerk eyeing them curiously through the window. Turning, they finally retraced their steps back to Mary's house. Mary was there, waiting for them with the report of her lack of success in discovering any openings in Pratt.

"That's okay," said Chris. "Ken tells us Peggy Lenge is getting married to Garland Vandiver."

A cheery smile that restored a hint of fullness to her face touched Mary's mouth. "Well, that's great. Bernie'll hire you in a second."

Chris looked at Paul. Paul looked at Chris. At the same instant they smiled. And for a timeless heartbeat they were alone.

With a little start Chris realized Mary was asking her about attending church the next day. She admitted she didn't have anything suitable to wear, explaining in a rush that she and Paul had married so precipitantly they'd gone off with scarcely more than the clothes on their backs. As she spoke she could feel both Mary's gaze of astonishment and Paul's of amusement on her and promptly determined to make him pay for this string of calumnies she was being forced to tell.

"Well, no matter," said Mary. "I've a shirtwaist dress I can alter to fit you with no trouble at all."

She bustled out before Chris could object. So, instead, she rounded on Paul. Wagging a finger in front of his nose, she hissed, "That's the last lie I'm giving voice to! From now on you can make the explanations."

He captured the flapping finger and nibbled gently on its tip. "But you look," he murmured as he teased his tongue over her nail, "so delightful when you blush."

"I wasn't blushing!"

"Oh, yes, you were. And very modest you looked too. Exactly like a newlywed."

How could she maintain a shred of temper when he looked at her with eyes that danced? When he spoke to her in a voice husked with humor? When he nipped playfully upon the very finger with which she admonished him? She couldn't. She didn't even want to.

Mary returned with an armful of thread, scissors, gauges, and a shortsleeved indigo dress with white collar and cuffs.

Paul watched as Chris put on the dress and turned this way and that at Mary's direction. He thought again how ordinary Chris looked. She was neither sleek nor sophisticated, neither sexy nor striking. And yet she was special. He had never before met anyone quite so special.

"What's there to do here on a Saturday night?" he asked after a time.

"Do? Here? Nothing," mumbled Mary around a mouthful of pins. She looked up in time to see disbelief flit over his features. She pulled the pins from her mouth. "If you want to go to dinner or a movie, you drive into Pratt. Here there's an occasional dance at the VFW hall, and there'll be a picnic on the Fourth of July, but the usual entertainment is television. Sometimes a card game or a dinner with friends, that's about it."

Paul began to think that even a week in Oscar would seem like a lifetime.

By Wednesday, he realized he'd misjudged. A week in Oscar seemed like an eternal lifetime.

Stumbling out of Vern Kilmer's pickup, he plodded across the yard and trudged upstairs to the rooms he shared with Christine. He collapsed onto the bed and simply lay, too tired even to groan. There wasn't a muscle he possessed that wasn't in revolt. He throbbed from head to toe, weary and worn out. The palms of his hands were scraped and sore. His lungs and nostrils were full of dust; his clothes full of dirt. He was certain that if there were any mercy in this world he'd expire before another day could rise to send him back out to the Kilmers' farm.

Six days in Oscar had been about five too many. The only reason people didn't complain about nothing to do, he'd concluded, was that they were too bored to care. The town revolved on work and gossip, and that, he thought with acerbic cynicism, was because there wasn't anything else. There was no culture, no couture, hell, there wasn't even a stop sign in the whole damn town!

"Paul?" whispered Chris, standing in the threshold. "Are you all right? Did you want to eat?"

He did not speak. He simply raised his arms and she came to him. The bed sagged as she lay beside him, nestling her head on his chest. The slow thump of his heart tolled in her ear, the slow breathing chorused with it. She gazed at his rough red palms and ached for his aches.

"Would you like me to put some salve on your hands?"

"Where did you get salve?" he roused himself to ask. They'd tried to buy some after his first day at the farm, but there was no pharmacy in Oscar and there'd been no salve to be found in the grocery store.

"Mary bought it for us when she went into Pratt today."

Again he didn't say anything. Chris started to rise, but he tightened his arms and whispered, "Stay."

"But your hands—"

"Just let me hold you, baby."

So they lay quietly, not speaking, not moving, simply sharing the silence. Calls of night creatures drifted up through the windows; muffled sounds from the television downstairs occasionally wound their way upward. His breath slowed, evened. Hers was scarcely drawn for fear of disturbing him. After a time, certain he'd fallen asleep, Chris shifted a little away from him. She tenderly took up each of his hands in turn and pressed a soft kiss on the abrased palms.

"That's much better than salve any day," he said drowsily.

She jerked, startled, then raised enough to peer at him through the shadows. "I thought you'd gone to sleep."

"Mmmm, almost."

Even in the darkness she could see the weariness etched

191

into his face. It made her heart ache. Love seemed to fill her every pore; she longed desperately to cry out her love for him. She said, "You need something to eat."

"I need you."

"You need," she somehow managed to say, "some food, some salve, and some sleep."

Not allowing him to protest, she slid from the bed and went down to the kitchen. She warned herself not to put too much credence in his words. She told herself any man as sore and tired as Paul would say he needed her. She knew the way her heart was soaring and her blood was pounding was ridiculous. She knew and yet she could not halt the excitement she felt.

When she returned to the bedroom with a mug of beef broth and a chicken salad sandwich, she found that Paul had gone to sleep. Sighing, she set the mug and plate aside and went to fetch the salve.

She eased onto the side of the bed and picked up his left hand. As she worked the salve into his palm, a wince crossed his face and a great sadness welled up within her. He'd obviously never gone through such physical labor. He wasn't made for it. She'd have to tell him to give it up and leave Oscar without her.

Definitely without her. Aside from the fact that she wasn't about to abandon her sole possession, Chris couldn't leave, not yet. She yearned to linger in this quiet place, to soak in its old-fashioned values and close-knit spirit. Having to drive fifty miles to get a tube of salve was, in her view, counterbalanced by never having to lock the front door. Imagine, never locking the doors! Imagine, living without the fear and stress of the city. It was the sort of life she'd always craved.

When she'd finished with both hands, she wiped the excess off with a tissue and recapped the tube. She unbuttoned his shirt and removed his shoes. Not wanting to wake him, she did not touch the rest of his clothes. She quickly undressed and snuggled naked against his warmth.

Staring into the night, she silently grieved. She grieved for all the nights they would not share. She grieved for all the laughter lost, for all the moments forfeited, for all the days never to be together. She had known, of course, that eventually their time would end, but she had not thought it would be so soon. She tried to tell herself it was best this way, best ended before she fell any deeper in love with him. In her sorrow she thought she would be lie tormented all night.

She woke to a ticklish feeling. Even as she raised a hand to brush the tickler aside, she realized it was Paul's mouth nuzzling the shell of her ear.

"What are you doing?" she whispered.

There was a pause. His breath curled around her ear to mist her cheek. "I didn't mean to wake you, baby."

"It—it's all right," she said unsteadily. "I'd probably have wakened anyway. It's so quiet here, I find myself waking at night and wondering where the traffic's gone."

He plopped back onto his pillow. "Do you miss it then? The traffic, the city?"

She heard the question behind the question and longed to say Yes, let's leave here and go back. But she couldn't bring herself to say it. She liked the measured pace, the secure simplicity here. She liked the unsullied sky and the uniform days. So she replied, "No. I'm just used to the noise. I don't miss it; I prefer the silence."

Paul held back a sigh. He wanted to leave, but he wanted to take Christine with him. When he'd awakened to the softness of her curled around him he'd reached for her, but halted as his stiffened muscles throbbed in protest. Each twinge and prickling pain reinforced his decision that it was time to leave, so he'd formulated arguments to convince her to forget the car and come away with him. He'd even considered telling her the truth and taking his chances that she'd forgive him.

And as he'd worked out first one conversation, then another, she'd mewed softly in her sleep and he'd been unable to resist kissing her, nibbling on her ear. But he now heard the determination in that single No, and knew none of his planned arguments had been strong enough.

"You like it here?" he asked, a hint of his amazement plain.

"Yes, don't you?" She waited a moment, then rolled over him, gazing down at his shadowed face. "All my life I've dreamed of a place like this. A real, honest-to-goodness hometown where everyone cares and—"

"Where everyone interferes, you mean."

"It's still better than the apathy, the lack of concern back in L.A. Can you imagine someone getting mugged here without half the town running to the rescue?"

"Are you saying you want to stay here? Chris, baby, is being a waitress at Dieble's Café what you want for your life? Do you think you could actually be happy with the slow pace here? Without anything beyond television for entertainment? You'll be bored to death in another week."

She lay atop him, her breasts flattened against his chest. Wisps of her hair feathered his chin as she shook her head. "I don't know. I honestly don't. I can't say I'd want to stay here forever. You're right, being a waitress isn't what I want to do with my life. And, yes, I'd miss the cultural advantages, the bustling array of the city. But, Paul, I've always wanted somewhere I could belong. This is the kind of place where people belong."

He wanted to tell her she could belong to him, but some last vestige of sanity stopped him. She wouldn't belong to Paul Richards, but to Preston Ridgeway, and he knew that was an impossibility. Aside from what his family would say, he wasn't certain she'd want to stay with Preston Ridgeway. And what was he thinking of anyway? He didn't want anything permanent, he just wanted her for a little longer.

Pressing his mouth into her hair, he murmured, "How can you think you belong in a place where people are still raving about how many garbage cans were knocked over on prom night?"

She giggled unwillingly at that. "I don't know. I really don't. But isn't that better than daily murder statistics?"

"Baby, can't you see we're like ducks out of water here? This isn't the kind of place where we belong."

With an abrupt jolt that spoke of her negation, Chris sat up and in so doing bumped into one of his bruises. He groaned. She immediately eased off him. He reached to pull her back, but she eluded him. Kneeling on the mattress, she looked down at him in consternation. "Oh, Paul! You're going to have to leave. You can't keep working on the farm. You're not suited to it."

"What do you mean, leave?"

"Leave here," she answered, confirming his worst suspicion. "There's no reason for you to hang around here for weeks on end, waiting for my car to get fixed."

"Neither of us has to stay," he said slowly. His heart hammered into the pause that followed. A hope rose that she was actually prepared to listen to reason. "We could take the bus out tomorrow and return when the car is ready."

She plucked at the patchwork flowers on the quilt, not looking at him. Finally she forced the words past the lump growing in her throat. "Like I said, I don't know if I belong here, but I do know that I'm staying until the Mav is fixed."

The ominous finality in her tone struck a chord of alarm in him. He raised up on his elbows. Within the shadows her skin shone a shimmery, insubstantial white, making her seem illusive, intangible. It fired his temper. "Damn it, Chris, be sensible! Waitressing in this one-horse town won't earn you enough to pay for the screws to put that

195

damn U-joint back on, much less—"

"I'm staying," she interrupted firmly, then swiftly softened. "But there's no need for you to. You don't like it here and, more, you aren't used to such work. It's not fair for you to go through such pain and effort on my behalf. It's my car and my responsibility. You needn't feel you have to stay on my account."

Faced with many of the arguments he had intended to raise himself, he perversely discarded them and leaped to the defensive. "I haven't said I don't like it here," he bit out, "and of course it's my responsibility. That you're here at all is my fault and therefore my responsibility."

"But I'm relieving you of that responsibility," she pointed out, surprised at the rough vehemence of his tone.

"I'll decide if I want to be relieved of it. Besides, I do like the town."

"I had the impression you thought it small and dull and peopled with busybodies."

He chuckled a little at that, for the stress of argumentation had gone from her voice. "Well, I do think those things. But I also think it's simple and clean and filled with honest people I'd be proud to call friends."

She studied him, trying to discern his expression in the darkness. "That doesn't put aside the fact that you're not suited for farm work."

"I'll get used to it."

"But the point is that you shouldn't have to get used to it, not for me, not for my car."

Heaving an impatient sigh, Paul silenced her in the most effective way he knew. He took hold of her shoulders and yanked her down to him, kissing her fiercely, determinedly. He privately doubted if he'd ever get used to working in the sun, hauling and lifting and pushing his body to the limit. But as long as she stubbornly insisted on waiting for that damn car, he was going to put up with it. He wasn't ready to do without Christine yet.

The ferocity of his kiss, the resolution behind it, elated her. He was staying, and he was staying because of her. She thought her heart might burst with joy.

He touched her with a new reverence, almost as if he couldn't believe she was real. From her brow to her chin his fingers traced the structure of her face, delicately seeking the arch of her eyebrows, the ridge of her cheek, the curve of her mouth. He stroked the line of her jaw and the length of her neck. Beneath his fingertips her pulse wildly thrummed. His own pounded savagely in response.

She wove her fingers into the soft thickness of his hair and let the passion of his kiss, his caress, sweep over her. With a soft moan she melted against him. Her breasts nestled into the mat of curls on his chest, her hips molded to the taut surface of his loins, and her legs twined with the length of his.

This was where she belonged!

His lips slowly followed the path of his fingertips down her neck to her breastbone. His hands skimmed over the sides of her breasts to her waist and back. He tasted the sweetness of her skin. He inhaled the scent of tuberose soap. He felt the rise and fall of each breath she took. He was wrapped within the enchantment of her.

Shafts of moonlight lanced the darkness. The pillow gleamed a ghostly white, emphasizing the black of Paul's hair. Chris gazed and felt awed by him. His eyebrows slanted into the shadows and his lashes formed crescents against his cheek. His lips curved into a sensual smile, a smile reflecting the pleasure she felt.

Pressing a quick, firm kiss onto that smile, she rose over him. He mumbled a protest which she ignored. She slipped his shirt from his shoulders, then slid down to straddle his knees. She ran her fingernail down his zipper and toyed with the snap.

He lay passive, enjoying the way her fingers teased his skin as she worked to free him of his clothes. His every

197

nerve seemed to leap at the lightest grazing of her fingertip.

Denim crumpled to the floor with a hushed rustle. Gliding her hands with deliberate leisure up his thighs, Chris bent to press her mouth onto the firm plane of his stomach. The stirring of his desire excited her past bearing. Her touch became more feverish, more impatient.

He moaned and set his hands on her waist. She resisted his tugging. Her kisses inched lower as her strokes climbed higher. "Baby, baby, I'm so sore, I . . . don't think I can . . ." he reluctantly rasped.

"Not even if I do all the work?" she asked on a breathy laugh.

"The spirit is willing, baby, God knows it's willing, but the flesh is too damn weak," he whispered hoarsely.

Her breath misted his skin with her husky laughter. "It doesn't look so weak to me. It looks . . . willing." She paused to drop another kiss upon his heated flesh. "And able."

He no longer cared if every bruise, every muscle, every damn cell he possessed, creaked and groaned in the morning. He ran his hands down to her hip. "So what are you going to do about it?"

"Lie back and see."

She fondled and played and drove him to the point of brain damage. Finally he could stand no more. He grabbed for her, begging her to take him. And when she did he thought he would pass out from the surge of excitement he felt.

Chris watched the play of passion over his features, delighting in it, in the knowledge that she was responsible for it, then closed her eyes to delight in the feel of his palms massaging her breasts. She worked to make him hers, creating the unspoken bond between them. To her, their rhythm sang of love—pure, strong, overwhelming love.

As she grew tired, new energy filled Paul. His body no

longer felt sore or fatigued. He felt gloriously alive, sensitive, enraptured. He locked his arms around her and rolled over, sinking her into the mold of the bed. Rather than draining him, each stroke brought him renewed strength. To him, their tempo raged of need, a racking need that would not be assuaged, not even when, at last, physical release came.

He tensed and she stiffened beneath him. Each one's pleasure merged with the other's, uniting them, before slowly they again became two separate beings. With a shuddering sigh Paul collapsed atop her. They lay tangled together, breathing deeply.

She skated her hands over his back, feeling the sweat cling to his skin, feeling the tension ease out of his muscles. When his breath evened, she asked quietly, "How do you feel?"

He flopped onto his back, then sought out her hand. Linking his fingers with hers, he replied drowsily, "Satisfied."

"Not sore?"

"If I am, I can't feel it." He brought her hand to his lips and tenderly kissed the back of it. "If I ever try to turn you down again, my dear Christine, have me committed at once. I must have been out of my mind."

She smiled, but it faded almost as soon as it touched her mouth. His physical need of her was exhilarating, but it wasn't enough to sustain a relationship. She felt she had to make him realize she wasn't trying to pin him down. "Paul, think about it. Really think about it."

He was drifting into sleep; his response to this was sluggish. "Think 'bout what?" he finally muttered.

"About taking the bus tomorrow."

That brought him to wakefulness instantly. He turned on his side and peered down at her. That she could think of sending him away after the wondrous love they'd shared made him so angry he could scarcely spit the words

199

out. "Don't start that again. The discussion is closed. Permanently."

She could see the thrust of his jaw outlined above her. She could hear the furious decision in his words. She licked her lips and ventured on a thin whisper, "We'll stay?"

"We'll stay."

CHAPTER TWELVE

August in Kansas sweltered with wet heat, heat that stuck
to the skin, heat that tracked relentless rivulets from brow
to breast to buttock. Hoisting a bale of cut hay, Paul flung
it onto the flatbed, no longer feeling the acrid sting of
trickling sweat down his bare back nor the sharp bite of
baling wire through his gloves. Perspiration matted the
dusty layers of his hair, hair grown haphazardly long. It
beaded over skin leathered by hours of labor under a hot,
unyielding sun; it dampened the denim of jeans fading to
gray beneath ground-in dirt.

Bits of hay flew through the air, sticking to his moist
skin. After tossing two more bales up to Floyd's eldest son,
Vern, he paused to brush impatiently at the prickling
straw. "I feel like I'm being tarred and feathered," he
muttered when Vern handed him a jug of water. He swallowed a long draught, then splashed some over his shoulders and chest.

"Wait'll it gets down your pants," drawled Vern.

"It has," said Paul.

A grin spread slowly over Vern's mouth. Paul received
it with a good-natured laugh. And as he laughed, he knew
a flash of amazement. For all his doubts that he'd ever get
used to the aches and pains, the calluses and cramped
muscles, the digested dust and inhaled dirt, Paul realized
he'd never felt so at peace.

Firmed, shaped, strengthened, his muscles no longer groaned. His roughened hands testified to the toil and sweat he'd put into the earth, but the tax on his physical abilities had purified him, cleansed his soul. His body had toned, his mind had settled.

He had wanted to find out who he really was, what he was really worth. He had. He'd found it here. Here he was accepted for himself, not for his name. Here he was respected for his accomplishments, not for his bank account. Here he wasn't part of an empire, but an individual who earned his own way.

He could almost believe he belonged here.

The simplicity he'd first scoffed at had brought him new serenity. For the first time in his life his restless frustration was gone. He looked about him and felt happy. He found enjoyment in the summer sun, the wind running through the wheat, the exchange of a smile with his friend. Simple pleasures, but true ones. And he owed it all to Christine.

He took another pull on the water jug and tried to cool the inner heat that always stirred at the thought of Christine. There wasn't a muscle in his body she hadn't eased with tender kneading; there wasn't a callus on his hands she hadn't soothed with loving kisses; there wasn't an inch of his body and soul she hadn't comforted with her own. The image of her body, softly molding to his, roused him, made him long for the shadows of the night when he could hold her, touch her. It surprised him, this increasing need for her. Rather than withering as time passed, his need for her had taken deep root, growing stronger, sturdier, surer.

He passed the jug back to Vern, wiped his mouth, and forced the thought of her out of his mind. He had work to do. He grasped the wires of another bale and glanced toward the sun as he heaved. Tonight would come eventually.

Would the night never come? Chris swept the back of her hand over her brow, then wiped it on the skirt of her shapeless once-white uniform. Air-conditioning was a luxury Dieble's Café could not afford. A ceiling fan lazily swirled, but the only real relief came from two oscillating fans set on the long Formica counter. Dieble's had six booths, three on each side of the door, eight stools at the counter, and one waitress to cover them all. Which wasn't much of a strain, thought Chris with a quirking smile. Scarcely more than a handful of customers were in the café at any time and occasionally, like now, there weren't any.

She was grateful for the respite from work. The heat was really getting to her today; she felt dizzy every time she turned around. She stacked the last of the dried glasses on the shelf above the sink, then propped her elbows on the counter and let the fan's breeze whisk over her face.

"Hot enough for you?" asked Bernice Iverson, the resident chef as well as owner of Dieble's. She made the same query day after day to anyone who passed through the doors. Chris swiveled her head to watch Bernie slouch against the frame of the door leading to the small kitchen, one plump hand teasing her short crop of silvery hair and the other lifting a tall glass to her smiling lips. Between sips of lemonade, she made the same observations she did every afternoon that it seemed the heat got hotter every summer and that it was a blinkin' wonder the whole darn town didn't pass out with sunstroke. Her comments were as predictable as the rising of the earth-baking sun. But that was just fine with Chris. She liked Bernie's predictability; she liked the never-changing routine of life in Oscar, Kansas.

"I'll be the first one to faint," Chris joked now. "The heat's got me so dizzy I'd thought I'd pass out when serving lunch."

Bernie eyed Chris steadily over the rim of her glass. "That so? You been dizzy much lately?"

Chris turned her face back to the fan's caress, letting it

203

whip her brown curls into indiscriminate tangles. "Oh, not much. Some. It's this heat."

"Is it?"

The roundness of Bernie's face usually gave her a cheery mien no matter what her mood, but at the moment Chris thought she looked suspiciously like a cat who's caught the canary. "Well, of course. What else?"

"Oh, honey, you just might think on that a moment. Or ask that handsome husband of yours what else."

"Ask Paul? What do you—" She broke off and stared in wide-eyed horror at Bernie's growing amusement. The implication hit her like a diesel truck heading for the interstate. It couldn't be! It was just the heat! It had to be! She saw the wrinkles in Bernie's multiple chins fold into the creases of her neck as she shook her head.

"You been married what, since the end of June? Seven, eight weeks? Honey, you'd better check your calendar before you go blamin' the sun for making you dizzy."

Somewhere deep down, Chris had known for days, had known she was changing and why. But she hadn't wanted to face the facts. The facts weren't pretty. The fact was she was completely, utterly in love with Paul. The fact was she was not married to him. The fact was he had never given the least indication of wanting to be married to her. The facts made her feel sick.

"Honey, what's wrong?" With an arm around her shoulder, Bernie guided Chris to the nearest stool and seated her. "You're white as a ghost! Don't you want a baby?"

"It-it-it's a bad time for us," she stammered. "Financially and all. We're—we're just getting started."

"You'll be surprised how things'll work out. Always do." Bernie lumbered behind the counter, puttered with ice and a glass and returned to press lemonade into her hand. "Drink this, honey, and don't you worry about it. That man of yours has broad shoulders. He'll take care of you. Both of you."

Her hand jerked and the ice jumped against the glass. "You won't tell anyone, will you, Bernie? I don't want Paul to—to suspect anything until I've seen a doctor. I mean, it's not even definite yet. It really could be the heat." She paid no attention to Bernie's disbelieving sniff. She gazed at the flecks of lemon sprinkled over the bobbing ice cubes and tried to keep her panic from rising. She failed. "You don't think anyone else suspects, do you? Oh, Lord, if Mrs. Huber knew, everyone will—"

"Don't carry on so," soothed Bernie. "There's no need to worry for a few weeks yet. You leave Lizzie Huber to me. Now why don't you go on home, rest a bit, then make an appointment with the doctor in Coldwater. Don't worry about me. If it gets busy, I'll call Sueanne in to give me a hand."

Normally Chris would have protested, knowing Bernie's daughter put in enough hours at the café, waitressing there each evening after she went home. But this wasn't a normal day and she couldn't make normal objections. She looked blankly at the lemonade, set it down, and left. For once she did not see the cracks in the crumbling sidewalks, did not hear the noisy meadowlarks and blue jays, did not notice the bright zinnias and marigolds sprinkled over yards on her short walk to Mary's house. She stumbled home in a zombielike daze.

Using their private entrance, she paused to pick up the letter one of the kids had tossed in the hall, then mounted the steps. Mail usually thrilled her. They didn't get much and it was a treat to see a letter or even a sales flyer lying on the hardwood floor. But today she didn't feel thrilled. She glanced at her sister's return address and felt guilty.

Turning into the bedroom, she dropped the envelope onto the nightstand and flopped to the bed without even bothering to kick off her shoes. She closed her eyes and lay without thinking. A door downstairs slammed. Eric yelled and Deirdre replied, an unintelligible sound that oddly comforted Chris. Though she doubted he'd admit it, Paul

205

was very attached to those two. She recalled how upset she'd been when he'd spent part of his first paycheck—the part she'd set aside for the car repair—on a tool kit for Eric and a set of clothes for Deirdre's favorite doll. Would he bring gifts for the new baby? Or would he resent it?

She opened her eyes. Fading clusters of forget-me-nots sprayed over cream wallpaper. She was reminded of another purple blossom and, stifled by the Kansas heat, almost felt the cool caress of a shaded breeze in an Arizona forest. Sighing, Chris sat up, her feet draped over the edge of the bed.

How had she been so stupid? Why hadn't she taken precautions? She'd always been so careful before. . . .

It was this sham of a marriage. She'd begun to believe it. She'd actually been thinking of herself as Christine Richards. To be addressed as Mrs. Richards had seemed so natural, so *right*. This had become the home she'd never had, filled with the love and the warmth and the giving she'd always yearned for.

There was only one problem.

She had forgotten she was play-acting. She had forgotten this was not her home, she was not his wife.

It occurred to her that if she remained with Paul for seven years she would be his wife, common law, but still his wife.

With another, more ragged sigh, she picked up the letter. The name Chris Casolaro leaped accusingly from the envelope. She'd told Mary she didn't want Theresa to know she was married until she and Paul were definite about what they were going to do. It would only, she'd said with somewhat more truth, cause her sister to worry needlessly. Mary hadn't seemed convinced, but being Mary, she'd neither prodded nor pried into what she considered none of her business.

The letter was short and cheery. Theresa wrote mostly about what the children were doing, how she felt about the one on the way. Each word seemed to slap at Christine.

206

She felt guilty and depressed and more than a little confused.

What was she going to do?

She would have to tell Paul. As little as she wanted to, as much as her first impulse was to say nothing, she knew she could not keep it from him. She loved him too much to withhold such news. It would be, after all, his baby too. But she was equally determined not to trap him into a marriage he did not want.

Unwilling to reflect upon his possible reactions, averse to looking further ahead than this one night, she resolutely thrust all thought from her mind and stood. On legs without feeling, she crossed the room to her dresser. From the far corner of one drawer, from beneath soft piles of underwear, she extracted the silver belt buckle she'd impulsively purchased that day in New Mexico and wrapped it in tissue paper. She'd been saving the gift for some special time, perhaps for when they eventually split up to go their separate ways. Now she thought a little honey might help him swallow the bitter news. She hid the wrapped buckle under his pillow and went downstairs.

"Hey, Chris, what's for dinner?" asked Eric as she walked into the kitchen. Sunshine poured through the windows, ricocheting off coppery glints in his golden hair. Daubs of red and blue paint smeared the front of his E.T. T-shirt and speckled his hands. Bits and pieces of a spaceship model were spread from one end of the kitchen table to the other. What a wonderful thing to be ten years old and free of worry, she thought wistfully.

She couldn't resist ruffling that towhead as she walked over to the cupboards. "What kind of a greeting is that? What's for dinner? You might try, hi, how are you?"

"Hi, how are you, what's for dinner?" he said obediently.

She responded with her first genuine smile in several hours. "I'm fine, thank you. Where's Deirdre?"

"Downstairs, playing with her dolls," he answered with

207

a moue of big brotherly disgust for a little sister's toys. "You gonna make sloppy joes? Make sloppy joes."

"If you had your way, all we'd ever eat is sloppy joes and burgers," she told him, but she pulled out the hamburger and the sauce mix. Though she was an unexceptional cook, she enjoyed doing her share of cooking. It was a homey task that reinforced her sense of being part of the family. It had been weeks since she'd felt like a boarder in the Sullivan home; Mary seemed like another sister to her and the kids were as dear as her own nieces and nephew. She truly felt as if she belonged with them.

But she didn't belong with them. It had been only a fantasy, nothing more. A gloomy cloud settled within her spirit, oppressing it. Her eyes didn't even water as she minced onion. As fervently as she'd previously rejoiced that the U-joint for her car had not yet arrived, she now cursed its continued delay. If she had to leave Oscar, she'd rather do so at once.

Because Paul didn't usually get home until the sun was down at nine or ten at night, Chris generally ate with Mary and the kids, then sat to talk with Paul while he ate his reheated meal. Occasionally she'd wait to eat with him, most often on Saturdays, the one night they felt able to linger because neither worked on Sundays. She normally enjoyed sharing the time with Mary and the kids, but on this Saturday night she counted each bite the children took and hoped her inability to sustain her end of the conversation went unnoticed as Mary chattered blithely about last week's church social.

She was wishing she could prod Deirdre into eating faster when she suddenly realized Mary had asked her a question. Biting her lip, she roused herself to mumble, "Pardon?"

Mary hesitated, an odd expression on her usually pretty features. Her natural beauty had begun to blossom again, particularly as she was always smiling. Now, however, her lips were puckered more in agitation than contentment.

208

"Um, I just asked if you might know who Ken took to Leah Holdhusen's dinner party last night? I mean, well, you hear everything at the café and, well, I was just wondering. . . ."

Her voice drifted away. Chris was surprised to discover she could still feel anything. Sympathetic concern actually pierced the numb shroud encasing her. "Well, yes," she reluctantly confessed, "I did hear he took that O'Donnell girl from Lake City."

"Oh? How nice," murmured Mary, then instantly rounded on Eric, telling him sharply not to chew with his mouth open.

"Ah, geez, Mom," he complained as Chris said on a rush, "Mary, you know if you'd just accept one of his invitations, Ken wouldn't take anyone else out."

"Oh, well, I didn't mean to imply—"

"It would be fun if we made a foursome to the scholarship dance," she suggested, not at all certain she and Paul would still be a twosome by then. Leaving Mary to think it over, she abruptly excused herself and retreated to the solitude upstairs.

Almost immediately her concern for Mary washed away in the floodtide of her own problems. Panic began rising; she tried to tamp it down by telling herself there may not be a reason for it. Perhaps she wasn't even pregnant. Perhaps it was the ceaseless humidity, the stifling heat. Perhaps she should wait a week or two before saying anything. Perhaps—

Knowing such thoughts were fruitless, she squelched them, refusing to allow herself the indulgence of rationalization. She bathed and changed, donning a clingy dress Mary had sewn for her. It had short sleeves and a V neck that dipped without revealing too much flesh. The waist was cinched with a fabric belt of the same rose-toned jersey as the dress. Feeling like a warrior girding for battle, she lightly brushed her cheeks with blusher, enhanced her lashes with mascara and her lips with a touch of pink.

209

Dropping the lipstick onto the dresser top, she grimaced at her reflection. *Coward,* her eyes charged. *Hiding behind a mask of femininity.*

She heard a door swing shut and heavy steps mount the stairs two at a time. She darted into the hall at the same instant Paul reached the top.

He halted, gaped, then pursed his lips in a wolfish whistle. "You look gorgeous, baby."

She could have said the same of him and meant every word. His unbuttoned shirt hung loosely, the ends flaring away from his bronzed skin. Flecks of hay clung to the dark tangle of hair on his chest, sinking into the jeans that rode so low upon his hips. From the thick dust that dulled the gloss of his shaggy hair to the dirt creased into the legs of his tight jeans, he looked fit and firm and gorgeous.

She took a step toward him, but he raised his hand. "I'll ruin that pretty dress of yours if you get any closer. Let me get cleaned up, then I'll greet you like I'm longing to."

He spun into the bathroom. She listened a moment to his cheery whistle, then went down to the kitchen to prepare a tray for him. She wasn't hungry. She set out cold fried chicken left over from the day before, a heaping plate of cole slaw and chips, and a frosted mug of beer. As she started upstairs with it Deirdre skipped out of the living room to hold open the door for her.

"Thanks, pumpkin," said Chris, smiling fondly at the curlyheaded girl who was a tiny, bright-eyed, buttonnosed replica of her mother. Deirdre giggled and twirled and Chris couldn't help laughing a little. She was still smiling when she set the tray down on the end table in the sitting room.

"I hope that smile's for me," said Paul from the doorway.

She wheeled and felt her heart start knocking against her ribs. He'd put on a clean white shirt and the gray slacks from his suit. Bluish streaks shone in his still-damp

hair and white gleamed in his engaging grin. "You'd better come eat," she said.

"First, sit down and close your eyes," he ordered.

Puzzled, she started to object, but noticed his hands
were behind his back. With a resigned sigh she sat down
on the brown plaid sofa behind the coffee table. She
squeezed her eyes shut and hoped he hadn't spent his
entire pay, as he'd shown a deplorable tendency to do, on
something frivolous. She heard the rustle of his slacks as
he came forward, and she inhaled the mingling soap and
cologne wafting from him.

"Okay, baby, take a look."

She opened her eyes, then blinked. Standing on the
coffee table beside the mug of beer, starkly staring, stiffly
smiling, was the kachina doll with the watermelon. Over
one red, straw-tassled horn of his hat, a bright band of
gold winked at her. It was a glint mirrored by Paul's broad
grin.

Looking from the doll to the ring to the smile, she
thought for one incredible bursting moment of joy that he
was proposing. "What?" was all she managed to whisper.

He chuckled and plucked the gold band from the doll's
horn. "Everybody's been after me to buy you a ring. If I
hadn't done it soon, I think Mary would've barred me
from the house."

So it was not a proposal after all. Chris could only hope
he couldn't see the disappointment that hurtled from her
heart to her toes. That one brief burst of joy left her
drained, listless. Her spirits felt as sluggish as her body
had earlier in the day and she had no energy with which
to resist as he picked up her left hand and slid the ring onto
her finger.

"I hope you like this one. I wanted to surprise you," he
was saying as he sank onto the sofa beside her. She said
nothing.

Lamplight danced over the smooth, plain gold, radiating a warm beauty distinctly at odds with the feel of it

upon her finger. It felt cold and bulky. It weighted her hand with an unaccustomed heaviness. The weight was laden with the burden of deception. The golden glitter reflected the tarnished luster of the lost meaning. She gazed dully at the ring, hating it. A wedding band should be a bond of love, not a shackle of deceit. If only their relationship were as real as the ring. . . .

Watching her, Paul's brows slanted ominously. What the hell was wrong? He'd anticipated this moment all day, visualizing her surprise, her pleasure. When he'd come home to find her dressed softly, wearing makeup, waiting for him, he had felt elated, certain that tonight would be a celebration.

But instead of surprised pleasure, Christine was eyeing the ring warily. She looked, he thought with rising resentment, as if she longed to yank it from her finger.

"What's wrong?" he inquired icily. "Don't you like it? Did you want a diamond? I wanted to buy you a diamond, but—"

"Oh, no, no, it's not that," she cut in hastily.

The eyes she lifted to him were misted. His annoyance ebbed as quickly as it had erupted and he said more softly, "If you don't like the band, baby, we'll get another one."

She shook her head. She lowered her gaze to her lap. "No. I—this ring is . . . Paul, you do remember that we're not actually married?"

He shifted, feeling uncomfortable. He didn't like being reminded that this wasn't real, that sooner or later his time with Christine would come to an end, that eventually Paul Richards would have to give way to Preston Ridgeway. He didn't want the intrusion of reality into the image of this as his home, of her as his sweet, sensible, loving wife.

But this wasn't real and she wasn't his wife.

Fixing his gaze on the brightly painted kachina doll, he expelled a long breath heavy with impatience. "Well, of course I remember it. What the hell has that to do with anything?"

212

The stab was so sharp, so fierce that Chris fleetingly wondered why she wasn't bleeding. She ran a finger over the smooth surface of the ring, over that mocking symbol of the marriage vows, and knew as she did so that she would not be telling Paul about the baby. Not tonight, perhaps not ever.

Out of the corner of her eye she saw his arm stretch toward the beer. She heard him swallow, heard the slap of the mug forcefully returned to the tray. "I thought," he muttered acidly, "that you'd at least like the damned doll."

She heard the resentment in his voice and knew what he really resented was her unmistakable hint at marriage. Well, she'd known all along that he wasn't the permanent kind. If she had forgotten that in the weeks they'd been in Oscar, he was not to be blamed for it. It was her own mistake, her own problem. She was strong enough to handle her own problems.

Summoning up a smile from some secret source, she said, "I do like the doll. I'm very touched. It's an expensive gift."

He twisted his head to look at her. He longed just then to tell her everything, to tell her that money didn't mean a damn to him and that she did. But he was afraid, afraid to risk losing what little time might be left to them. Days had somehow stretched to weeks, weeks to months, and still he wanted a few weeks more. If he told her, he risked everything. As he'd once said, he was in too deep to tell the truth now.

"You're not exactly bubbling over with excitement," he said, but the tartness was gone from his tone.

"I *am* pleased. Really."

She sounded about as warm as tepid tap water. He tried to cover the depth of his disappointment, but he wasn't any better at disguising his feelings than Chris was at hiding hers. They spoke a little while he ate, but the mood had soured. Chris was sorry she'd spoiled his surprise,

213

ruined the evening. As soon as he'd finished and pushed the tray away she knelt behind him on the sofa and began kneading her hands over his knotted muscles.

"God, that feels great," he grunted after a time. "How did you learn to do this so well?"

"Practice. I used to rub my mother's shoulders. I had no idea what I was doing, but she was usually too tired to resist. She worked two jobs and it seemed like she was gone more than she was around. I guess it was a way I could get closer to her."

"You don't have to rub my shoulders to get closer to me." He threw her a teasing smile over his shoulder and the air between them crackled with new electricity.

She fastened her gaze on the flexure of her hands. "You're not at all close to your family either, are you? You never speak of them and I sometimes wonder why not."

"No, I'm not close to my family. You can't get close to them. You get frostbitten if you try. I've never felt close to anyone in my life. Not until now. Not until I met you." He swiveled abruptly, catching hold of her waist as he faced her. "Whatever else I've told you, whatever else has happened between us, that's the one truth. You're the only person who has ever meant anything to me at all."

"And . . . what do I mean to you?" she asked on a bare thread of a hope.

"This," he said and pulled her to him. His mouth sought hers. "Let me get close to you, Christine," he murmured at the corner of her lips.

"This isn't close?" she retorted breathily.

"I could never get close enough. I want to lose myself in you. Over and over and over." As his husky words whispered down her neck, his rough hands rubbed over the folds of her dress, molding to the curve of her hips, then pressing into the swell of her buttocks, bringing her closer and closer.

It was almost painful, the way her body sang in response to his touch. Her pulse leaped to beat against the warm caress of his lips on her neck. Her heart jumped to hammer against the pounding force of his. Her back arched to force her softness against the firm length of his body. But from the pit of her very soul a hurt rose up to pierce the joy she felt in his embrace.

He did not wish to marry her. He had never said he loved her. He had just told her that all she meant to him was the physical gratification she could give him.

All this flayed her. But she needed to savor the brief time left with him. She ignored the sadness dimming her joy and gave herself up fully to the pleasure his hands, his lips, his body, could bring. Weaving her fingers into the thick layers of his hair, she surrendered her mouth to his with a shuddering need.

When that tremor raced from her to him, Paul's hunger to taste the special fragrance of her skin could no longer be restrained. He lifted her off the sofa and carried her down the hall to their bedroom. His tongue plumbed the depths of her mouth, thrusting eagerly against the grainy softness of hers. Whatever else had gone wrong with his plans for the evening, this was still right. This was always right between them.

Chris had already turned down the quilt, folding it as she did every night neatly at the foot of the bed. He pressed her into the crisp sheets and braced himself a mere whisper above her. Her warmth rose up to heat his body. Her breath kissed his mouth. Her soft stillness settled in his blood. As he had once before, he asked slowly, hoarsely, if she would let him love her.

"Yes, my darling, always," she replied, knowing he meant one thing and she another, but no longer caring. To have him now, this moment, was enough.

He bent his head to nuzzle her skin along the edge of the V neck. He played with the belt at her waist, teasing her.

She retaliated by skimming her fingers over his shirt buttons, by nibbling lightly on his earlobe. She felt the ripple that ran down his body and quivered with him.

Suddenly they were no longer playing. They were touching and tasting and kissing fiercely, possessively, each anxious to take, each eager to give.

Paul struggled to restrain his urgent need to take her, wanting to give of himself, to please her. But Christine grasped him with such compulsion, kissed with such feverish desperation, he felt himself losing control. The jarring note of ripping cloth rent the darkness. Neither paused, neither cared.

Their clothes ended in a heap on the floor. The quilt was kicked in a tumble from the bed. The sheets were rumpled as never before. When Chris thought she would go mad if he didn't ease the ache throbbing within her, when Paul thought he would explode if she didn't appease his thunderous craving, they were together, rocking in a frenzied rhythm. They loved with unbridled recklessness, a turbulent intensity, as if their passion could commit them in ways their words could not.

At the final moment Paul burrowed his mouth into her neck, muttering unintelligibly. They tensed together, then lay still. Two hearts thumped wildly, then gradually steadied. Reality slowly intruded. They were half off the bed and slipping farther over the edge.

"We're going to fall off if you don't rescue us," Chris pointed out. He lay atop her, his sweat-slicked body sticking to hers. She pushed vainly at his chest. He didn't move. "Are you listening? We're falling off the bed. Hey, you, are you dead?"

"Died and gone to heaven," he murmured.

They slid another inch. "Paul!"

With a groan redolent of his reluctance, he shifted, hauling her back onto the bed with him. "I'd have happily fallen off the earth pressed to you like that." He dropped back onto his pillow and yelped. "What the hell—"

"Oh, I forgot," she said. She reached under his head and withdrew the present. "For you."

"For me, ummm? You think after what you just gave me I need anything else?"

She waved the tissue under his nose. "This seems to be our night for gifts. Take it."

He bunched his pillow together with hers, nestled back, and drew her into his arms. With her snuggled to him he didn't need gifts. He didn't want anything but this quiet time together. It was such a contrast to the furious passion raging between them moments before. He'd never been so out of control.

"I tore your dress," he said. "I'm sorry."

"If you hadn't, I would have," she laughed huskily. "I was mad with wanting you. Delirious."

The ripe resiliency of her breasts crushed into his chest, rousing an urge to make love to her all over again. He ran his callused hand over the pliant swelling. "You're so soft, baby. I'm almost afraid to touch you. Are my hands too rough?"

"No. I like the feel of your hands," she whispered, kissing his jaw. "They're honest hands. You've earned those calluses."

He stopped caressing her. Abruptly, jerkily, he took the package, then turned on the bedside lamp. In the muted glow her tawny skin shone like melted honey. The glimmer of the ring on her finger caught his eye and, not wanting to remember her earlier disappointment, he turned his attention to the gift. He tore the tissue away. Shiny etched silver sparkled around inlaid turquoise. He had no idea what to say. He knew what money meant to Chris. He knew how much the buckle must have cost. He knew he'd never in his life felt more moved by a present.

Her fingers crept into the hair on his chest. "I hope you like it. I wasn't going to buy it, but then an impulse hit me and . . . well, I wanted you to have it. To remember me by."

He tightened his arm around her shoulder. "Of course I like it. My God, it's—hell, Chris, what do you mean to

217

remember you by? You're not going anywhere." It was a statement that held the hint of an anxious question.

She rolled over on top of him to silence his question with a kiss. That question was something she had no strength to face, not yet. Between several hot little kisses, she asked him if he thought Ken would convince Mary to go out with him. "I know she worries because she's older than he is, which is silly but—"

"At the moment, baby, I don't care about Ken or Mary or anything but this." He returned each of her kisses with interest while swirling his hands over her back, down her sides, then up again. He tugged at her lower lip with his teeth, coaxed with his tongue. "Tell me you're not leaving," he ordered gruffly.

"I won't go unless you want me to," she murmured, not certain she was telling the truth.

He lifted her, poising her over him. "Don't you know yet what you do to me? God, a sip and I thirst to drown in you."

It was the closest he had ever come to saying he cared. She sank to him, became part of him, feeling a new joy. If they weren't meant to have forever, at least they had this sweet time together. Surely it was worth whatever bitterness might follow. She held on to that thought as she melded herself to him.

They swayed together in a gentle antithesis of their earlier passion. Leisurely they lingered in love, delighting in each slow kiss, each lazy caress. Paul watched the beauty of their fusion pass over Christine's face and ached to hold this moment forever, to be part of her forever. He deliberately held back as long as he could, wanting to extend her pleasure, wanting to watch that pleasure fill her. She stiffened against him and a pain pierced him even as he felt the sweetness of release.

The moment had not lasted forever. Nothing lasted forever. The day was coming when he would have to let her go.

CHAPTER THIRTEEN

Oscar, Kansas, was not the place in which to try to keep a secret.

On the day Chris borrowed Mary's car and drove into Coldwater, ostensibly to do some much needed shopping, Peggy Lenge Vandiver happened to leave Dr. Neuberger's just as Christine went in. Her cheery hello was not heard and Peggy left wondering what could be wrong with Bernie's new waitress. When she arrived home she called Bernice to find out, but she had slipped out of the café to run down to Myrtle Hanson's to have her hair done for the big dance at the VFW hall that night. Bernie's daughter, Sueanne Miller, had no idea what could be wrong. Both women decided to call around and see what they could find out.

Christine learned all this when she walked into the house late that afternoon. Mary dashed out of the kitchen in a swirling blizzard of flour and powdered sugar and intercepted Chris before she could retreat upstairs.

"Why on earth didn't you tell me you were going to see a doctor? What's wrong? I've worried all afternoon!"

Chris peered around two large sacks filled with socks and underwear, new shirts and jeans for Paul, and gaped at her friend. Sprinkling flour as she moved, Mary rushed forward to yank the bags from Chris and dump them on the dining table. "Come sit down and tell me what's wrong with you. I about died when Sueanne called and asked me why you were visiting the doctor over in Coldwater. Chris, why didn't you tell us you weren't well?"

Allowing herself to be thrust into a chair, Chris said blankly, "But how did Sueanne know?"

"Peggy Vandiver saw you. She was at the doctor's today to get fitted for a diaphragm and saw you entering. Well, you know how it is, there's nothing to keep people occupied in Oscar but what goes on with everyone else. I reckon half the town knows by now that you went to the doctor's and the other half will know by sundown."

"Oh." Chris bent her head. The wedding ring shone accusingly at her. She twisted it nervously. "I haven't . . . adjusted well . . . to the heat. I went to see about . . ." She glanced up. Mary's green eyes were clouded with obvious concern. It touched Chris to the quick. Since first acknowledging her suspicions to herself, she'd suffered an agonizing sense of loneliness. Unwilling to tell Paul, she'd longed for someone to confide in, someone to share her burden. For two weeks she'd prayed for a miracle that had not come. Now, seeing the sympathy, the worry of her friend, her eyes misted and she blurted, "Oh, Mary, that's a lie. I went because I'm pregnant."

Flour flew into the air, coppery waves billowed as Mary leaped from her chair to hug Chris. "That's wonderful! Oh, that's terrific! Wait'll Paul hears this!"

"No!"

The abrupt shriek snapped Mary's torrent of joy. They stared at each other, eyes widened in pain and shock.

"Paul's not to know anything about it," Chris insisted, her face stonily set.

"But he's—"

"He is not to be told. Promise me that."

After another short, tense silence Mary whirled and marched into the kitchen. Chris sat staring blindly at the cast iron radiator along the far wall, wondering rather dully how her life came to be so impossibly messed up. She didn't come up with an answer. Her mind seemed capable of absorbing only two facts. She was pregnant and the long-awaited U-joint had finally arrived.

Ken had flagged her down on her way home and given her the news. It had been expected for so long that its arrival took her by surprise. Instead of pleasure she'd felt only shock. Now she felt sadness. It brought her departure from Oscar—and from Paul—all too close.

Eventually Mary returned with two tall glasses of iced tea. "You don't have to tell me about it if you don't want. Between us, Bernie and I can make 'em believe it's the heat. If that's what you want."

Chris pressed her head into her hands. "I'm not sure what I want." She pulled her hands away. "Except that I do not want Paul to know yet."

She watched as Mary visibly swallowed back the impulse to ask why. If the truth of her relationship with Paul were her secret alone, Chris would have opened her soul to Mary just then. But it was Paul's secret, too, and she couldn't reveal it without his knowledge. Instead, she haltingly told Mary that there were problems that had to be worked out first.

"Problems? You and Paul?" Her disbelief rang shrilly. "You love him. He adores you. What could be wrong?"

"Sometimes things aren't what they seem," whispered Chris, unable to meet Mary's clear green eyes.

"Well, that's true enough. But even so, you can't keep the truth from him for long."

A fly buzzed noisily. The ice cracked in Mary's glass. The back door swung shut with force and Eric called out "Mom, I'm home" as he ran through the kitchen to his room in the basement.

"You do plan to have the baby," said Mary.

"I don't know," said Chris.

A low hum gathered force and burst into an angry shriek. "Oh, hell," muttered Mary. "That's my pies." She jumped up and headed toward the sound of the screaming oven timer. At the door she hesitated and said without looking back, "It's none of my business, but that's not a decision you should make on your own. It's Paul's decision too."

"It's *my* baby," returned Chris on a furious hiss. She collected the sacks with a crinkling swoop and ran upstairs. She pitched the new clothes onto the bed, feeling angry with Mary, with Paul, with life. Most of all, Chris felt angry with herself. Two and a half months ago her life had been a dull, uncomplicated routine of school, work, and Theresa's family. Now it was a mess so tangled she doubted she'd ever get it unraveled. And she had no one but herself to blame for the knot.

After bathing her face with cold water, she clipped the tags from an off-the-shoulder pastel peach blouse she'd bought and slipped into it. The crisp freshness of it felt cool and clean after the damp wrinkles of her old lilac top. Tucking it into her jeans, she headed downstairs, determined to apologize to Mary. She hadn't been thinking rationally. If she had, she'd have realized immediately that Mary's first concern had been for her. Chris could feel only thankful she had several hours in which to compose herself before having to face Paul.

At the bottom of the stairs she heard screeching tires and a slamming door. She looked out the side screen door to see Paul hop out of Vern Kilmer's black pickup. Before she had a chance to assimilate that he was home in the middle of the day, he bounded up the porch steps and flung open the door.

"Chris! Are you all right? What the hell happened?" He cupped her head in his palms and frowned down at her.

Shouldn't she be asking him that? What happened? Why was he home? He didn't look ill. His unbuttoned shirt and creased jeans were covered in dirt and sweat. Dust clung to the hair on the chest that was heaving rapidly. The palms pressing into her cheeks were damp. The eyes searching hers were dark with worry.

222

"What are you doing home?" she asked.

"Floyd came out to the field saying you'd been taken to the doctor's. Jesus, I nearly broke my leg leaping off the flatbed to get the hell home. What happened?"

He let her go and stepped back. Other than the twin patches of dirt he'd smeared onto her cheeks, she looked perfectly normal. Every brown curl tumbling exactly as it should, every tawny-colored limb whole and healthy. She looked a bit pale, but not hurt or ill and certainly not dying. His racing heart began to slow and his concern turned to irritation. What the hell had he barreled home for?

"You don't look sick," he accused.

"I'm not exactly sick," she said.

"Then what's going on?"

Beneath all the dirt he looked comically belligerent. She took in his lowering frown, his accentuating brows and suddenly gave way to an explosive volley of laughter. She sank to the steps and laughed until she cried. The harder she laughed, the more he scowled, making her laugh all the more. Half-recognizing her near hysteria as a much-needed emotional catharsis, she did nothing to stem the tide. She simply chortled and chuckled and held on to her aching sides. He swore vividly and Mary came out of the kitchen to gawk at them both before vanishing to leave them alone.

"I do trust you'll share the joke—at your convenience, of course," he said acidly. He'd damn near killed himself to reach her and here she was, hale and hearty and laughing her head off at his expense.

"Oh, Paul, I'm sorry," she gasped. "It's just, it's just—" Her speech disintegrated into another hearty guffaw and he stamped off to get a beer from the refrigerator.

Slowly the frenetic locomotive of laughter ran out of steam. As she calmed, Chris wiped the moisture from her eyes and inhaled deeply. She felt better. The emotions she'd tried to tamp down had briefly run amuck; the mo-

223

mentary release steadied her, left her feeling more collected, more able to deal with the situation she was in.

When she regained complete control of herself, she went into the kitchen and stood meekly waiting for Paul to acknowledge her presence. He leaned against the edge of the kitchen sink. He saw her come in, raised his beer can to his lips, and swallowed. Mary glanced her way, then continued rolling out dough for pie crusts. The hot aroma of rhubarb and apple drifted from pies already cooling on racks by the open window.

"I'll never," said Mary to the world in general, "get all these pies baked in time for the VFW dance tonight if I don't get some elbow room."

"You love having a man underfoot," said Paul.

He sounded remarkably calm. Chris chanced taking a step forward. He looked up at her and she halted. He held out his arms and she ran into them.

"You through laughing at me?" he inquired tenderly into the curls tumbling over her ear.

"I wasn't laughing at you, never you." She threw back her head to look at him and he brushed her hair back from her smudged face. "I thought I was being so secretive and I came home to have Mary jumping all over me, and Sueanne Miller and Peggy Vandiver calling all over town and then you dashed in and—" She buried her head into the comfort of his shoulder, sighing and inhaling the strength of him. "And it all seemed so ridiculous. I might as well have taken out a full-page ad."

"Damn it, Chris, why didn't you tell me you were going to a doctor? How long have you been feeling unwell?"

"I didn't want to worry you."

"Worry? Hell, I damn near had a heart attack. I envisioned you mangled, dying. . . ." As his voice trailed away he gave her a little shake and set her from him. "Now why did you go to the doctor? Mary's as tight as a drum on the subject."

"I've felt . . . dizzy sometimes, that's all. Nothing to

224

worry about. It's just this heat." She could feel Mary's eyes skate over her but refused to meet them.

"You're sure? You're going to be okay?"

"Yes, I'm sure. Who'd have thought this heat wave would last into September?" Unconsciously twisting the wedding band around her finger, she licked her lips and said slowly, "Paul, I stopped by Ken's on the way home and he says he got the part in this morning. The Mav ought to be ready in a day or two. We—we need to talk about leaving."

The aluminum beer can crumpled in his fist. He studied it for several seconds before dropping it into the trash sack on the other side of the sink. "Yeah, sure. Look, since I'm home, I might as well take a bath and start getting ready for this thing tonight. We'll talk later."

He strode out and Mary immediately turned on Chris. "Are you serious? Are you really thinking of leaving?"

"Well, you know we never meant to stay," said Chris feebly.

"Yes, but that was before. I mean"—Mary looked around the room, her frustration stamped on her face—"I kind of thought, we all thought, that you two might be settling down here. To stay."

"I don't think that's possible. No matter how much we might like to stay in Oscar, we're going to have to leave." Chris spoke with gentle sorrow, thinking that in a more perfect world she and Paul and the baby-to-be would be staying here, a real family surrounded by real friends. But the world was not perfect and they were certainly not a real family. They would have to leave Oscar and soon.

Upstairs, Paul was telling himself the same thing. He'd known for weeks that he was living on a razor's edge. He had never expected to stay for so long. Somehow time had slipped away, but now, apparently, the sand was running out of the hourglass. They would have to leave. He would have to return to the real world, to the work of shuffling

225

paper, to the rounds of meaningless parties, to the world of the Ridgeways.

Impatiently his gaze swept the bedroom, focusing on the faded wallpaper, the handsewn quilt, the mismatched dressers. An image of his luxuriously sterile New York penthouse apartment rose up to taunt him. He struck out aimlessly, anxious to dispel the haunting vision of his past meeting up with his future, and accidentally knocked over the kachina doll. It toppled from the scarred wood top of the vanity to the frayed rag rug on the floor. An utterly absurd jealousy filled him. Christine loved that damn doll. He bent to pick it up and the pink patchwork flowers on the quilt draped over the bed once again caught his eye.

He could count each hour of sweet passion on that bed. Each hour he had shared himself with Christine, giving as well as taking. The nights when simply holding her was enough. The mornings when waking together was the peak of his day. How long, he wondered, had he been in love with her?

For weeks. Months. Probably from the very first, only he'd been too damn dumb to see it.

He saw it now, clearly. He loved her. He loved her so much, his stomach clenched at the thought of losing her. His fright today had been the worst of his life. On that mad drive from the farm his only thought had been to reach her, to care for her, to love her. Recalling it, he knew a moment of incredulity. My God, how had he failed to realize just how much she meant to him?

His fists clenched. He felt the sandpaper roughness and slowly unfurled his hands. Honest hands, Christine had called them. He stared at his callused palms, seeing the same long, slim fingers, the same lines tracking the center. But the patrician smoothness had been replaced by a laborer's hardened thickness, a tough grainy texture he had toiled to earn. His clothes, too, were no longer custom-made suits and designer shirts. The well-worn jeans that hugged his hips tightly had no impressive designer label on the back pocket. The sweat-soaked shirt was of a durable cotton, made to be worn more than once.

The idle, empty man who wore the designer silk was gone forever. Paul curled his fingers around the doll and slowly straightened. He stared deep into the painted gaze of the kachina doll and came to a decision.

He was not going back.

My God, it was so damn simple. By staying he would not lose Christine. By staying he would not lose himself. By staying, added another insistent voice, a life of luxury and leisure is lost. A generous slice of a staggering fortune disappears. Fast cars and fast women pass out of the picture.

For one heartbeat his hand shook. The straw tassels whisked at the top of the doll's hat. He set the kachina on the vanity and mutely demanded that it tell him what to do. The doll only smiled, a secretive smile that was at once fixed and free of doubt.

Gradually, a centimeter at a time, his lips curved into a smile as defined and certain as the watermelon god's. With a jaunty snap of his fingers, he consigned his birthright and inheritance to the devil. Who and what he was would be precisely what he made of himself and nothing more. With an equally jaunty flourish, Paul gathered together clean clothes and sauntered into the bathroom.

By the time he'd bathed, shaved, and dressed, he felt drunk with excitement. For the first time in his life he had a future to plan for, a future of his own design. If he had to struggle and do without, his achievements would be all the sweeter. Looping his leather belt through the inlaid silver buckle, he grinned over the prospect of the evening to come. He would lay the foundation of his destiny tonight, with Christine and the truth.

Standing at the top of the stairs, Chris watched him through the open door. His hand went to the buckle and her mouth went dry. He was so unbelievably handsome. The blue-striped shirt had a tapered Western cut that accentuated the breadth of his shoulders, the narrow line of his waist. It hurt to see his beauty. It hurt to know that all too soon she'd never again see that heart-melting smile. Steeling herself, she hid her agony beneath a careful mask and entered.

"What's made you so cheerful, handsome?" she inquired pertly, determined to play out her part to the end.

"Loving you," he answered, stopping her dead in her tracks.

Before she could summon up a laugh at what must be a teasing joke, he grabbed her by the waist and twirled her round the room.

"I love you, and if you don't declare your own undying passion for me with the utmost alacrity, I won't be held responsible for my actions." As he set her down he kissed the top of her head, then rubbed his hands over her bare shoulders. "Ummm. I like what there isn't of this blouse. Even better, I like what there is under it. Well?"

"What?" she said stupidly. She was certain her ears had malfunctioned and were sending the wrong messages to her brain. It was the only explanation.

"Well, do you love me? Answer correctly and the little lady wins a lifetime of dirty laundry from the man of her choice."

"W-what are you saying?"

"That's the incorrect answer, but as a consolation prize, the little lady will receive fifty years worth of sexual fulfillment." He tossed her lightly onto the bed and plopped down beside her. Blinding her with his most dazzling smile, he leaned over her and prompted, "You get one more chance at the big prize. Do you love me, baby?"

"I—" Chris expelled a gust to steady herself. "Yes. Madly. Adoringly."

He brought his lips to hers so softly, so sweetly that she wasn't certain she hadn't conjured the tender caress up out of her own imaginative cravings. Then he moaned and kissed her hotly, thoroughly. When he finally came up for air, she knew she hadn't imagined the bruising intensity. Her swollen mouth was proof positive of it.

He raised himself slightly away from her. "As soon as Ken has the car ready to go, we'll drive to Oklahoma—"

"Oklahoma?"

"Miami, Oklahoma, to be exact."

She stroked his jaw with feathery fingertips, almost as if to reassure herself he was really there, this was really happening. She didn't understand what had loosened the miserable knot tangling their lives, but she didn't care. All that mattered was that Paul loved her. Knowing that, she knew she would go with him to the ends of the earth.

"Okay, I give," she whispered in a voice still smoky with passion, "what's in Miami, Oklahoma?"

"Wedding chapels."

Her fingers stilled against the warmth of his cheek. "What?"

He put his hand over hers, pressing her palm into his skin. "Chris, darling, I want to make our marriage real. I don't want to pretend anymore. I love you. I want you to be my wife."

She was stunned speechless. A horrible suspicion filled her. Had Mary told him after all? Her eyes darkened with troubled thoughts. She wouldn't want to marry him if he were marrying her just because of the baby. She wanted to be loved for herself, not for the sake of the baby. A marriage without a complete commitment of love on both sides could only fail.

Watching her, Paul's happiness faltered. She was going to refuse, he could see it in her darkened eyes. He hadn't expected this, nor had he suspected how piercing the pain of it could be. The urge to reveal himself died stillborn. If she didn't want to marry Paul Richards, she sure as hell wouldn't want Preston Ridgeway. The thought stabbed him.

"Why?" she asked.

"Why?" he repeated, eyeing her blankly.

"Why are you asking me to marry you? Why now?"

His heart threatened to catapult right out of his chest. Her voice was absolutely colorless. It was obvious she had no intention of accepting him. Somehow, he didn't know how, but somehow he would find a way to change her mind.

"I'm one big idiot, that's why," he said, choosing his words carefully. "It's taken me all these weeks to realize how much you mean to me. When you said we could leave town soon, all I could think of was how much I needed to stay with you. The thought of being without you . . . I realized I loved you. I love you and I want you. Permanently."

Christine thought she might burst with the volcanic eruption of her happiness. He loved her! He wanted to marry her! For herself alone and not because of the baby! Oh, dear God, the baby. Her elation braked to a bone-rattling halt. She had to tell him about being pregnant. That might change everything. . . .

Her face mirrored her worry like a streetlight changing from green to red. Paul saw it and clearly read the stop signal.

"Don't answer me now," he said, speaking quickly before she could actually verbalize her refusal. "Think on it, love, before you make a final decision."

"But I don't need to think on it," she protested.

He silenced her by capturing her mouth with a fierce kiss. When her mouth parted to submit to his unspoken demand, the sharp ache eased and he softened the impact of his kiss, coaxing instead of commanding her response.

She melted against him, mewing throatily. He moved restlessly over her and she sank farther into the mattress beneath her. She could have been sinking into oblivion and she would not have noticed. The tantalizing thrust of his tongue against hers and the sensual shift of his hands over her body were all she noticed, all she cared about. For, this time, she knew he gave out of love, not just need. She accepted and returned his love, multiplying it beyond measure.

He bent his mouth to her collarbone. She shoved her fingers through the thickness of his hair and pressed his head against her breast. His breath warmly whispered over her flesh and she arched toward him, wanting all of him.

He tasted her honey-warm skin, feeling her acquiescence in the way she molded herself to him. He knew a brief, bitter triumph. All those years of practice in the art of seduction had paid off. If in no other way, he could make Christine submit in this most elemental way.

But he wanted more than her body. He wanted her heart.

With a silent curse that he had not come to his senses sooner, he gently nuzzled one last kiss at the edge of her sweet, full mouth, then raised his head. "If I don't leave you alone, you'll never be able to get ready for the dance." He rolled away before she could stop him. "We'll talk again later, after you've had time to think it all over."

"I honestly don't need to think—"

"Don't argue with me, baby," he said with a credible air of light banter. "Even as a make-believe husband, I expect my make-believe wife to obey me."

She sat up, her heart pumping overtime. She hoped that particular organ was strong enough to withstand her furious joy. Otherwise this new warmth of his just might be the end of her. "You're way behind the times. They took *obey* out of the wedding vows years ago."

"Not out of my make-believe vows. Obey was most definitely a part of those."

"Humph!" she retorted, aiming a pillow directly at his head. He ducked and the pillow slammed into the doorjamb, sliding to the floor with a muffled thump. A white speck of a feather floated lazily through the air.

"Lousy shot," said Paul. He winked and stepped over the pillow.

231

When he had gone Chris sat for several minutes simply hugging her happiness to herself. She couldn't believe how the upside-down dilemma of her world had righted with such sudden ease. She was almost afraid to take a breath for fear of tipping it over again.

The fact that he was about to acquire a family as well as a wife would have to be broken to him delicately. Knowing he loved her would make telling him easier, but she thought it wouldn't hurt if she knocked his socks off first. So she dressed with special care, wearing the red silk dress he'd bought her in Vegas. The memories she donned with it eliminated the need for blusher, but she carefully applied some just the same, as well as mascara and lipstick to enhance her features. She lightly dabbed perfume on her temples, throat, and wrists, then added the finishing touch of gold hoop earrings, borrowed from Mary for the occasion.

Her efforts were well rewarded. Upon her entrance into the dining room, all conversation ceased. A long, low whistle prefaced Ken's remark that she was going to set the town of Oscar on its ears. "I do trust, Mr. Huber, that that is a compliment?" she said lightly, coming forward.

"You trust right, Mrs. Richards," he replied. He looked her up and down once more and expelled a sigh. "What a pity about the Mrs. If you weren't married—"

"You'd better stop while you're ahead," said Paul pleasantly, but with a definite note of warning, "or you'll be swallowing several of your teeth."

A happy thrill bolted through Chris at this display of jealousy, this evidence of his love. Though previously she'd been quite restrained about demonstrating her feelings for him in the presence of others, she now skimmed directly into his arms. Setting her hands on his shoulders, she sighed breathily. "Does that mean you don't think I'll set the town on its ears?"

His dark eyes smoldered as they inched over her curves.

"God, I'd forgotten how you looked in that dress," he muttered, his tone low and pulsing with sexuality.

Looking at the two of them with an amused smile, Mary coughed discreetly. "As much as we'd love to stay and see the show you two could put on, we do have an obligation to deliver several pies to the hall."

Paul suppressed the temptation to tell her to go on without them and released Chris to heft a wicker basket delicately stacked with fruit pies. Ken picked up a similarly loaded cardboard box and commented that he had a particular weakness for pies.

"You have a weakness for anything that's edible," retorted Mary and they all laughed. Even in a rural community famed for hearty eaters, Ken's appetite was a source of wonder. Muttering mock warnings about just what he'd do with his armload of pies, he followed Paul outside. As the screen door banged shut behind them, Mary issued a silent question to Chris.

"Not yet," she said in reply. "Don't frown, Mary. Why do you think I wore this?" She waved a hand over the shapely skirt. "I want to butter him up before hitting him with the news."

Rolling her eyes, Mary let it be known in no uncertain terms that if there was one man Chris did not have to butter up, it was Paul. "He's as good as melted every time he looks at you."

Flushing, Chris turned the subject by remarking how well Mary's jade sheath clung to all the right curves. Her friend accepted the new topic, but with a knowing look that said all too clearly she understood the tactic for the cowardly evasion it was. Though Chris had seen the molten response in Paul's gaze, she couldn't entirely shake her fear that her joy would not last. She was terrified her news would shatter the fragile love he'd discovered for her; she didn't want to face the thought of it until forced to do so.

Prying a reluctant Eric away from the television, they received a grudging hug and kiss in turn before submitting

233

to an overeager embrace from the chubby Deirdre. After giving last minute instructions to the pigtailed, gum-cracking baby-sitter, they finally left to join the men.

Once in the car, Mary twisted a little to send a smile toward the two in the back seat. "Thanks for getting this washed while you were out today, Chris. It looks brand new."

"Yeah," said Ken as he backed out the drive, "Looks great. I heard you went over to see Doc Neuberger in Coldwater. Nothing wrong, is there?"

Christine groaned. "Doesn't anybody in this town have anything better to do than advertise *my* doings?"

"It's just concern, baby," soothed Paul. He wrapped an arm around her and squeezed. "You should be flattered they care."

She could have laughed at that. Imagine Paul defending the very busybodies he'd scorned!

He bent his head, whispering, "You're sure you're okay?"

Was all that love and warmth really for her? *Oh, God, oh, God, please don't let it disappear when he knows the truth,* Chris begged silently as she reassured him that she was fine, just fine.

Ken winked at her in the mirror. "You'd better be prepared. You're going to be bombarded with questions once we reach the hall."

"Maybe I could borrow the band's microphone and make a general announcement to save time," she joked, but with a sinking heart as she realized this was going to be one long night.

The VFW hall was a rectangular brick building on the far edge of Oscar, squatting in the shadow of the grain elevator between an empty pasture and the railroad tracks. Long shafts of lowering sunlight slanted a rosy glow over the dingy whitewashed walls and gilded the metallic tops of cars and trucks scattered over the field. A colorful parade of people, laden with boxes or baskets of food and arrayed in their Friday night best, streamed into the hall. Several called out and waved when Ken drove onto the grass to park beside Emmett Iverson's Bronco. Before they had rolled to a complete stop, Emmett slapped a tobacco-stained hand on the roof and peered in through the open window.

"'Lo, Mary, Ken. Hey, glad to see you could make it, little lady. Heard you went to the doctor over in Coldwater. You okay?"

From the back seat Chris managed to focus a pretty smile somewhere in Emmett's direction. "Yes, I am, thank you. Just the heat. Is that sister-in-law of yours here yet?"

"Oh, yeah," he said, standing back to hold open the car door. "Bernie probably directed the unlocking of the hall. I swear that woman could direct traffic in Times Square on New Year's Eve."

They joined the flow to the hall and Emmett loped along beside them, talking all the way. From the size of the turnout, he reckoned the fund-raiser would be a success and they'd be able to increase the amount of the senior scholarship this year. He also reckoned a dance would be just the thing to perk Chris up. She tried to reassure him and everyone else that she was perfectly fine. But as they paid and had their hands stamped with a purplish ink, queries about her visit to the doctor came at Chris with frightening frequency. Instead of getting easier, the lie was getting harder to repeat, having to be forced past her constricting throat each time.

When Wilma Admires joined the crowd swelling around her, Christine didn't at first notice the tiny, withered old woman. Grasping Paul's sleeve, she was about to escape to the main room when Wilma's clawlike hand fastened over her wrist. She glanced into pale, watery eyes and said automatically, "It's just the heat. I'm fine really."

"I know you'll do fine, girlie. It's the best time for you," said Wilma in a voice that rasped like crackling paper.

Chris exchanged a quizzical look with Paul. He

235

shrugged and she faced the old woman in bewilderment. "I'm sorry, but I don't know what you mean."

Wilma bobbed her snowy head knowingly. "It's proper. It's the way of nature to birth in the spring. Yes, spring's the proper time for birthing."

CHAPTER FOURTEEN

The floor seemed to spin dizzily. Clutching Paul's arm, she felt the rigid shock ripple through him and somehow yanked the spinning room to a halt.

"Whatever do you mean?" she asked. Her voice was high-pitched, unnatural, totally unlike her own.

A wheeze that may have been a laugh issued from the old woman's wrinkled lips. She ran narrowed eyes once over Christine's figure, then moved on, shaking her head and wheezing.

Perhaps he hadn't understood Wilma's innuendo. Perhaps he'd put it down to an old woman's senility. Perhaps he wouldn't make any connection to her at all. Christine took a deep breath of courage and looked at him.

There was no doubt at all that he had fully understood what Wilma was driving at. Nor any that he believed her.

His brows were held at his most intimidating slant. His eyes were snapping darkly. She could see the swift calculation pass through his mind. She could see he didn't like the sum. It was her worst fear come true. She wanted to fling herself on him and wail, but some sense of pride held her back. Smiling stiffly for the benefit of the crowd, she waited for him to unleash his volatile temper on her.

Retaining a firm hold on her, he shouldered a path through the oncoming tide of arrivals, reassuring several that his wife was just fine, that they'd simply left something in the car. But outside he turned away from the field to yank Chris across the railroad tracks. Stumbling in her heels to keep up with him, she thought the shattering of her heart echoed through the night. Once past the tracks, he pulled her down the cracked, sunken sidewalk to a dark, narrow gap between the deserted gas station and the drygoods store. He shoved her into the shadows, pressing her against the wood side of the drygoods building, and braced himself in front of her.

A crazy fear that he intended to murder her loomed, then vanished as he spoke.

"Why didn't you tell me?"

His whisper was so soft, so endearingly tender, the noise drifting from the hall almost drowned it out. She licked her lips and even in the fast-falling darkness, saw his eyes follow the movement of her tongue.

"I—I was going to. Tonight. I didn't know for sure myself until—until I'd gone to the doctor's today. I had to get used to the idea before I told you."

He pressed closer. His chest flattened her breasts and his belt buckle bit into her waist. His breath fanned over her face with each husky word he uttered. "I don't know what's going on in that head of yours. I don't think I'll ever know, but file this away up there because it's a fact. You're going to marry me, Christine. As quickly as we can arrange it."

"But—"

"No buts. I asked you before. Now I'm telling you. We're getting married. I love you. You say you love me. You're pregnant with my child. So far as I can see, that makes us man and wife in the truest sense. Now we're going to make it legal. Got that?"

"Got it," she sighed obediently.

"I'll talk to Floyd and see about getting away next weekend. We'll drive to Miami, get married, and come home."

238

Home. Yes, she thought, this was her home, *their* home. She felt dazed with the happiness of it.

Home. God, he loved the sound of that. He loved the feel of the woman in his arms. She was his home.

He flicked his tongue over her parted lips, deliberately tempting her. "Tell me, my darling, delectable, make-believe wife, were you planning to reject my proposal?" She did not reply and he brushed his mouth against hers. "Well, were you?"

"I didn't want you to marry me just because of the baby," she said finally. "And when you said you loved me, I was afraid you wouldn't want to marry me because of the baby. I was so mixed up I couldn't think."

"So stop thinking and just feel."

Wreathing his neck with her arms, she complied, giving herself up to her feelings. She felt the sure perfection of his mouth on hers. She felt the thrusting need in his tongue slipping between her teeth. She felt the urgent heat of his body melting against hers and the rising warmth of his desire.

A tremble quivered down the length of him and he slowly pulled away from her. "There's something I've been waiting to tell you, too, baby. Something I've wanted to tell you for a long time."

Missing his warmth, she wriggled herself closer to him and tilted her head back, offering her mouth to him. He accepted it with a low groan. His palms pressed at the base of her spine, his touch burned through the red silk. She wound her hands around his neck and knew by the frantic leap of his pulse that he was as aroused as she.

"Later," she murmured on a smoky rasp, "You can talk later. Right now you've got more important things to do."

"Oh, God, Chris . . ." He half-growled her name. Cupping her buttocks in his hands, he lifted her against him.

A startling streak of light flashed over them, accompanied by a blaring horn and the sharp pierce of wolf

239

whistles. "Go get her, buddy!" called out an unseen masculine voice as a truck whizzed past.

Paul jerked his head up and stared toward the road dazedly. As reality returned, he glanced down at her apologetically. He sighed. "I suppose we'd better get back before tongues really start wagging."

"I suppose so." The sigh she heaved was equally reluctant.

"We'll have time . . . later . . . for talk."

"And other things," she pointed out breathily.

"And other things," he agreed on a thickened note.

With one last, lingering kiss, he gently righted her on her feet. Hand-in-hand they strolled through the darkness, back to the brightly lit bustle of the VFW hall. Displaying the ink stamped on their hands, they slid past those knotted at the entrance and into the open expanse of the main room. At the far end, on a raised dais, speakers and instruments awaited the band. On both sides of the room tables laden with food, including a great variety of baked goods, were interspersed with folding chairs filled with those already weary of mingling. One table had an enormous ring of bodies, mostly male, circled around it and it was toward this table that Paul now guided Christine.

Fluorescent light radiating off a golden head told her why Paul had beelined this way. As they drew closer the crowd parted and she smiled up at Ken. He grinned back. "You want some Coke?" he asked, gesturing toward a motley array of soft drink bottles on the table. He held up a brown bag and winked. "Or something stronger?"

Liquor by the drink was illegal in Kansas and those wanting something more spirited than soda or cola had brought their own refreshment. Several bottles were pulled from paper sacks and proffered to Paul. He reached over to pluck a ginger ale off the table, which he handed to Chris. Then he asked casually, "What have you got that's suitable to celebrate becoming a father?"

In the act of handing over his bag, Ken did a double

take, then let out a yelp. "Hell and be damned! Is that what all this doctoring was about? Congratulations!"

Within minutes they were the center of a loud, hearty babble. While Chris stood flushing to a shade rivaling the color of her dress, Paul was punched repeatedly on the shoulder. "You sure didn't waste any time," said more than one backslapper. A bottle of whiskey was thrust into Paul's hand and he raised it with a broad grin. He sent Chris a half-lidded look that stopped her heart. "To my wife," he said before swallowing deeply amid another round of knowing whistles and ringing slaps.

The news raced around the hall like wildfire sweeping over the prairie. The women descended to drag Christine away. She was inundated with advice, all of which she accepted with a glowing delight. This was a perfect world after all. These were real friends and soon they would be a real family.

Her eyes were drawn to where the men were offering more than mere advice with their congratulations. Paul tilted yet another bottle against his lips, then lowered it with a laugh. There was no vestige of the harsh bitterness she had first responded to in him. The deep unhappiness had been cleansed, washed away in the joy of their love. Yes, this was a perfect world.

"Well, honey, I see you quit pickin' on the sun and placed the blame for your dizzy spells right where it belongs—on that man of yours."

"Don't go blaming it all on that boy, Bernice," put in Nadine Dixon. The solemnity of her expression was belied by the sparkle in her eyes. She glanced at Chris and almost smiled. "Takes two, you know. He must've had a little cooperation sometime or the other."

When the group of women burst into laughter, Chris felt herself blushing madly. Mary took pity on her and changed the subject by complimenting Bernie on her hair. It looked like the same closely cropped cap of silver to Chris, but Bernice preened, her plump jowls sinking into

241

her extra chins, while averring Myrtle could make an old duck look like a peacock. When discussion turned to clothes and sewing patterns, Mary took hold of Christine's arm. "Come on, let's get in on the cakewalk. I never win, but I never give up trying." As soon as they were beyond earshot of the others, she gave Christine's arm a squeeze and whispered, "I'm so happy for you. Aren't you glad you listened to me and told him?"

"I didn't exactly tell him," confessed Chris. She explained what had happened, declaring that Wilma Admires must be a witch. "She took one look at me and bingo! How could she do that? How could she know?"

"There's no mystery to that," laughed Mary. "Wilma's cousin's daughter Lou is Dr. Neuberger's receptionist."

Christine sputtered. "That's breaking a confidence. That woman shouldn't be allowed to keep her job."

"You could never prove she told and, anyway, it's all worked out for the best, hasn't it? I told you there wasn't anything to worry about. Paul's so proud, he's about to bust."

"You'd think he was the only man who'd ever done it," she conceded, laughing.

"That's just the way Tim was." A sadness flickered over Mary and her eyes wandered toward where Hazel Sullivan was dispensing coffee from a gigantic aluminum urn. Chris followed her gaze and then looked back at Mary to see the frown imprinted on her brow.

"Something wrong?" she queried.

Mary shrugged and paid her quarter to join the next circle of the cakewalk. "Not really. Tim's mother was less than thrilled that I came with Ken. I'm not sure which offends her more, the fact that he's so young or simply that he's so male."

Paying her own quarter, Chris stood in place beside Mary, waiting for the circle to fill and the music to start. "You aren't going to let what she thinks affect how you

242

feel about Ken, are you? She can't expect you to become a nun. Age is a state of mind anyway."

"Now *that* I've heard before, more than once. Rather like a broken record, in fact. Are you in league with Ken?"

The tinny sound of an Olivia Newton-John song began playing and they shuffled over a chalked circle of numbers. With a billowing wave of her lush golden-red hair, Mary threw a smile over her shoulder at Chris. She returned it, wishing she could as easily return the happiness she was feeling. But happiness was something you couldn't give. People had to make their own happiness. Ken and Mary would have to choose for themselves, as she and Paul had, whether or not to share their love and life, whether or not to be happy together.

The scratchy record cut off abruptly and the line halted. A number was called out, the winner cheered, and the circle broke up while the lucky one made her selection from a table spread with an appetizing variety of cakes.

"Another loss. One of these days . . ." muttered Mary.

"You probably make a better cake than any of them there."

"That's not the point. It's winning one that makes it special."

"You want to try again?"

"Of course. Don't they say a sucker's born every minute? Here I am."

They went around twice more, without winning, before their men showed up to rescue them from the folly of walking around "just one more time." Ken whisked Mary off onto the dance floor, where the band had just launched into an amplified rendition of "Heartbreak Hotel." Paul leaned unsteadily toward Chris and with breath reeking of alcohol, informed her that she had, indeed, set the town on its ears.

"Better than setting it on its rear," she returned pertly. "Which is what I think you're trying to do. You, my dear man, need coffee. By the gallon."

243

He laughed, sending another gust of boozy breath her way, but meekly permitted her to lead him to the table where Hazel Sullivan poured coffee into plastic foam cups and Joan Miller, Sueanne's mother-in-law, handed out paper plates piled with sandwiches cut into triangles amid a smattering of potato chips. Christine took a cup and a plate, then located two folding chairs in a relatively secluded corner. She gave him one half of a ham sandwich and bit into the other half.

"Having fun?" he asked.

Chewing, she nodded. She was having fun. In fact, she was having the time of her life. When she swallowed, she told him this. He smiled crookedly.

"So am I. Must be the company." He looked around. His dark hair fell over his forehead as he shook his head. "It sure isn't the entertainment."

Mostly young couples shifted in a rhythmic tempo, dancing to take advantage of the opportunity to hold and touch. The band made up in volume what it lacked in talent, drowning out the cakewalk record, forcing the walk coordinators to signal frantically when it was time for everyone to stop. Over by the soft drinks loud guffaws roared intermittently, indicating a round of ribaldry. Knots of women were dotted about, talking about babies and recipes, old-fashioned topics in an old-fashioned setting.

Chris's hand clenched the sandwich, imprinting her fingermarks in the soft white bread. She stared down at it. "Do you think you'll get bored living here?"

She spoke so softly, he had to bend to catch her words submerged by all the clashing noise. When he realized what she was asking, he loosened her fingers from around the sandwich, dropped it onto the plate, and hauled her to her feet. Though his gait rolled slightly, his path was sure. As they reached the undulating flow of dancers, he wrapped his arms around her and swayed with her, nuz-

244

zling his lips into the tendrils of brown hair curling over her ear. Then, and only then, did he reply.

"It doesn't matter where we are, as long as we're together. I won't get bored with you."

It was what she'd needed to hear. The hoarse fervency in his whisper sent her blood crashing through her veins. "I love you," she murmured, her breath caressing his jaw and her body molding tightly into his.

He ignored the upbeat tempo of the music and continued to move leisurely with her, his arms clamped around her waist and hers pressed into the muscles of his shoulders. His heart thumped against hers, repeating the message of his love for her, his need of her. Chris wondered vaguely if anyone else there was aware of the magic flowing in the VFW hall. Or perhaps the magic passed only between the two of them. Had it ever been quite this special for any other souls on earth?

The music ended with a jarring clash of cymbals. "We're gonna take a break, folks," announced the group's singer. "But don't go away. There's gonna be a blue-ribbon auction. As you all know, Mary Sullivan bakes the best darn pies in the county, and you can bid on takin' one home."

There was a shuffle of anticipation and people began to crowd around the dais. The band members discarded their instruments and filed off the stage, to be quickly replaced by Bernie and two other Auxiliary women. The auction got under way with the offering of one of Mary's specialties—rhubarb pie.

It soon became apparent that Ken Huber intended to outbid every other person for every pie offered. By the fourth pie, a cherry with a criss-cross crust, Mary was writhing in acute embarrassment, suffering the daggered looks of her mother-in-law and trying desperately not to show how they affected her. Christine attempted to talk sense into the younger man, but too much whiskey ruled his senses and he wouldn't listen. Seeing Mary pull her lower lip between her teeth as Ken upped the bid yet again, she whispered fiercely to Paul, "Do something! He's upset Mary and he won't listen to me. Make him stop!"

It was, she soon realized, a mistake. But she couldn't deny that her plea was effective. Paul looked from Chris to Mary to Ken and back to Chris. He gave her a reassuring smile and called out a bid. He then reached over, tapped Ken on the shoulder, and, as Ken turned to look, Paul sent his fist into the targeted jaw. Ken sank like a wrecked ship.

The commotion was brief. Gasps competed with laughter until Bernice shouted out over the clamor. When a sufficient quiet returned, she said calmly, "I'm glad someone had the sense to do that, I was about ready to myself." She acknowledged the laughter with a terse nod. "Now which one of you wants this pie? Last bid was five dollars."

Together Mary and Chris managed to get Paul and Ken out of the hall without any further fuss. The faint hint of a breeze swished the leaves of the cottonwoods behind the hall, bringing a welcome relief after the suffocating density within the building. A garish floodlight cast a surrealistic glow that shriveled before the looming shadow of the grain elevator. With a swagger that closely resembled a stagger, Paul sauntered into the darkness. Occasional off-key notes of a jaunty whistle wafted back to the trio progressing slowly in his train.

"I thought," muttered Mary over the slackened form between them, "fresh air had a sobering effect."

"I think the only thing that'll sober these two is a solid night's sleep."

They exchanged a look, then a laugh. "I'm sure the Women's Auxiliary has never had a more exciting fund-raiser. What with your"—Mary grunted as they heaved Ken into the back seat of her car—"news and these two providing free entertainment."

"They were better than the band." Chris nudged Paul into the middle of the front seat and got in beside him. He grinned happily. "Do you always slug people when you're drunk?"

"Only for you," he replied.

"I do not recall, Mr. Richards, ever asking you to punch someone out on my behalf." She giggled, destroying the effect of her lofty tone. "But the look on Ken's face was priceless."

"I could price it," said Mary under her breath. She shoved into gear and they bounced out over the grass. "I know I was laughing, but I'm really angry at him. Drunk or not, he knew just what he was doing. He was making an announcement that we're . . . oh, you know. And it's not true. Not yet. I'm not ready for anything like that. But who'll believe that now? By God, if Paul hadn't already decked him, I would have."

They made the short drive in silence, Mary obviously still fuming and Ken snoring in the back. Paul was awake, but quiet, and Chris couldn't help wondering what was going on in that gorgeous head of his. She herself felt torn between sympathy for her friend and a selfish elation that permitted little to intrude on her happiness.

At the house Mary came in only long enough to check on the children and pay the baby-sitter before leaving to drive both the sitter and Ken home. When Chris inquired whether she could manage on her own, she said with a tight smile, "Oh, yes. I'll just roll him out into his yard and drive on."

She left and Chris slowly mounted the stairs in Paul's weaving wake. Inside their bedroom he dove onto the bed and lay still. Chris switched on the bedside lamp and the muted radiance glossed over the black of his hair, shining in vivid contrast to the white of his pillow. She kicked out of her heels and peeled off her hose. He lay motionless.

"Have you passed out?" she inquired with interest.

He flopped over onto his back, his arms and legs sprawled over the quilt. His smile gleamed at her. "Not yet."

"Well, that's a relief. You can help me get you undressed."

"Yes, ma'am." He obediently stuck a leg into the air. She grabbed hold of the foot and pulled off one boot. She let go and the leg plopped back to the bed. With effort he presented his other foot to her.

"I do wish," she grunted as she yanked off the boot, then removed his socks, "you'd realize you can't hold your liquor."

"I held plenty," he contradicted.

"That's what I'm talking about."

"It wasn't the quantity," he protested. "It was the mixing. I never should've mixed all those different kinds of liquor."

Her brows disappeared beneath her rippling bangs. Shaking her head, she crawled over the bed atop him, straddled his legs, and began undoing his belt buckle. As she worked at the belt, then the snap and zipper of his jeans, he slowly inched his hands up the satiny thigh beneath the silk of her skirt.

"You feel great, you know that? I love to touch you."

"Well, that's good," she said as she backed down his legs and stood at the end of the bed. "Seeing as how you've committed yourself to a lifetime of touching me."

He moaned and told her thickly to get the hell back on the bed. She laughed and tugged his jeans off. "Help me out a little, will you? Lift your butt. Thank you." Folding his jeans, she glanced at him. "Underwear on or off?" she asked.

"Off."

She couldn't resist snapping the waistband before sliding them down his long legs. He swore revenge and she sighed. "Is that a promise?"

"Damn right it is. Come here, baby." His voice dropped to a husk of desire. "Let me touch you."

She lay down beside him, facing him. To her surprise he did not stroke her breasts or shoulders or hips. Light,

248

feathery fingertips followed the curve of her cheek, the plane of her jaw. One by one she undid his shirt buttons, but when she spread the shirt open he made no effort to remove it. Instead, he traced the full curve of her lips with his fingertip, then skimmed over the short snub of her nose.

"Don't you want your shirt off?"

"You know what I like about this place?" he asked in answer.

She shook her head; her earring danced into the pillow. His eyes followed the merry motion. His lids drooped lazily. When he raised them to look at her, she almost stopped breathing. The passionate glint of love poured over her. She lay wide-eyed and wordless, wondering if he intended to look at her like that often. If he did, she'd go through life in a permanent daze.

"You're in it," he told her.

The noisy serenade of crickets drifted through the open windows. Chris could barely hear them over the wild drumming of her heart, the crashing rate of her pulse, the labored pattern of her breath. How could a body survive such an explosion of love?

"My, my," she said unsteadily, "how the liquor in you does flatter."

"That's not the liquor," he contradicted her, dropping a breathy kiss on the corner of her mouth.

She flapped her hand before her wrinkled nose. "Whew! That's certainly not ginger ale on your breath. Why you must've drunk—"

He devoured her words with an impassioned kiss. All the love that had simmered within him throughout the long evening boiled over. His mouth moved feverishly over her lips, her throat, her jaw, her ears, and back again. His hands stroked flames from her shoulders to her breasts to her belly. He paused there, swirling his fingers over her stomach. His child was growing in there, inside Christine.

249

His child, his woman. He lifted his head to gaze at her in wonder.

Her hair rippled over the pillow, her lashes flickered over her cheek. Her lips parted, quivering in anticipation. He brushed the lightest of kisses once, twice, three times over her.

"Stop teasing me," she pleaded hoarsely.

"That wasn't teasing," he corrected in an injured tone. "That was cherishing. I was showing how much I adore you."

"*That* was teasing. *This* is adoring." She thrust her hands into his hair and clamped his head down, forcing his mouth to linger over hers. Nibbling on his lower lip, she played her tongue over each soft bite, then plunged deeply. She let her hands drift down, sliding them under his open shirt, weaving through the soft hair to explore the muscled contours beneath. She arched, lifting to him, meeting his hardness, inflaming it.

His breath met hers on a heated groan and his hands rose over her rib cage to cuddle the undersides of her breasts. Silk rustled between his palms. It felt pleasantly soft. But he wanted to feel the exquisite pliancy of her breasts, the grainy pucker of the crest as he tempted it to rigidity. He raised himself a bit and shrugged out of his shirt. "Unless you want the most expensive dress ever worn in Oscar, Kansas, to be ripped to shreds, you'd better take it off. Quick."

She mocked a frown. "That's a lousy attitude for a lover."

"I'm not a lover. I'm a husband."

"Not yet," she reminded him. "There's still time to escape."

His reaction startled her. She'd just been teasing, continuing the banter. But Paul pounced on her, shoving her into the mattress, grasping her wrists, and pinning them above her head. His solid weight pressed down on her,

250

trapping her. A dark stain rushed into his face and his mouth narrowed to an invisible line.

"That's not funny," he said without seeming to move those tightened lips.

It didn't do, Chris silently told herself, to forget the short fuse to his temper, particularly when he'd been drinking. She wondered if he would actually get violent. Aloud, she said quietly, "I'm sorry. I wasn't being serious."

He stared down into her widened eyes and slowly the tension eased from him. He loosened his hold upon her wrists, stroking his thumbs gently over the pulse points. "I'm sorry too. I have a hell of a temper, especially when I care about something. I care about you, Christine. You mean so much to me, it almost frightens me."

"It frightens me too," she said, chancing a teasing smile.

He groaned and kissed her and held her tightly. Somewhere in the blurry depths of his mind he knew he had to talk to her, but the dizzying whirl of his emotions had caught up with him. The fright of thinking Christine ill, the pain of contemplating leaving her, the elation of realizing his love for her, the gut-wrenching fear she would not have him. And the stunned, overwhelming tide of feelings when he'd discovered she was carrying his child. It was too much, too quickly. He couldn't face another upheaval of any kind. He wanted nothing more than to lose himself in her comforting embrace. Tomorrow he would tell her; tomorrow would be soon enough. For tonight, he swore aloud never to frighten her again and proceeded to do exactly that by passing out so abruptly, she thought he'd had some sort of an attack.

Reassured, however, by a gust of stale breath that he still ranked among the living, Chris entwined her arms about him and drifted to sleep with the warmth of his breath unconsciously caressing her. Her last alert thought was that she'd never felt happier. Life was perfect.

* * *

At about four in the morning her opinion of life suffered a drastic reversal. She woke, hot and nauseated. The night breeze that had striven to alleviate the stultifying heat had ceased to stir. The room was smothered in sultry, motionless air. A sticky sheen of perspiration coated her skin, particularly wherever Paul touched her. She pushed at him, then regretted the action. It made her head spin violently. She lay still, but it did no good. Her vertigo got worse. It moved from her head to her stomach. It threatened to move from her stomach up her throat. With a muffled groan, she shot from the bed and bolted to the bathroom, arriving at the toilet bowl just in time.

She had finished heaving and was simply holding on to the cool porcelain, trying to steady herself for the effort of rising, when a pair of arms lifted her. Propping her up by the sink, Paul dampened a washcloth with cold water, then tenderly rinsed her flushed cheeks. "Poor baby. Is it morning sickness?"

A feeble smile trembled over her lips. "Uh-uh. Middle-of-the-night sickness."

Chuckling, he swung her into his arms. "Do you think you're all through?"

"I hope so. It isn't fair," she muttered as he carried her back to the bed. "You do all the drinking and I'm the one that gets sick."

"I'd trade your stomach for my head in a flash."

"Aching?"

"Pounding like a drill hammer."

"I'd think a man who suffers hangovers the way you do would avoid drinking."

"I'd think a woman who suffers morning sickness at four A.M. would avoid pregnancy."

They looked at each other and simultaneously grinned. Chris felt remarkably better. He stood her by the vanity and slid her wrinkled dress to the floor, removed her bra, and tossed it onto the crumpled heap. He changed the sheets before letting her get back into bed. "Your side of the bed was literally soaked," he explained as he worked. "Is that part of being pregnant or is that something else?"

She heard the thread of anxiety and responded with as much calmness as she could, wobbling nearly naked by the dresser. "I don't know. Probably. It could be the heat partially. It's so humid here, I feel like I'm being wrung dry all the time."

Her voice had escalated to a whiny note she'd never meant to use. He hadn't seemed to hear it, for he came back, picked her up, and laid her gently down without remarking on it. What he did say was, "We'll have to get some books on having babies, so we'll know what to expect."

He turned out the light and she heard him puttering around the room. Then the bed sagged as he pressed into place beside her. His hand found hers in the darkness and clasped it. "We'll have to plan for the future. Our future."

Our future. She liked the sound of that. Yawning, she murmured drowsily, "Isn't it funny? Two months ago we didn't know there'd be a future for us. Now there's a lifetime ahead of us."

"I don't think it's funny, darling. I think it's destiny. I've been waiting all my life for you." He paused and inhaled deeply. "Baby, there's something I want to tell you. I've wanted to for weeks, but I couldn't quite find the right time, the right words. I just want you to know that no matter what, my feelings for you are true and real. I love you. And I hope you love me enough to forgive me. You do love me, don't you?"

She did not answer. Paul leaned over in the darkness, then fell back into his pillow with a sigh. Once again his timing had been wrong. Christine had fallen asleep.

CHAPTER FIFTEEN

The ceiling fan completed another lethargic rotation. The clatter of forks scraping across plates pinged above the constant whirr of the electric fans. In the back, Bernice sang as she grilled hamburgers and slapped together a corned beef sandwich. In the front, Chris smiled as she refilled a coffee cup.

"Don't look so glum. You'll live," she said with an attempt to cheer that brought Ken's golden head up from where it had lain in his palm.

"Is that supposed to comfort me?" he asked with a rare asperity. He glanced around the café, looking rather as if he longed to use the other diners as punching bags. His eyes slid back to Chris. "I blew it last night, didn't I? I made a fool of myself. I got so caught up in your happiness, I thought I finally had a shot at it myself. And all I did was show Mary I'm as immature as she's always thought."

"It's got nothing to do with maturity. Paul's nearly ten years your senior and he was as big a fool as you last night."

He didn't respond to her teasing smile. She moved away to refill other cups, take dessert orders, and hand out checks, and all the while she was wondering what she could do for her two dearest friends. She hadn't seen Mary before leaving for work, but Ken had been at the café the

254

moment they'd opened up, hung over and miserable, begging for coffee and aspirin. When he returned for lunch, his headache had abated, but his depression had deepened. Obviously whatever had passed between Mary and Ken on the drive home the night before had not been pleasant.

The cash register rang as Chris accepted payment from two of her regulars, then she slammed the money drawer shut. She returned to Ken. This time she didn't attempt to tease him from his mood. She said on a somber undertone, "You've loved her a long time, haven't you?"

A mirthless bark of a laugh answered her. Then, seeming to need to speak against his will, he said harshly, "For as long as I can remember. She was my baby-sitter. We used to joke about my growing up faster for her. At least *she* joked. I was serious. But by the time I got into high school, she'd married Tim and already had Eric. I told myself it was a childhood infatuation. Hell, every boy falls in love with his sitter. I thought I'd grow out of it."

There was a silence in which the mumbled conversation from one of the booths drifted by. Chris swiped a cloth over the Formica, waiting. Ken pushed the coffee away with an angry jerk that sloshed some over the rim. "I didn't. I kept on loving her. Every girl I dated, I compared to her. I'd kiss them and wonder, did Mary feel this warm, warmer? Did she kiss Tim the way I was kissed? Touch him the way I liked to be touched?" His handsome face clouded with despair. His voice filled with self-loathing. "I wanted to hate Tim, but I couldn't. Nobody could hate him. He was a real nice guy. And when he died, my first thought wasn't what a great friend I'd lost. Oh, no, I thought, *Now's my chance.*"

Chris held her breath, not daring to interrupt the flow of rage and sorrow he needed to release. He expelled a gust of air and continued more calmly. "For months I've been telling myself, go slow, go easy. The difference between us isn't so great now. Now she'll see I'm a man. Then last

255

night I turn around and prove I'm the same dumb kid she used to watch over."

"I don't think it's as bad as you think. You're magnifying it out of proportion. You can't give up just because you once—"

Ken spun off the stool. He didn't bother any longer to keep his voice down. "You didn't hear what she had to say to me. She made it more than clear what she thinks of me." He dug into his overalls and tossed money without looking at the counter. Coins rattled to the floor. Heads riveted on him. He didn't notice. "I'm getting the hell out. What do you think's kept me in this town? The cultural assets?"

"Running away doesn't solve—"

But he had wrenched open the door and stormed out. After a stunned moment Chris bent and retrieved the coins from the linoleum floor. When she straightened, the customers had ostensibly returned their attention to their meals.

Bernie came out of the kitchen and pursed her lips in a silent whistle. "Puts on quite a show, don't he?"

"He's suffering."

"Oh, I know, I know. He's got it bad. Always did. And if you want to know the truth of it, Mary's felt just the same. That girl loved him for years, but was afraid of robbing the cradle. Maybe it wouldn't mean much elsewhere, but in a town like this, it would cause talk, snubs, hurtful doin's. I'm not saying she didn't love her husband, mind, but her feelings for Ken Huber ran too strong to ever be called friendly."

"We have to help them somehow," declared Chris. She met Bernie's raised brows with a determined thrust of the chin. All through the afternoon she worked out what to say to Mary when she got home. If she had to drag her by that gorgeous mane of hair, Chris was going to get Mary into Ken's arms. He loved her, he loved her chil-

256

dren; he would be perfect for her and if Mary let him go, she'd be a fool!

That, Christine decided for the umpteenth time, was just what she was going to say. She slid another piece of fresh German chocolate cake into the glass dessert case, then glanced at the round-faced clock on the wall behind her. Four-fifteen. Just forty-five minutes until she confronted Mary. The door opened and she removed her gaze from the clock. Her smile of welcome dissolved to a curve of curiosity.

The two gentlemen coming into Dieble's Café were almost like a species from another planet. The men who usually came into the café wore overalls, jeans, heavy-duty khaki creased and dirtied with the day's labor. They picked up menus with roughened hands that bore calluses and broken nails. They laughed loudly and spoke to her with easy familiarity. These men would never, she was certain, descend to such a level with a mere waitress. Identical dark blue suits, perfectly pressed and fitting as only tailor-made suits could fit, draped forms that didn't look as if they'd ever known a bead of sweat, a speck of dirt. Both had dark hair, cut in conservative styles, and both bore the same studiously blank expression. After one exploratory examination of the small interior, they moved as one to the left corner booth.

Trying not to reveal her amusement at the oddity of their presence in this café, Chris plucked up two plastic menus and crossed to them. She paused to ask her sole customer if he needed anything else, then greeted the two men with a friendly smile. As they took the menus, she absently noticed their hands, immaculate hands with neatly trimmed nails tipping long, slim fingers. It floated through her mind that they looked like Paul's used to look—smooth, polished, patrician.

A prickling of unreasoning fear coursed down her back. She gaped at those hands, saw them set aside the menus and pause, waiting. Slowly she drew her gaze upward to first one face, then the other.

"Are you Christine . . . Richards?" inquired the first.

Her eyes swung back to him. How, she briefly wondered, could anyone possibly appear so cool in this heat? Not a sign of perspiration dared touch that bloodlessly pale face. The nose had a hint of breadth, but the rest of his features were thin and perfectly tapered. Custom-made lips, she thought inanely, and felt her apprehension escalate. She realized his pause in her name had been deliberate. She wiped her hands on the sides of her uniform and wished she hadn't betrayed her agitation. "Yes."

The men exchanged a look. She read derision in it, dismissal. A seed of anger blossomed. She stiffened her back. "May I help you?" she bit out.

"I am Sterling Ridgeway, Miss Richards," announced the first. "And this is my brother Gerard."

Another shock of dismay hit her at his use of the title *Miss*. She forced herself to meet that cold, contemptuous gaze directly. His eyes were darkly brown, but without the warm, rich depth of Paul's. They were, she told herself, as warm as a puddle of mud.

"It's Mrs. Richards actually," she said, keeping her tone void of the rising fear and anger she felt. "Now what would you like?"

"We should like, Miss Casolaro—"

She drew in her breath sharply, hissing above the hum of the fans. Those sculpted lips curved in the slightest of smiles.

"We should like for you to get out of our brother's life. And this"—Sterling Ridgeway reached inside his suit jacket and extracted a long, bulky envelope. He tossed it in her direction— "should prompt you on your way."

She didn't pick up the envelope. Her lips parted a little, and she gripped the edge of the booth. He knew! Somehow he knew she hadn't married Paul! But how? And what did he mean, get out of his brother's life? She made herself speak. "I'm sorry, I don't know what you're talking about."

"Preston, we're talking about Preston," said Gerard. He spoke quickly, nervously. Christine swiveled her gaze from one to the other, landing on Gerard. He did not meet her eyes.

"I don't know any Preston. I don't know what you're talking about." A shrill pitch began rising in her voice. "Really, I think you've made a mistake."

"I think not," countered Sterling. He looked at her with the warmth of a man eyeing a cockroach. "You are Christine Casolaro. Age, twenty-six. Occupation, former cocktail hostess at a disreputable establishment known as The Scarlet Lady. You have spent the past two months masquerading as the wife of *Paul Richards.*"

She licked her lips. She opened her mouth. Nothing came out. This was a nightmare.

"You don't expect us to believe you don't know that Paul Richards is Preston Paul Ridgeway." He extended a hand and tapped one manicured fingernail on the envelope. "This will, I am certain, more than compensate you for having provided my brother with . . . shall we politely say, companionship?"

The sneer in that chilled tone snapped Chris out of her stupor. "You can believe what you like. I haven't the least idea what you're talking about. And I don't care. I'm not standing around letting you insult me." She pivoted, then flinched as a smooth, cold hand circled her wrist. Her eyes traveled from the polished hand up the tailored sleeve to Sterling's austere face. Not so much as a single hair was out of place.

"Forgive me. If you do not know about Preston, then you should let us explain," he said, and she didn't believe that apology for a moment. This man didn't have sincere emotions. This man had calculated reactions. She didn't believe he gave a damn if he shattered her world with his well-modulated words. He only cared that she hear them.

But neither could she doubt the truth of what he was saying. It was there, plain to be seen, in the furtive, sympathetic glances from the one called Gerard. She shook her wrist free and walked blindly to the register. Bernie appeared, cast a searching look at the corner booth, and disappeared, leaving behind a cream-topped carrot cake to be sliced and added to the dessert case. Numbly, not daring to think, Chris took Herm Vogel's money, cleared his plate and glass, and wiped the booth clean.

The low murmur of the men's voices reached her, though not the content. Her heart banged so savagely she thought it would break her rib cage. She did not think she could bear to hear what they wanted to say to her. Yet she found herself returning to the booth, heard herself saying, "Well?"

Later she wished she hadn't gone back to that booth. Later she wished she'd run from the café, run to Paul, asked, begged, demanded, to be told it wasn't true. Now it was too late. Now she knew it was all horribly true. The brothers revealed too many little truths—how he had a way of charming people into doing what he wanted, how his explosive temper ignited with a mere look, how women seemed to melt at his slightest smile. Tonelessly they told her about Preston's monied background, his important position, his restless inability to settle down, his continual string of discarded women. She sat stony-faced through it all, not revealing by a single flicker of expression the havoc they were wreaking inside her.

At the end of it, Gerard cleared his throat and nudged the envelope toward her. His eyes would not settle on her. It was obvious she was an embarrassment. His words confirmed this. "Take it. You're entitled to it. You're, ah, different from his usual, er, type. It's inexcusable, the way he's used you."

This time she picked it up, opened the flap. Crisp bills, dozens of them. She closed the flap.

"It's, ah, twenty-five thousand," explained Gerard. "Yours. All you have to do is leave Preston alone."

"We do ask, Miss Casolaro, that you sign this." Sterling took a folded sheath of papers from his inside pocket and handed it to her. He laid a gold pen beside her hand.

Was it real? Of course it would be. The son of Ridgeco Oil wouldn't use a Bic. *Funny, how the mind works. While they've been destroying my love, my life, I've been thinking how the sugar needs to be broken up. The humidity's lumped it together.*

"What is this?" she heard a voice ask. Was it hers?

"A contract. You agree that neither you nor the child— should you indeed decide to have the child—will ever make a claim against the Ridgeway family or their holdings. You also agree never to attempt to see Preston again. It's all perfectly forthright."

"Have a stack printed up on the ready?" She picked up the pen, flipped to the bottom sheet of three and poised her hand above the line marked payee. Was that what she was? A payee? What an ugly, empty little word. Why play such word games? Why not ex-mistress? That's what she was and they knew it. She raised her eyes. "How did you find us? How did you know about me?"

"We've had detectives searching since the morning Preston's Lamborghini was discovered abandoned at that bar. They learned immediately of the incident there, of your disappearance with him. He called us from Albuquerque, but we were unable to pick up your trail out of New Mexico. We might never have found you." Gerard stopped abruptly.

"But then my brother made one of his typical errors," said Sterling. "A few weeks ago he sent a letter assuring us of his well-being. The postmark was Coldwater, Kansas. A small town, Coldwater. It didn't take long to learn he'd purchased a ring at a jewelry shop there."

Christine looked down at the gold wedding band. When

she realized those muddy eyes had followed hers, she shoved her fist in her lap.

"It was easy enough to track him from the jeweler's to here," Gerard finished. "We flew out this morning and got an additional report, including the news that you are—er, well—"

"I see," said Christine. Her fingers tightened about the slim, gold pen. The document should be read, she knew that. But she couldn't face having the love she'd given Paul dismissed in precise legalese, with empty, ugly words like *payee*. She dashed her signature across the line and dropped the hated instrument. She stood. Somehow her legs still supported her.

"You can put your minds at ease, *gentlemen.*" The emphasis she placed on the last word left no doubt as to what she would really have liked to call them. I'll be out of Pau—Preston's life by tonight. Then he's all yours."

She turned to walk away, but halted as Sterling called her name. Looking over her shoulder, she saw him hold out the envelope. "You forgot this," he said.

"I didn't forget it," she said, then kept walking. She went to the tiny bathroom at the end of the kitchen and locked herself in. She ran cold water over her face, but didn't feel it. She felt nothing at all. How could she? She had died in bits and pieces out there. Nothing was left but this shell in which she moved.

There was a rapping on the door. "You okay, honey? If you're not feeling well, you go on home. Sueanne oughta be here in a shake of a lamb's tail."

"Thank you, Bernie," she said, and wondered where the strength to reply so steadily had come from. She dried her face and hands, then left. Not wanting to risk another meeting with the Ridgeways, she went out the back door. She took a step, and another. Then she broke into a run and kept on running. She was puffing with a pain in her side when she darted into the yard.

Chris ignored the pain, racing up the steps and into the

house. Upstairs, she collapsed onto the bed, but she did not cry. She was past tears. You had to feel to cry and she felt nothing. She was glad. If she felt it, the agony would rent her soul.

Downstairs, the dining room door opened. "Chris, I'm off to drive the kids to Hazel's. I shouldn't be too long." A stretch of silence, then, "Chris, are you okay?"

"Fine, Mary, I'm fine. Getting ready for a bath. Drive carefully."

Where did that collected voice come from? Surely not from within the raging desolation of her mind, her heart, her soul? She heard Mary's blithe 'bye, then the doors closing.

Time inched by.

Eventually she rose and with a deadened calm began folding her clothes into a cardboard box she had taken from the closet. Reaching for a blouse, her hand grazed the silk of the red dress and she angrily flinched. She would not take that with her! As she furiously shoved the dress out of her way, a golden flash caught her eye, taunting her. With an abrupt jerk she wrenched the ring from her finger.

Her gaze darted wildly and found the bright watermelon doll. Disdainfully, as if she could not let go of it soon enough, she dropped the ring over the doll's horn. The kachina doll and the ring, like the dress, would not go with her.

Suddenly leaving was vitally important. She could not stand another second in this room she had shared with him. She quickly changed into a royal blue blouse and jeans, then ran downstairs to call Ken.

Her conversation was brief. She asked him to bring the repaired Maverick by. He agreed. She hung up. Unexpectedly she began shaking. She wrapped her arms about herself and fought off the urge to run from the house and keep on running. She could not do that, not yet.

Just today she'd told Ken running away didn't solve

anything. But now she knew there were some problems beyond resolution. Sometimes walking away was the only solution left. But she knew she had to stay a little longer. She had to stay until she heard Paul—no, she bitterly corrected herself, Preston—tell her himself just why he had used her so cavalierly. She wanted to watch his face as he twisted the knife his brothers had driven into her heart. Then she could leave.

When Ken brought her car he did not, as he would normally have done, come in through the front. He knocked on the side door and blatantly refused to enter until she assured him Mary wasn't there. "She drove the kids over to their grandparents' for the weekend and I expect she's staying for supper there."

He came in and dropped the car keys into her palm. In turn she gave him the check she'd written out while waiting for him. It would be the last time she signed Christine Richards. She told herself she was glad of it. Ken rippled the check through his fingers, then said hesitantly, "I'm sorry I blew up at you today. I know you were only trying to help."

"Don't worry about it."

An awkward silence permeated the tiny hallway. Ken said something about the spiffy strangers he'd seen driving around town. Chris clenched the keys so hard, grooves were cut into her palm. Wouldn't the whole town buzz when they knew who those strangers were? When they knew who Paul was? Who she wasn't?

"Oh, really?" she choked out. He started to leave and she stopped him with a question. "When do you think you'll be leaving town?" She was asking just to help pass the time, to keep from tormenting herself with bitter reflection. His answer, however, startled her into paying attention.

"I'm not going anywhere. I was just spoutin' off steam. It wouldn't make any difference if I did go. My love for Mary wouldn't go away no matter where I was. I can't run away from that. So I'll stay and hope one day she'll realize I've grown up."

No, you can't run away from love. Her own painful love would go with her. But she could run away from the humiliation, the torment. She realized Ken was waiting for her to make some sort of response. "I—I'm sure she will," she stammered.

This time she made no move to impede his departure. Even before the door closed she forgot about him, forgot about Mary. All the compassion, all the distress she'd felt for them had been overwhelmed by the tidal force of her own heartbreak. She had no feeling to spare for others. She stumbled upstairs, wishing desperately she had not spoken to Ken. It had dented the safety shield she'd shrouded herself with. No longer did a vast numbness protect her. She felt sick and hurt.

She lay on the bed, coiling into the fetal position. From the very first he'd lied to her. And continued to lie. She had forgiven him and he'd strung her along with more lies. Charming, meaningless lies. What else had he told her that had no substance? Had he lied about loving her? Had he proposed just for the fun of it? Because he'd found out she was pregnant? Had he intended to marry her at all?

Questions without answers battered her, drove her finally from the bed to seek escape in a flurry of action. She loaded the packed box into the Maverick's trunk. She checked the map and marked out a route to Los Angeles. She wrote a note to Mary, saying good-bye, conveying her love, explaining nothing. When she ran out of things to do, she went to the sitting room and curled in the chair, waiting in the dark for the sound of a stopping car, a door opening and closing, footsteps. At some point it occurred to her that the brothers may have gone directly to the Kilmers' farm, that Paul—Preston, damn it!—might have left with them, might not even consider coming home—to this house!—to say good-bye to her. At that moment she thought she hated him.

And at that moment she heard the car, the door, the steps.

"Chris? Baby, you home?" he called.

She did not answer. A light flicked on. She heard him go into the bedroom. Long strides echoed down the hall. He was in the frame of the door. She knew the instant his eyes discerned her in the shadows. His tense form relaxed. His breath was released in a soft sigh.

"What're you sitting in the dark for?" he asked, switching on the overhead light as he entered. "You're not feeling sick, are you, baby?"

"No," she said flatly. "I'm not feeling sick, Preston."

He froze in the act of squatting beside her chair. The few seconds of immobility seemed eternal. Then he slowly crouched on his haunches, at eye level with her. "How did you know?"

"A little birdie told me. Two, in fact. Named Sterling and Gerard." She spat the names as if the taste of them upon her tongue sickened her. She was glad when he blanched beneath his deep tan. She was glad when his dark eyes turned opaquely black. She hoped he was hurting, and was sorry only that his pain could never equal hers.

"How the hell did they—" he began, then stopped. The cold, set disdain on her face made him feel ill. He leaned toward her. She flinched back. "I was going to tell you myself."

"Were you?"

"Yes! Of course I was! I've tried, many times."

"Funny, I don't recall a single instance."

"Last night, damn it! I tried last night. We were interrupted, then I got too drunk and you feel asleep and this morning we woke too late, so there wasn't time. But I swear I was going to tell you."

"Tell me what? More lies? I wouldn't believe you if you told me the sun is hot!"

She leaped up so suddenly, he tipped back on his heels.

266

She was at the door before he came to his feet. She faced him, but something in her expression held him back.

"I've waited all evening, something in me still hoping you would deny it. That it was all some stupid mistake. That you were the man I thought I loved." She gave vent to a dry laugh without humor. "I guess that was my stupid mistake."

She whirled and took a step. Preston launched himself at her. The wood floor groaned beneath his weight as he crashed into her. He thrust her against the wall, pinning her with his body. The grime from his shirt imprinted the front of her blouse. The pungent odor of dried sweat assailed her nostrils. His heartbeat battered into her breasts.

"I never lied about my feelings for you."

All the hours of despair and pain and rage came out in icy sarcasm. "Ah, come on, Mr. Ridgeway, tell me another one."

"It was just a name! So I gave you the wrong name. Is that such a crime?"

"It's not the name, it's the deceit that makes me sick. I could forgive the initial lie—in fact, I did. But even as you promised not to lie to me anymore, you were adding lie onto lie. I trusted you and you betrayed me."

"I thought you were trying to get rid of me!" He saw she didn't believe that and throbbed with frustration. This was a nightmare! This cold, hostile woman was not his warm, loving Christine. He tightened his grip about her arms, as if by basic contact he could make her see reason. "I didn't think you could love Preston Ridgeway, but I thought Paul Richards had a chance with you."

"And so you lied to get what you wanted. That's typical of you. You're selfish, Mr. Ridgeway. You've been brought up to think of no one but yourself."

"I can't deny that. I was selfish. I never cared about anybody else. But I've changed—"

"No. No, you haven't. If you had, you'd have told me the truth long before this."

267

Christine hurt as she had never hurt before. It was true—if he had loved her the least bit, he would have ended the lie before this. But he did not love her. He was incapable of it. He was too selfish to know how to give love. How could she possibly survive this torment? The feel of him, the scent of him could no longer be borne. She had to get away, now, before she shattered into splinters before him.

"Let me go. You're hurting me."

He visibly hesitated, then, seeing the implacability in her clenched jaw, released her. She stood stiffly waiting, and finally he stepped aside. She started down the hall. He followed. "Where the hell are you going?"

She'd left her purse at the edge of the steps. Now she hefted the voluminous bag onto her shoulder. "Home. I'm going home."

"This is your home."

She ignored that and started down the stairs. He came behind her, step by step.

"You can't leave," he said firmly.

"Watch me."

"Damn it, Chris, we have to talk!"

"You don't know how. Your expertise is in fabrication, not communication."

"We're getting married."

"No, we're not."

"What about the baby? My baby?"

At the bottom step she turned and eyed him without expression. "I think not," she said coolly.

"What the hell does that mean?"

"*My* baby, Mr. Ridgeway, not yours."

He grabbed her wrist and yanked once, hard. "Don't you ever say that again. And quit calling me Mr. Ridgeway. You make it sound like a social disease."

His hand was rough and clammy with heat. She thought of the cool, smooth touch of that other hand upon

268

her earlier and felt sick. Why had she stayed? To torture herself?

He saw the flicker of distress that crossed her features and softened. "Let's talk it out, baby." He felt her tremble; she tugged on her wrist, trying to be free of him. He would not, he could not let her go! "Christine, I need you."

"Too bad. I don't need you," she lied.

She wouldn't have thought it possible that skin tanned to the shade of aged leather could bleach utterly white. But his did. His hand fell away from her wrist.

"You don't mean that," he said bleakly.

"Would it make any difference to you what I felt? It's only your needs, your wants that matter to you, *Mr. Ridgeway,* and I'm tired of accommodating you."

On legs too leaden to feel a step, she walked through the dining room into the living room. She heard him behind her, but did not turn around. As she reached the front door, instinct warned her and she skittered away just as his hand shot out. Whirling, she glared at him, daring him with her gaze to touch her.

"Don't do this, Christine. Not without giving me a chance to explain."

"You've had over two months. Nothing you could say could explain away that." She reached for the doorknob.

"Chris! I love you. You can't just run away from love."

She wrenched open the door, then paused, looking over her shoulder at him. "I'm just glad I can run away from *you!*"

The door slapped shut. She was gone.

CHAPTER SIXTEEN

Despondency crashed over him in waves. He stared at the wood of the door, immobilized by an oppressive hopelessness. She was the only truly good thing to touch his life and she was gone. My God, to face a life without Christine . . .

It was this thought that spurred him to action. Nearly hauling the door off its hinges, he yanked it open and clattered down the porch. The Maverick was parked in the drive; Chris was sliding in behind the steering wheel. He made a frantic dash and threw open the side door just as the engine roared to life.

Chris cast a shocked look at him. He sank onto the seat. "What are you doing?" she asked shrilly.

"Going with you," he bit out.

"This isn't funny."

"So who's laughing?"

"Get out of my car."

"Not until you do."

Their eyes met in a blistering duel. Hers were the first to drop. She stared at a bit of foam just visible beneath a rip in the vinyl and thought she just might give vent to an ear-splitting scream. Why wouldn't he leave her alone? Hadn't he hurt her enough? Did he enjoy making her sick with misery?

Preston took a deep breath and started talking. He

spoke with an urgency that rattled his heart in his chest. He felt like a convicted man pleading for a stay of execution.

"I admit I've made mistakes. Anybody can make an error in judgment. Mine was in waiting too long to tell you the truth. But in the beginning I thought it was just for a week or so, and if I told you, you might run to the newspapers or my family. I never expected to fall in love with you. But I do love you, Christine."

"You don't know how to love," she insisted coldly. "If you had loved me, you'd have told me the truth long before this."

"I was afraid of losing you."

Her reply to this was a cynical expulsion too jarring to be called a laugh. Only with great effort did he keep himself from physically assaulting her. He'd never felt like hitting a woman more than at this moment. He longed to knock some sense into her.

"By the time I knew I wanted to tell you, you'd made it more than clear what you thought of people like me. I knew you'd hold my background against me, so I held back telling you."

She told herself not to listen to him. She told herself he would say anything to get what he wanted. And still her heart gave a dangerous little leap because he wanted her. "Are you through?" she inquired icily.

"No.

"Leave me alone," she demanded through gritted teeth.

"No," he repeated.

She rounded on him, shaking a furious fist in front of his nose. "You could talk yourself blue in the face and I wouldn't listen. Now get out of my car."

"Not a chance, baby. Whither thou goest . . ."

With a sinking heart Chris gazed out the windshield. She did not really see the moonlit street or the opaque silhouettes of houses across the way. And she could no longer permit herself to glance in his direction. He was undermining her will to resist him. She was weakening and she knew it. Oh, God, didn't she have any pride? Any sense of self-preservation?

The lance of headlights thrust through the darkness. A sleek, black limousine emerged out of the shadows and slid with a purring sigh to a stop. Seeing it, Preston uttered a coarse oath and Christine shook with the effort not to laugh hysterically. She couldn't preserve herself, but the cavalry had come to the rescue. She turned off the ignition and sat waiting.

The Ridgeways approached with slow, sure confidence. Their dark suits rustled as they neared. Despite the pervasive humidity, they'd somehow managed to remain crisp and cool. Above all, they looked civilized.

"By all means, let's be civilized," muttered Chris under her breath.

"What?" Preston slewed his eyes her way.

"Nothing. Don't you think you should get out to greet your brothers?"

He fought to ignore her acerbic tone, fought for his self-control. He knew he'd much rather run them over and keep on driving. "I'm staying put as long as you are," he said tightly. "You want me to get out, fine. We'll both get out."

She did not argue. She was certain Sterling Ridgeway was more than capable of bringing his younger brother into line. He'd obviously had plenty of practice. How many other "contracts" had he arranged for? How many other "embarrassments" had he removed? Groping blindly for the handle, Chris clenched her jaw so hard, her teeth ached. She found the metal bar and made her escape from the suffocating confines of the car.

Slowly Preston got out, keeping one hand firmly on the door. Though he looked toward where his brothers stopped just feet away, he wasn't thinking of them at all. He was thinking, as always, about Christine. What could he say to convince her of his love? Say too little and it

272

might not be enough. Say too much and it might seem insincere. Two months ago he'd have said to hell with her; he'd have said he didn't need anybody but himself to get by. But he knew now that wasn't true, had never been true. He'd always needed someone. He'd always needed Christine.

"Well, Preston, I wouldn't have thought it possible, but you've astounded even me with this escapade of yours," said Sterling by way of greeting. His words were softly spoken, but Chris could feel the tension radiating from him even on the opposite side of the car. "Do you have any idea of the time and expense you have cost us?"

"No, but I'm certain you've got it calculated down to the last cent," replied Preston with an ease he was far from feeling. Would Chris be able to see he didn't belong with these people? Would she see that he belonged with her? "I don't know why you bothered. I'd have thought you'd be relieved to be rid of me."

"Preston! This isn't the time for jokes!" Gerard moved from behind his elder brother to face his younger one. "You can't imagine the worry we've been through."

"I'm sorry, but I told you when I called not to worry."

"*Four days* after you disappeared! Do you realize how frightened we were?"

"To be honest, I didn't think you'd give a damn," he told Gerard with a bitterness he could not mask.

Christine drew in a sharp breath. All three men glanced at her. She wished she could simply disappear. This was a scene she didn't want to be witnessing.

"Ah, Miss Casolaro, we certainly didn't expect to find you here," murmured Sterling. His soft voice carried without difficulty over the night songs of cicadas; his pale hand gleamed in the moonlight as he gestured toward the car.

Somehow both the tone and the gesture implied an insult. She thrust up her chin. "I was just leaving," she said in a firm manner she hoped was intimidating.

Sterling wasn't the sort to be intimidated. "But not

273

alone. I am disappointed, Miss Casolaro. I had thought, when you signed this . . ." He removed the contract from his inner pocket. The white sheath waved with ghostly suggestion as he held it up.

"What's that?" demanded Preston roughly. He took a hostile step forward.

His brother handed over the papers without hesitation. "A contract. The usual sort," he added, piercing Christine to the quick. "Read it over for yourself. The signature should be one you recognize. The amount was twenty-five thousand."

He was utterly still. He couldn't draw a single breath. Then, slowly, insidiously, his head bent over the document, his eyes narrowed against the darkness, his hands shuffled to the last page. Even in the deep shadows he saw the signature. His heart stopped. His world collapsed. No wonder she'd been in such a hurry to leave. No wonder she'd taken time to heft that damn purse of hers over her shoulder. It was weighted with twenty-five thousand dollars.

He had to hear it from her own lips. He had to hear that she had been bought. He forced the question out.

"You took the money?"

For two heartbeats, she did nothing at all. Then she stiffened. How could he think that? How could he claim to love her and think her capable of taking that kind of money? How could he?

"Perhaps, Preston, we should go inside where you can clearly see the signature." As he made the suggestion Sterling took his brother's arm and prompted him toward the house.

Preston allowed Sterling to guide him for precisely one step before halting abruptly. He furiously shook off his brother's hand as he whirled. "How could you do this, Christine? I love you! I was going to marry you! How could you sell my love like that? Our future?"

His voice rang eloquent of anguished despair. Then he

spun and barked "Come on" as he strode toward the silently waiting black limousine.

"No," said Gerard. He blocked his brother's path.

"Get out of my way," snarled Preston even as Sterling hissed a remonstrative, "Gerard!"

"No, Preston. She didn't take the money. She did sign the contract, that's true, but she didn't take so much as a dime."

"Gerard, you fool!"

"If he really loves her, if he intends to marry her, then we've no right to interfere, Sterling. I'm not excusing his behavior, but perhaps his motivations were—"

"Is this true?" Preston cut in unceremoniously.

"Well, of course it's true. I don't tell—"

Preston shoved both brothers from his path and strode ominously around the car. Chris didn't have to see his expression to recognize the menace in him. She backed until the metal door handle cut into her buttocks, then shakily tipped her chin up. His hands descended on her shoulders and began shaking as he began interrogating her.

"What the hell were you doing, making me think you'd taken a payoff? Why didn't you say you hadn't? Did you want me to leave, is that it?"

"How could you think I would take that money?" she responded in between short, sharp jerks. "How could you think that of me?"

He ceased rattling her and hauled her to his chest with a deep groan. "My God, my God. My whole world's turned upside down in the course of an evening and you expect me to *think*? I've only had one thought since I got home, and that was how to keep from losing you."

"As touching as this little scene of undying love is, we still have a legal agreement, signed by Miss Casolaro, to the effect that she will leave you alone."

Her breath was knocked from her by Preston's constrictive squeeze. "I don't give a damn for your legalities, big

275

brother. You don't have anything saying I will leave her alone. And believe me, I'm not leaving her alone. I'm marrying her."

"You really think father will permit you to throw yourself away on . . . her?"

"What father will permit doesn't concern me. I'm a big boy now. I don't need his permission to get married."

"Think about it, Preston," said Sterling quietly as he strolled toward the pair of them. "Think about the penthouse in New York, the condo in Florida, the villa in Nice. Think about the casinos of Monte Carlo, the Alpine skiing, the beachcombing in Molokai. Do you really believe you can give all that up? Do you believe you can give up the sports cars, the women? Do you think she's worth all that?"

"Easy come, easy go," he said, but she felt his muscles tense beneath her fingertips.

"Paul!" she cried without thinking. "You can't mean that. You can't give up all that for me."

He stood back and cradled her head between his palms. Silvery strands of moonlight streaked through his black hair and slanted ribbons of shadow over his straight nose, his full mouth. Christine gazed at him and felt herself drown, as she'd once longed to do, in the fathomless dark pools of his eyes.

"You're right. But I'm not giving all that up for you. I'm doing it for me. I don't want to inherit my future, I want the satisfaction of building it myself. Up to now my life has been empty and meaningless. Over the past two months I've discovered this is the life I want, for me, for us."

"But I'm just—"

"You're just the woman I love. You're the only thing I need, the only thing I want."

"B-but Paul, it's so much . . ."

"You mean so much more . . ."

He brushed his lips as lightly as the night breeze over

her upturned mouth and thought he'd never tasted anything so sweet. A clear splinter of a tear straggled down her cheek. He flicked the crystal drop away with his tongue and savored the salty flavor. There was nothing about this woman that he did not cherish. He could feast on her forever and still have room for more.

"Just how do you expect us to explain all this? How do you expect Father to react?"

Somewhat dazed, Preston pulled himself from his immersion in Christine. He released her, only to pull her within the circle of his arm as he faced his brothers. "Father will bluster and bellow and forget all about me at the first hint of a possible takeover here or merger there."

"How the hell do you think you're going to survive here? You of all people!"

"It may come as a surprise to you, Sterling, but I plan to survive by my own sweat. It's called working for a living, and I don't mean pounding tables in a boardroom with a title as phony as the job. I mean earning an honest living."

"Doing what? Baling hay for some farmer?" His sneer was barely visible in the weak light.

"Actually I'm thinking of running my own farm." He looked down at Chris and added quickly, "It's one of the things I wanted to talk to you about, darling. I want to sell off what I own—the cars, the apartments, everything— and purchase a farm over to the west of Kilmer's. Floyd'll lease me about six hundred acres to plant wheat and eventually I hope to buy them outright. It's not much, but it would be a start."

"You want to stay here?" Her voice rose in disbelief. It was happening too quickly. She couldn't absorb what he was saying.

"I did," he admitted, trying not to be disappointed at her negative response. "But if you don't, we won't. I'll be happy wherever you want to go."

The blinding flash of headlights threw the figures on the

277

driveway into stark relief. A car pulled up behind the Maverick and paused, idling as the beams glinted over the immobile tableau. Then the lights cut abruptly, darkness fell once more, and Mary climbed out, saying uncertainly, "Hello."

Preston stepped forward at once. "This is our landlady, Mary Sullivan. Mary, these are my brothers. They'd love to talk to you, I'm sure, but they were just leaving. Give my regards to the rest of the family."

"You can't be serious," Sterling began, only to be interrupted by Gerard.

"Let's go. I don't think we have anything more to do here. He's made his choice. Don't forget he's Father's son too."

Sterling wavered, seeming inclined to protest. Gerard thrust out a hand to Preston. "Congratulations and good luck. Let us know when the baby's born, will you?" After one quick handshake, he turned and strode to the limousine without looking back. Sterling hesitated another moment, then followed him.

"Whew," said Mary. "What a car! They're your brothers?"

Preston grinned. "Yup. Look, Mary, could you do us a favor and make a pot of your terrific coffee? Chris and I have some things we'd like to discuss with you."

Her red hair flamed in the night as she nodded and left them alone. Chris traced a pattern on the hood with her finger, feeling unaccountably shy. Knowing Preston's identity was one thing, knowing he was willing to sacrifice all that money, all that influence to stay with her was another. She felt awed. What could she possibly give in return for that?

"Baby," he whispered. He inched closer behind her. He had to work not to grab her and smother her in kisses. He knew that if he did, she would respond. But he wanted far more than that from her. He fought for patience. "Baby,

278

you do forgive me, don't you? I swear my tongue will shrivel up before I ever tell you another lie."

The heat of his words drifted over her nape, distracting her all the more from thinking rationally. His world had tipped upside down, he'd said. Well, so had hers, and then righted with dizzying speed. Her brains had been scrambled in the tumble. How could she trust him?

"Do you really think I should?" she asked on a hush.

"No. But I'm hoping like hell you will."

His breath drifted over her skin, distracting her. "H-how can I trust you?"

"Take it day by day and let me prove that you can. That's all I'm asking for, Christine. The chance to show you I won't betray you. The chance to give you my love. Let me give to you, darling. I ask nothing more than that."

Forgiveness always came easily to Chris, and much more so with the man she loved more than life itself. She did love him. With all his faults, she loved him to distraction. He could be selfish and demanding, but he could also be generous and caring. And he wasn't demanding now; he was asking. Knowing in her heart that she could deny him nothing, she peered over her shoulder at him.

"You'd ask nothing? Ha! I know you. A day and you'll be demanding clean shirts and a home-cooked meal."

The breath he hadn't even known he'd been holding rushed out in a long sigh. "Oh, God, baby, I love you!"

She turned fully into his arms, the arms she'd longed to lose herself in all during this miserable day, the arms that brought joy and warmth as no other arms could.

He received her eagerly, tenderly. He rained intense little kisses wherever his lips would reach, in her hair, on her brow, over her eyes, her nose, her mouth. He caressed her shoulders with a fiery fervor, stroking the length of her arms, the smooth plane of her back. As if to assure himself she was real, he paused to simply stare hungrily.

"Pau—Preston—"

"Paul. I like the sound of it on your lips. It sounds . . . worthy, real."

"Paul, then. I think we'd better go in. Mary's waiting."

He was reluctant to let her go, even momentarily, and told her so. She laughed with breathy delight and said she'd hold him to that later. They started toward the house, but she stopped. "Should we bring in the stuff?"

"What stuff?"

"My clothes and things."

He frowned. "You carried all your belongings down the stairs all by yourself? Damn it, I don't want you doing anything that stupid again. You could've hurt yourself, hurt the baby."

"I'm not made of china, Paul."

"Don't argue. Get in there. I'll bring up your clothes."

That tone was his not-to-be-denied tone. Now he was demanding! With a secret smile she handed him the car keys and went on into the house. Mary stood waiting in the dining room, trying vainly not to look eaten alive with curiosity. It became impossible as Paul entered, bearing a large cardboard box stuffed haphazardly with Christine's clothes.

"What's been going on here?" she demanded of Chris. "Were those men really Paul's brothers? Were you leaving? Why?"

Not certain what to say about the Ridgeways, Chris evaded this barrage of questions by sinking onto a chair and, bracing her elbows on her knees, she propped her chin on her hands. "Can't talk without coffee."

Paul clattered down the stairs, walked over to her with a savage scowl marring his features. "Here," he snapped, thrusting the wedding ring under her nose. "Put it on and keep it on." When she had complied with this directive, he strode out, not even bothering to glance at Mary.

The thump of Mary's coffee mug onto the table echoed in the silence he left behind. Chris toyed nervously with the band, spinning it on her finger. It felt good to have it back in place. Her finger had felt so empty, so naked without it. But then, so had she. She realized Mary was staring at her. She stopped twirling the ring. Mary still stared.

"We, um, had a little spat," she finally mumbled.

"I'd gathered that, only I don't think it was so little."

Up went Christine's chin. "Don't sound so critical. You're not exactly in the position to throw stones. Until today I'd never seen Ken go ten minutes at a time without grinning. He wouldn't even enter the house tonight until I told him you'd gone. Whatever you said to him, you said it but good. He was even talking about leaving town before —"

"Leaving? Ken?"

Every vestige of color deserted Mary's face. Her green eyes stood out like bright stones in a bleached setting. Chris reached out and put her hand over her friend's trembling fingers. "Oh, Mary, he didn't mean it!"

Mary shucked the hand and jumped to her feet. "He's just a pig-headed fool and I'm going to tell him so! He can't leave when we've just begun to—" She cut herself short.

"That's just what he told me," put in Chris quickly. "He said he can't leave town because he loves you. The age difference really isn't all that great, Mary. You'd be the pig-headed fool if you let that ruin your chance at love."

Mary slowly sat down again. "I have been a fool, haven't I?"

"I think we all are when it comes to love."

"I—I do love him," confessed Mary. "I think, in a way, I always have."

"Tell Ken that. He needs to hear it, Mary. He needs it badly. He needs *you.*"

A hint of amusement glinted in the green eyes. "Isn't it amazing how good we all are at handing out advice to someone else? I was going to say that Paul needs *you.* "

They were giggling when Paul came in, arms overflow-

281

ing with a miscellaneous array of clothes on hangers. He dumped the load in an untidy heap onto the sofa and joined them. He looked from one woman to the other, then he held out his hand to Chris. She gave him a mug, which he set down. He reached for her left hand and tapped a fingertip against the gold there.

"That's where that belongs. I'll let it go this time, but after Saturday, you'll be in big trouble if that's ever off your finger again."

"Yes, sir," said Chris meekly, loving him madly.

He picked up his coffee and sipped. Mary waited until he lowered the mug. "Saturday?" she said then.

"Our wedding day."

Mary's mouth opened, sputtered soundlessly, closed, and finally opened again. "Wedding day?" she squeaked.

He turned a dining chair around and straddled it, resting his arms along the back. "That's what we wanted to talk to you about. My name isn't Richards and we're not married. Yet."

While Mary revived herself from the shock with strong coffee, they proceeded to tell her the whole story, interrupting each other several times, clarifying or disagreeing over a point. At the end there was a stretched hush in which a faraway motorcycle rattled the windows. Paul was the first to break it.

"What I'd like to know, Mary, is whether you think the people of Oscar will show the kindness they've done from the beginning and accept the truth?"

She hesitated. "You don't have to tell the truth. You could just go on as you were."

"No way," he said firmly. "From here on out I'm playing it straight. I promised Christine never to tell another lie and I mean to keep that promise."

"Paul—"

"Baby, it's the only way." He turned to Chris, his face filled with such earnest love that her breath stopped. "Those that don't accept us, don't accept us, but I'm willing to risk losing everything else to have you openly, honestly, with pride."

"Those who'd hold it against you wouldn't be much of a loss." Mary nudged her coffee cup first one way, then another, took a deep breath, and asked on a rush, "Do you think there'd be room for a couple of passengers when you drove to Oklahoma?"

"To witness the wedding?" asked Chris happily.

"Actually I was thinking more of a double wedding."

Paul whooped and Chris cried, "Oh, Mary, that would be absolutely perfect!"

"That's if he'll still have me. I'm going to ask, but that's no guarantee. He may say no."

"Keep asking," advised Paul. "Persistence pays."

"He won't say no. There's not a chance of it." Chris leaped from her chair to tug Mary to her feet. She shoved her toward the door. "Go on, go and ask him right now, right this minute, before you confuse yourself with stupid second thoughts. Drive right on over there and tell him you love him, won't stop loving him, and that he'd better make an honest woman of you."

"But he hasn't—I mean, we haven't—"

Chris quirked her brows and smiled coyly. "Ah, but you take care of *that* before you ask him."

Flushing, giggling, looking like a young girl, Mary hugged them both and flew out the door. She raced back and yelled through the screen. "I'll call. I'll let it ring twice, then hang up if it's good news!"

They stood at the door, watching and waving as she backed out of the drive and gave a happy honk as she sped off into the distance. And still they stood, neither daring to break the spell, afraid that this happy ending was a dream that would vanish in a poof.

For Christine the happiness was muted by a twinge of doubt. What could she give to reimburse Paul for his enormous sacrifice? She stared out over the moon-buttered lawn and racked her brain. What was a home and child compared to millions and the ability to have anything, anytime? What was she? She didn't have beauty or sophistication to keep him interested.

For Paul the happiness was yet so new, so fragile he could scarcely bear to believe in it. He had run off to find himself and had found love. He gazed down at the profile glowing like honey in the moonlight and wondered anew at the incredible feelings she engendered in him. She was so special. He would spend the rest of his life treasuring her.

"Shouldn't we go upstairs?" he inquired finally. "You've got some unpacking to do."

Chris touched a fingertip to the wire mesh, rubbing the screen lazily. "Paul, are you sure? Are you really sure?"

"I'm sure that I love you."

He nuzzled his lips into the disheveled brown curls above her ear. She felt the moist warmth of his mouth and knew a second, sharper stab of fear. Would his contentment last? How long? She swiveled her head, brushing away his tender caress.

"I'm serious. Are you sure you won't regret giving up all that wealth? All the luxury and leisure?"

Turning her fully around, he pressed her against the wood of the open door and leaned back to study her. The moonlight checkered through the screen door to pattern her face, oddly masking the pleasant features, the clever, capable features that he loved so much. He lightly touched his fingers to her cheeks.

"There won't be any regrets, baby. I've made my decision. I'm not the kind to look over my shoulder at what's behind me. It's the future—our future, yours, mine, our child's—that matters to me. I look forward to a lifetime of sharing love and laughter and tears and disappointments and all the minor everyday ups and downs with you. Those are the things that really matter, Christine. Those are the things I would regret losing."

The swirl of his fingertips worked into her blood, where

it sang so loudly she thought she would faint from the roar. "But if you should suffer one regret—"

"If I do, then I'll face up to it. We'll work it out together." He pulled her into his arms. She heard the singing of her blood mimicked in the wild pounding of his heart. "I'm through running away, Christine, from anything. You taught me that. You taught me to face up to responsibilities. If we have problems, we'll stand up to them. Together."

She tilted back her head to gaze into that handsome face she so adored. "Dearest, you're giving up so much. What can I give you in return? How can I make all that up to you?"

He drew a shuddering breath that trembled from his head to his toe. The look on her face was the one he'd longed to see. It was the look of complete commitment. "Just love me, darling," he whispered hoarsely. "Love me and don't stop loving me. That's all I need. All I want."

"I do love you. I'll always love you." She pressed scalding kisses into his chest, his throat. He groaned and she felt it ripple through him.

He swept her into his arms and kicked the door shut with his heel. Carrying her toward the stairs, he murmured that she was the best, the loveliest, the most wonderful woman on earth. She clasped her arms around his neck and dampened his shirt with joyful tears that flowed unchecked as she repeated over and over that she loved him.

They were halfway up the steps when the phone jangled. Paul paused, lifting his head to listen. She raised her head, sniffed back tears, and tensed. On the second ring they both unconsciously held their breaths. After a full thirty seconds of silence, they shared smiles. After sixty, two smiles melted into a single kiss.

They continued up the stairs to their bedroom and their future. Together.

When You Want A Little More Than Romance—

Try A Candlelight Ecstasy!

 Wherever paperback books are sold!

NEW DELL

CANDLELIGHT
Ecstasy Supreme

TEMPESTUOUS EDEN,
by Heather Graham.
$2.50

Blair Morgan—daughter of a powerful man, widow of a famous senator—sacrifices a world of wealth to work among the needy in the Central American jungle and meets Craig Taylor, a man she can deny nothing.

EMERALD FIRE,
by Barbara Andrews
$2.50

She was stranded on a deserted island with a handsome millionaire—what more could Kelly want? Love.

NEW DELL

CANDLELIGHT
Ecstasy Supreme

LOVERS AND PRETENDERS,
by Prudence Martin
$2.50

Christine and Paul—looking for new lives on a cross-country jaunt, were bound by lies and a passion that grew more dangerously honest with each passing day. Would the truth destroy their love?

WARMED BY THE FIRE,
by Donna Kimel Vitek
$2.50

When malicious gossip forces Juliet to switch jobs from one television network to another, she swears an office romance will never threaten her career again—until she meets superstar anchorman Marc Tyner.